Saving
Christmas
in the
Little Irish
Village

BOOKS BY MICHELLE VERNAL

Michelle Vernal

Saving Christmas

in the

Little Irish Village

bookouture

Published by Bookouture in 2024

An imprint of Storyfire Ltd.
Carmelite House
50 Victoria Embankment
London EC4Y 0DZ

www.bookouture.com

Storyfire Ltd's authorised representative in the EEA is Hachette Ireland
8 Castlecourt Centre
Castleknock Road
Castleknock
Dublin 15 D15 YF6A
Ireland

ISBN: 978-1-83790-807-3
eBook ISBN: 978-1-83790-806-6

May peace and plenty be the first
to lift the latch on your door,
and happiness be guided to your home,
by the candle of Christmas.
May you always have walls for the winds,
a roof for the rain, tea beside the fire,
laughter to cheer you, those you love near you
and all your heart might desire.

— *IRISH CHRISTMAS BLESSING*

PROLOGUE

Eight-year-old Hannah Kelly opened today's window on her snowman advent calendar and popped the chocolate behind it in her mouth. Usually, the calendar made the long wait from 1 December until Christmas Day more bearable because it was the only time of year she and her sisters were allowed chocolate before breakfast! This morning, Hannah barely tasted it because she had far more important things on her mind this year than what she'd scribbled down on her Christmas wish list.

Hannah's world had shifted since the day she won first prize for her recyclable art project at school. The prize, a book titled *Save the Planet*, had opened her eyes to the fact that due to humans' lack of care, Earth was slowly dying. A fire had been lit within her, a determination to do whatever she could to make a difference.

Hannah placed the cardboard calendar back on the sideboard in the kitchen alongside her older sisters Imogen's and Shannon's equally festive gingerbread cottage and reindeer ones. Then she sat at the table to scoff the warming bowl of porridge her nan had set down. There was somewhere else Hannah needed to be, and her eyes flitted to her school bag, which was stuffed not with her books but with the tools to put her plan in motion – a skipping rope, her lunch, a drink bottle and the sign she'd painted at school during break time. It had been touch and go as to whether it would dry in time before her classmates piled back in, and a few of the letters had smudged in her haste to hide it in her backpack, but it wouldn't matter. She'd use her voice, too.

Her family was oblivious to what Hannah was plotting as the familiar morning routine played out with twins Grace and Ava, the youngest of the five Kelly girls, being tag team fed by Mam. Dad was stealing a few minutes to skim the morning paper while Imogen and Shannon chatted over their oats about whether their letters would have reached Father Christmas's headquarters in the North Pole yet. Hannah, however, was quiet as she shovelled her breakfast down, eager to be on her way and begin putting her plan in motion.

'Slow down, Hannah. No one's going to take it off you,' Nan tutted, sitting down with a cup of tea.

But Hannah was already scraping the bowl.

She excused herself and got up from the table. The next time her family saw her, she was rugged up for the walk to school. Slinging her bag on her back, she was out the door before they could question her eagerness to get to class so early.

Hannah barely registered the snow that had settled on the ground overnight as she hurried up the laneway running between her home at the Shamrock pub and the row of village shops onto Main Street. There wasn't a soul in sight, which was just as well because the last thing she needed was a busybody like Mrs Tattersall wanting to know why she wasn't on her way to school.

In her haste to get to where she was going, she nearly skidded over in a slushy puddle but managed to stay upright, and then she was there. The village square. It was empty save for the troughs filled with flowers in spring and summer, but within a matter of days, Hannah knew an enormous Christmas tree would fill it, and it was the cutting down of that same tree she was going to protest. She might not be able to save the world, but she could try to save a tree.

She unhooked her backpack, pulled out the skipping rope, wrapped it around the signpost at the square's edge and tied it around her waist because she wasn't going anywhere. Then Hannah fetched her hand-painted sign, and holding it up high, she shouted at the top of her lungs, 'Save Ireland's trees!'

One by one, heads popped out of the colourful doors lining either side of Main Street to see what all the noise was about.

Hannah Kelly shouted even louder.

1

Hannah's eyes closed as she envisaged the roaring open fire at the Shamrock Inn. Then, picturing the welcoming warmth of the kitchen in the Kelly family quarters attached to the pub, her nose tingled. She sniffed, breathing in the cinnamon, citrus, cloves and ginger aromas that signalled Nan was baking up a storm for Christmas. What was truly special about home, though, was the sense of belonging as she barrelled back through the door.

The realisation that things would be different this year made her eyes pop back open, and she was almost surprised to find herself not in Emerald Bay but in the Cork City branch of Feed the World with Bees. Instead of delicious home baking, the office space smelled of coffee and damp wool. Through the half-misted windowpane beside her desk, Hannah could see the sparkling Christmas decorations lighting up the streets beyond. Inside, someone had half-heartedly draped tinsel around its frame. She decided it was probably Sonya, who'd been wearing cute little candy cane earrings in a nod to Christmas yesterday.

Hannah's gaze settled longingly on her colleague Dylan. He'd just asked her when she'd begun to feel passionate about the environment because he was updating the staff profiles on the Feed the World with Bees website. She'd told him the story of her 'Save Ireland's trees' one-child protest, and as he input this into the computer, she admired the determined jut of his jaw, signalling a kindred spirit.

'OK. So you tied yourself to the signpost, and what happened then?' Dylan's fingers had temporarily stopped flying over the keyboard, and his cocoa-brown eyes locked on Hannah. 'Did you stop the villagers cutting down the tree?'

'No. I wasn't made of as strong stuff as I am now. I eventually got cold and hungry and howled for Mam to come and snip the skipping rope because I couldn't undo my knot. But don't you dare put that under my bio! You'll ruin my tree-hugger street cred.'

'So you gave in?'

'I did.' Hannah nodded, even now not liking the sense of failure. 'And I felt bad about it for a long time. I cried myself to sleep every night in the lead-up to Christmas that year and vowed to help make the world a better place when I was bigger.' She remembered her eight-year-old self standing in front of the bathroom mirror, giving a solemn Brownie salute as she promised to always stand up for her beliefs. Hannah liked to think it was a vow she'd kept.

Dylan went back to his typing, and she shifted in her seat. Her bum was going numb. What she needed was one of those standing desk yokes like he had there, but the problem was she couldn't be arsed with all that standing. It was a conundrum. On her desk in front of her, packets of wildflower seeds were scattered along with a sky-high stack of Christmas cards featuring a bee with a Santa hat on. Today, her task was to stuff a seed packet inside each card and put it in an envelope ready for purchase.

The seeds and cards were a great money spinner when it came to saving the bees, and the non-profit organisation also did an Easter and birthday range. That was Hannah sorted on the present-buying front for the year! She glanced at the box full of envelopes she'd already stuffed. Was RSI imminent? she wondered, flexing her fingers, and rather than continue working, she said, 'My mam says I feel things more deeply than others.'

That piqued Dylan's interest, and basking in the glow of his attention once more, she continued.

'I was always the kid who'd bring the dead bird home and insist on a proper burial ceremony.' Nora Kelly also said she was one of life's blurters who would do well to think before she spoke occasionally. Right at this moment, for instance, she desperately wanted to blurt, 'I think I might be in love with you,' to Dylan because at least then he'd know how she felt. This bubbling sensation of things hovering between them unsaid was so unsettling. It took a determined effort to zip it for the sake of her job, and she was grateful when he intruded on her thoughts.

'Byline?' he asked, fingers hovering over the keyboard.

'Erm.' She thought for a moment. 'Why don't you say something like, "Hannah passionately believes that healing our sick planet is not an ideal; it's a necessity"?'

Her reward was seeing Dylan's impressed, slow nod. It warmed her insides like she'd been given a cinnamon-sprinkled hot chocolate with marshmallows floating on top. His opinion of her mattered because he was the real deal in her eyes. While he worked with her at Feed the World with Bees during the day, he was also the frontman for the Climate Guardians action group he'd established in his student days.

Hannah stared out the window again as he typed this in. The building where she worked had once served as a home. It now served as a second home – well, third home for her if you counted the Shamrock and the flat she currently shared, given how much time she spent here. The office was one of many in a colourful row converted into businesses in the city centre.

She watched a woman laden down with shopping bags hurrying past, and her mind snapped back to Christmas. Usually, she'd count down December's days until the twenty-fifth, a habit stemming from the advent calendars of her child-hood. This year, though, the anticipation that would be building about now had deserted her because she would be the only one of her five sisters without a partner to snuggle up to over Christmas. Hannah would be the odd one out, but what made her even sadder was knowing she was just as loved up as her sisters. She stole a glance at Dylan. Only hers was a pathetic one-sided affair.

2

Hannah trudged under the wing of a golden angel and glanced up. The illuminated decoration, arms reaching to the heavens, spanned the width of the street. Her sisters said she was a Christmas Grinch because she didn't believe in rampant consumerism, but that didn't mean she didn't appreciate how lovely the festive streets looked. She was making her way back to the office and being careful to avoid the puddles of water glistening on the pavement. They looked like mysterious rock pools under the twinkling fairy lights, she thought somewhat romantically, feeling a pang for Emerald Bay. She'd always loved exploring the rock pools down at the bay when the tide went out, leaving behind an arc of wet sand and rocks to clamber over.

The rain hadn't lasted long, thank goodness. Hannah had taken shelter inside a cafe playing Michael Bublé's Christmas album until the downpour had passed. Now, humming 'Santa Claus is Comin' to Town', she shivered despite her thrift-shop wool coat. Her breath was white on the frigid air, and she thought, kudos to Sonya, for whom she'd stepped in. It was hard work freezing your arse off flogging cards. She'd felt like Hans

Christian Andersen's Little Match Girl these last few hours as organised people weighed down with parcels, getting in early before the last-minute Christmas rush, filled the pavements.

Nonetheless, it had been a successful afternoon because she'd offloaded the entire box, touting the cards stuffed with seed packets as a great little stocking filler for an important cause. 'Christmas was a time for giving' being her line that sealed the deal. She also fancied that people felt sorry for her loitering on the street in arctic weather. It was also easier to hand over a tenner than have her stand in their way, giving her spiel with the same zealousness as a religious fanatic sharing the good word.

A tenner was an exorbitant price for a Christmas card and packet of wildflower seeds, but she'd say it was a small price to pay in the grand scheme of things. Think about how those seeds would impact the bee population and the world's food chain. Oh yes, Hannah had her sales pitter-patter down pat.

It had been her idea to swap places with Sonya for the afternoon because she needed to put space between herself and Dylan.

As she reached the office, Hannah paused and looked in the window to see him on the phone and Sonya wearing a fed-up face as she sat there card/seed stuffing, lit by the harsh yellow glare. She could have headed back to her flat. The day was nearly done, but sometimes Dylan suggested going for a team-building drink on Fridays at the end of the day. She hadn't wanted to miss the opportunity of squeezing into a snug alongside him. So here she was back at Feed the World with Bees, staring in the window with the same longing as a child outside a sweet shop.

Suddenly mindful of not getting caught on the outside looking in with her tongue lolling like an eager puppy, Hannah moved toward the door.

Dylan raised his brows in greeting as she stood stamping her

Doc Martens-booted feet on the mat. Sonya, obviously glad of an excuse to down tools, stopped card stuffing and asked how she'd got on.

'All gone.' Hannah held out the empty box.

'Well done.'

Hannah grinned. 'Thank you.' She perched on the edge of the desk, picking up a card and packet of wildflower seeds. 'What have you got planned for the weekend, then?'

'I'm heading up to Dublin for the anti-gold mining protest. If you've no plans, you should come.'

Hannah would have gone in a flash if her finances were flush enough for a weekend in Dublin. As things stood, she couldn't even stretch to a weekend dossing on someone's couch in the capital city. It was all right for Sonya, who still lived with her parents and paid a token gesture toward her keep. Working for non-profit organisations like Feed the World with Bees meant scraping by. Not that she was complaining. She loved working with people who lived and breathed environmental causes and, more often than not, spent their weekends holding placards, trying to draw attention to what was happening in their country and the world. Dylan was especially vocal, and Hannah admired him for it.

'If my share of the gas and electric wasn't due, I'd be by your side, Sonya. This proposed mining up north is bad news, all right. We don't want it.' Hannah gave a vehement shake of her head.

Before Sonya could reply, Dylan, who'd finished his call, beckoned her over and gestured at his computer screen. 'Hannah, c'mere to me. Have you seen this?'

Hannah was glad of an excuse to stand in Dylan's personal space. She leaned over his shoulder, and her body tingled in response to his minty breath and the clean scent of soap. There was something else, too. It was musky and giving off some serious pheromones, so she had to summon all her inner strength to focus on what Dylan wanted her to look at and not begin snuffling around his neck like a truffle-hunting dog.

'Proposed garden centre and Christmas tree farm for Emerald Bay,' Hannah read out loud before skimming over the article Dylan had dredged up from one of the news pages. When she'd finished, she reread it more slowly, this time trying to make sense of it, then continued to stare at the screen as her mind whirred. Surely not? But it was there in black and white. Some bigwig developer was pushing for the West Country's largest stop-shop garden centre, complete with a Christmas tree farm, to be built behind Emerald Bay. There was even a quote from the architectural project manager – or arse, as Hannah immediately retitled him – about the boost this would bring to Emerald Bay's local economy and tourism blah-de-blah.

'It's in the middle of nowhere, for feck's sake.'

She didn't realise she'd spoken aloud until Dylan said, 'That land is all blanket bog, right?'

'Right. Most of the land is a nature reserve, but not far from the edge of the village, there's an abandoned farm with a famine cottage still standing. I'm picking that's the proposed site.' She shuddered, picturing a hideous monstrosity plonked on the landscape she knew so well. 'This can't happen.'

'And you've not heard so much of a whisper about it until now?'

'Nothing. It's obviously been kept hush-hush.'

'What are you going to do about it then?'

'What I always do in times of crisis.'

'What's that then?'

'Phone my mam!'

3

'The Shamrock Inn. This is Kitty Kelly speaking.'

'Nan, it's me, Hannah.' There was an urgency in Hannah's tone as she plucked at the denim of her dungarees for want of something to do with her free hand.

'Oh, Hannah! 'Tis lovely to hear your voice. How're you?'

Hannah couldn't help but grin despite her state of agitation. Nan had a knack for making it sound like it had been months instead of days since she'd last heard from her granddaughter. However, before she could get to the crux of her call, Kitty Kelly ploughed on, 'Now, what I want to know is, are you eating properly? I thought you were looking thin when I last saw you.'

'I told you the other day, Nan, I'm after eating plenty of greens.'

'And meat. A woman needs her iron, you know, Hannah.'

'And meat.' She wasn't, but sometimes it was easier to fib. Besides, meat was pricey. It suited her to be vegetarian whilst in Cork.

'I'm glad to hear it. What colour is the hair this week, then?'

'Same as when I FaceTimed last week on Mam's iPad, Nan. Green.' She'd thought she'd heard the end of the hair lectures when she cut off her locs earlier in the year, but now her vibrant hair colour choices were a bone of contention.

'I'm not sure about the green, Hannah. It's unnatural. Sure, you're not a leprechaun, and there's you with those pretty chestnut highlights like your mam's and Shannon's if you'd only leave your hair alone.'

'You weren't sure about the red either, Nan, and I don't want to look like Mam or Shannon. I want to look like me. And would you let me get a word in?'

Kitty blithely carried on. 'Christmas is nearly upon us again; sure, I'm counting down the days. I suppose when you think about it, green's a festive colour. It puts me in mind of a holly wreath.'

Hannah, rolling her eyes, decided she'd had enough. 'Nan, I didn't ring to chit-chat about my hair colour and Christmas.'

'Well, that's charming, so it is. What was I just saying? Holly's prickly and all.'

'I rang because I'm after reading a news story about a proposed garden centre with a ridiculous Christmas tree farm attached to it behind Emerald Bay.'

'What are you on about garden centres and the like? Sure, the closest one's in Galway, and why would you want to go to a garden centre this time of year? Unless it's for a poinsettia. I bought your mam a lovely one once, but while Nora might well do a lovely job with the window boxes, she's cack-handed when it comes to indoor pot plants. The poor thing had withered by the time the new year rolled around. As for a Christmas tree farm, I think someone's after pulling your leg. We've already got the Shaughnessys' place, where your dad goes each year. They do a grand Nordmann fir, so they do.'

Hannah tried to keep her voice even. 'Nan, would you please listen to what I've got to say because it's serious? A developer wants to build this monstrosity I've just told you about on the abandoned farm's land behind the village.'

'What was that?'

Hearing her nan's bewilderment, Hannah slowly repeated herself.

'I'm not an imbecile,' Kitty snapped. 'And that can't be right. The farm was deserted during the Great Hunger, and building on it would mean knocking down the famine cottage. Sure, that's part of Emerald Bay's heritage.'

'It's in the paper, Nan.'

There was no sound but that of Kitty breathing as she processed what she was being told.

'Nan?'

'I'm still here.'

'This can't go ahead because what you said about it being part of our village's heritage is true. We can't have a stranger barrelling into town destroying our history.'

This time, Kitty didn't beat around the bush. 'No. It can't go ahead. That place should be left alone with its ghosts. So what are you going to do about it?'

'Me?'

'Well, the middle granddaughter with the green hair I know and love wouldn't stand by and let some bigwig developer walk all over us.'

'You're right, Nan, she wouldn't.' Hannah's blood was beginning to boil.

'So then? Are we agreed?'

'Erm, did I miss something?'

'You'll come home early, and together we'll make sure this garden centre/Christmas tree farm malarkey doesn't get the go-ahead.'

Hannah picked up on the 'we'. This wouldn't be a one-woman protest like the last time she tried to take a stand at Christmas. Dylan would be OK with her finishing a week earlier once she'd explained what was at stake because they both knew how these things worked. He had to be because the developer would be trying to rush planning permission through before everything shut down for the Christmas holidays. Red tape was easier to snip through when people were desperate to clear their desks before the holidays.

'We're agreed, Nan.'

'Grand. Your mam's just after walking in.'

Hannah heard her asking which of her daughters was on the phone.

'It's Hannah, Nora. She was after ringing to tell me the news. Have you heard about this ridiculous garden centre/Christmas tree farm business?'

'The pub's been abuzz with it since Isla Mullins closed half an hour early and stormed in waving the paper. I had a feeling Hannah would be on the phone as soon as she got wind of it. Can I have a word with her?'

'I'm just passing you over, Hannah. I'll see you soon.'

'You will. Bye, Nan.'

Nora Kelly didn't bother with pleasantries. 'It's caused a right to-do with the local business owners. The consensus amongst them is it would be the death knell for their shops because everybody knows garden centres don't just sell plants and the like; they've a finger in the gift line, and sure, you know yourself, they always have a cafe thrown in there, too.'

Hannah hadn't even considered that side of things. She'd been focused on the cottage's historical value and its surrounding land, but those with shops on Main Street had every right to be up in arms.

'And what about you and Dad? How do you feel about it.'

Her mam's reply took her by surprise.

'We're keeping an open mind for the time being.'

'Mam!'

'You asked, and we're entitled to our opinions. The Shamrock's our livelihood, so it is, and if it brought more people to the village, then that would be good for our business. We're not sure there isn't room for everybody.'

Hannah held the phone away from her ear in disgust. However, she could still hear her mam prattling on about how progress frightened people sometimes and how easy it was to let emotions override good business sense. She pressed the phone back to her ear in time to catch the end of her one-sided conversation.

'Your dad and I would like to know more about the project is all I'm saying, Hannah. Now we've a full bar, so I've got to love you and leave you.'

A kiss was blown down the phone, and Hannah's, '*But, Mam,*' fell on deaf ears.

There was no point in sitting here feeling irked, not when she needed to get home to Emerald Bay. So, after running through how to broach leaving the organisation in the lurch with Dylan at the busiest time of the year, Hannah ventured downstairs to the office, her fingers crossed behind her back as she cleared her throat.

Dylan looked up from whatever he'd been doing. 'Hannah, I wondered where you'd got to. Sonya's after reminding me it's the second-to-last weekend of GLOW in Bishop Lucey Park. We flogged a heap of our Christmas cards there last year.'

'I remember. I was doing the hard sell so I followed this fella onto the Ferris wheel thinking he was a shoo-in for buying a wodge of cards.' The 'Twelve Days of Christmas'-themed festival's big draw card wasn't just its lights; the thirty-metre-high Ferris wheel also pulled in the crowds. Never again, she thought trying to shake off the wave of nausea the memory of rocking back and forth at the top of the wheel for what felt like forever invoked.

'And did he?'

'Nope, but he did ask for my phone number. I gave him short shrift obviously.'

'Obviously. The thing is, Sonya's in Dublin this weekend.'

'I know.' Hannah squirmed, not liking where he was heading.

'And the Climate Guardians rally is happening tomorrow night. We've got something big planned that's going to highlight the lies being told about the financing of fossil fuel in Ireland. It's going to show not just Cork but the nation the Climate Guardians aren't just mouthpieces. We mean business.'

Hannah was sidetracked as she pictured paint bombs being lobbed or someone scaling the National Monument and pouring tomato soup over it – quickly changing the mental image to minestrone with all its lumpy bits because tomato was her favourite – before asking him what was going to happen.

'I can't say anymore right now, but trust me. People will be talking about this Cork City protest for a long time.'

Whatever was planned, Hannah knew this much: Dylan wasn't messing. She'd heard the stories of him having being strip-searched, held in the cells for hours and the numerous court appearances he'd made in his quest to draw attention to what he believed in.

'So I wondered if you'd mind heading along?' The maniacal gleam in his eyes disappeared as he fixed her with his puppy-dog gaze, and Hannah, realising he wanted her to go to GLOW, dug her nails into her palms because no matter how much she wanted to please him by saying yes, she knew she needed to go home more. She took a deep breath and was as surprised as Dylan by what came out of her mouth. 'No. I can't, Dylan.'

He blinked, clearly a little taken back.

'I'm going home tomorrow. I'll need to take early leave because I'm not going to let this proposed monstrosity destroy my village. I won't let planning permission be rushed through because some eejit who doesn't give a toss about Emerald Bay wants to sign off for Christmas.'

The steel in her voice brooked no argument.

4

A clear, frosty Saturday morning saw Hannah hit the road home to Emerald Bay early. Outside, it might be a wintery December day, but inside her beloved old banger, Doris, the temperature was tropical, thanks to the heater being stuck on the highest setting. Hannah, cooking, had whipped her jumper off and was stripped down to her vest as she puttered along the coastal road. Annoyingly, the radio station kept crackling in and out of reception. Still, it was better than juddering along alone with her thoughts.

Without the musical distraction, her mind would begin to tick, tick, tick, her thoughts turning to the world and all its problems. Global warming, capitalism, the threat of nuclear war, the refugee crisis, hungry families. The images she'd seen online would crowd in, her feelings welling up until she'd feel like all the air had been squeezed from her chest like a wrung-out sponge. Then she'd have to pull over and breathe slowly into the sick bag she kept in the glove box. Panic attacks. She couldn't pinpoint when they'd started and was loath to go to the doctor for fear of being stamped with a label; there were so many these days. Nor did she want to be issued with medication. If that were to happen, and she allowed herself to be softened and soothed, then she'd stop being Hannah, and she didn't want that. Not when she had so much to do. So much to fix.

There she went again. Overthinking.

To distract herself, she began drumming her fingers on the steering wheel to the crackling beat of some poppy song she hadn't heard before. It didn't work, though, and her mind flitted to Dylan and what she fancied was an admiring glint in his eyes as she'd laid down the law about going home for Christmas early. Her fingers had itched to reach out and touch his face for no reason other than to feel his skin beneath her fingertips. Of course, she hadn't.

A rabbit bounding across the road just then saw her slam her foot on the brake. Feck! That was close and would teach her to daydream about Dylan while driving. On Doris's back seat, the hold-all she'd stuffed her gear into had slid off the seat. At least the Feed the World with Bees Christmas cards filling Doris's boot were in boxes jammed in alongside one another with no room to move. Selling the cards while she was home was a condition of being granted early leave. Determining to stay focused, Hannah eased her foot off the brake.

On her right, the Atlantic ocean frothed and churned, its roar a constant battle cry as the white horses charged into shore. Then, rounding the bend, she counted off the familiar land-marks, signalling she was nearly home. Kilticaneel Castle, the fishing boat harbour, Benmore House, the row of pretty thatched cottages (one of which Shannon and James were now the proud owners of), and then finally, she was passing under the Merry Christmas banner strewn across Emerald Bay's Main Street.

'Happy Holidays' was painted on the window of the art gallery's jewellery shop, Mermaids. Hannah soon saw that the rest of the village shops had gone to town with tinsel and displays of colourful hanging bells, paper snowflakes, faux miniature Christmas trees and gift-wrapped boxes with bows piled on top of one another. The usual fairy lights were draped like a magical arbour across the street, and the Christmas tree stood tall and proud in the square.

'Home sweet home,' Hannah announced as she clapped eyes on the Shamrock Inn with its cheerful door, candle stubs in the window and the window boxes that Mam had planted with seasonal, lush green foliage and berrying plants to add a splash of winter colour. It was always so comforting to arrive at the Shamrock and see that only the window boxes had changed. There were no surprises, which was part of its charm in an ever-changing world. This was why the garden centre and Christmas tree farm couldn't proceed. It would change everything, she thought, parking around the back next to her dad's hulking yellow wagon.

There was no sign of her mam's car, she noticed, pulling up the handbrake. She must be out and about.

As the heater died in the car along with the engine, Hannah bent to retrieve her jumper from the floor of the passenger seat. She'd have to clean the car at some point, she thought, eyeing the rubbish hidden by her jumper.

A tap at the window saw her snap upright like a piece of elastic being pulled too tight and suddenly let go. Jaysus! Then, registering the black cap pulled so low that its wearer's face wasn't visible, fear stabbed her.

Cop yourself on, Hannah, she told herself. Carjackings were uncommon in Ireland and unheard of in Emerald Bay. Besides, why would anyone want to steal Doris? She was one of the most easily identifiable cars in this part of the country, covered in stickers for everything from Greenpeace to Stop the Gold Mining, not forgetting her beloved bees. Accordingly, she wound the window down and registered the familiar face beneath the cap with an annoyed huff.

'For feck's sake, Imo, don't sneak up like that when you're

dressed like a criminal. And why are you panting and jiggling about like so? You know where the toilet is.'

'I'm jogging on the spot, you eejit.'

'More fool you then.' At least that explained her sister's head-to-toe designer activewear. Imogen never did anything by halves. Since she'd shacked up with Ryan back in Emerald Bay, she might not be quite the Dublin designer label fiend of old, but a leopard never really changed its spots.

'I've taken up running. I'll seize up if I stop. I saw you rattling your way in. No one mentioned you were home this weekend,' Imogen puffed indignantly.

'Because I didn't want Dad doing his *Ice Road Truckers*, ten-four, little buddies, what's your ETA bit.' Liam Kelly worried about his girls driving on the open road and expected regular route updates.

Imogen managed a breathy laugh. 'Fair play. So are you taking your holidays early then?'

'Yes and no. I'm here on a mission.'

Imogen cocked a brow. 'If it involves bees, then I don't want to know.'

'Not bees. Garden centres and Christmas tree farms.'

'With bees?'

'Forget the fecking bees for a minute!'

'Well, get to the point then – it's not easy this jogging on the spot business.'

'I'm home to ensure the proposed garden centre and Christmas tree farm on the abandoned farm site don't get approval.'

'Right. Well, good luck with that.' Imogen clocked what Hannah was wearing. 'Why are you wearing a vest in December?'

'Because Doris's heater is faulty. It's like the Costa del Sol in here.'

Imogen's fitness tracker began beeping. 'My heart rate's

dropping. I can't stand about arguing the toss with you. I'll catch you later.'

Hannah thought her sister's running style was more penguin than gazelle as she watched her go. Then she slipped her jumper back on, grabbed her bag off the car floor and made her way to the kitchen door. She'd get Dad to help fetch the boxes in the boot later.

The small but industrious kitchen and dining space the Kellys all managed to squeeze into was empty, and the savoury aroma wafting from the oven made Hannah's tummy grumble. It was comforting to know that wherever Nan and Mam had got to, lunch was sorted.

Hannah glanced about, trying to put her finger on what was different. Something was missing.

Napoleon. Shannon's Persian cat, who'd had a temporary home here at the Shamrock, would have appeared to greet her by now, but the cat with attitude had moved to the cottage with her sister and James.

Hannah lugged her bag to the bottom of the stairs. Resting one hand on the bannister rail, she called out in case anyone was upstairs. There was no reply, and so she trooped up the well-worn treads and down the landing to her old room.

The bedroom she'd shared with the twins had had an upgrade since they'd all moved out, their mam insistent on Cape Cod style with its beachy vibe. Hannah missed the fairy theme of her childhood, though. Not that she'd admit it. She missed the twins' presence in the room on the occasions she found herself home alone, like now. Still and all, they'd be home in under two weeks for Christmas.

After offloading her bag onto Ava's bed, she flopped down on her identically made-up one. The walls in here echoed with secrets shared and laughter, even though there were also plenty of times she'd stamped her foot over having to share with 'babies'. There were seven years between her and Ava and Grace. It was nothing in the grand scheme of things, but as a teenager, the gap had seemed huge. Sure, look at the way things were panning out, Hannah thought. She kicked the little voice into touch, whispering how pathetic it was that while her little sisters were madly in love and settled, she was floundering after a fella who'd not shown any sign of fancying her.

'You're not here to moon after Dylan, Hannah Kelly,' she told herself. 'A hot shower, that's what you need.'

The floorboards beneath the carpet creaked as she made her way to the bathroom, and in the time it took for the water to begin steaming, she'd stripped off. Finding the sweet-smelling shower gel, which Imo must have left behind, was an added bonus.

As a rule, Hannah didn't take long showers, but on this occasion, she made an exception, standing beneath the hot jets for an age before stepping out of the shower and wrapping herself in a fluffy towel. When she picked up her jeans, she noticed a brown stain near the zipper. Coffee, she realised, cursing her sloppiness silently. Ah well, there was no point in putting them on; they could go straight in the wash. The corduroy trousers her sisters said should see her strung up for fashion crimes against humanity would have to do. She'd nip back to her bedroom and dig them out, and then she'd be good to go.

Clouds of steam billowed out as she opened the bathroom door and stepped onto the landing, guilt pricked at her excessive hot water usage. Her feet refused to budge as she heard a sound that shouldn't be there. A throat clearing. It took a second for the haze to clear sufficiently for her to see the man on the stairs and to realise that the glass-shattering scream she could now hear was coming from her own mouth.

5

In the moments after the scream, Hannah's reflexes kicked in, and she covered her lower half with the scrunched-up jeans. Logic kicked in.

It was highly probable this wasn't a case of stranger danger but rather a guest making his unsuspecting way upstairs to Room 5 only to encounter her standing here like Taylor Swift emerging on stage through clouds of dry ice. Though instead of wearing a sparkly leotard and shiny tights, she'd a woolly jumper, plain old cotton knickers and lily-white legs to boot.

The stranger, whose face was shadowed in the dim light of the staircase, was holding his hands up, warding her off. Hannah guessed that she must have given him as much of a fright as he'd given her. Her heart rate was returning to normal, and fright had been replaced by mortification. 'Sorry, I, er, I, uh, I didn't mean to startle you.' Light bounced off the man's glasses. 'I'm staying in Room 5.'

'I didn't know anyone was staying,' Hannah mumbled, beginning to back away. There was no chance she was going to turn around and expose her bottom.

It was a bad move because she dropped the jeans as her heel

connected with the ruck in the carpet that Mam had been on at
Dad to sort forever, along with all the other handyman jobs he
never got around to. Her arms flailed like a Dutch windmill as
she tried to steady herself, knowing that awful way you do
before you hit the ground that it was futile.

'Oof!'

'Are you OK?' The man took the remaining stairs two at a
time. 'Jaysus, you hit the ground with a terrible thud.'

Hannah, lying sprawled on the carpet, blinked several times
in shock. She was winded and would likely be bruised; as for
her dignity, that was well and truly in smithereens.

'I'm fine,' she lied as he loomed over her. She stared through
the lens of his glasses into a set of intriguing smoky-grey eyes.

He held his hand out to help her up. Before she could grasp
it, however, her mam's voice rang out, breaking her trance.

'Hannah Kelly, what are you doing at home? More to the
point, what are you doing rolling about on the floor in your
knickers like so? Are you all right, Thomas?'

Charming, Hannah thought. She was flat on her back, and
Mam was concerned about whoever this Thomas was staying in
Room 5. It was hardly surprising, though, given that she'd never
been any different regarding guests of the Shamrock. They
could do no wrong. When Hannah had pointed this out to her,
Nora had quickly replied of course that was the case. The
guests paid their way happily, unlike her five daughters, whom
she'd had to wheedle the board from every week back in
the day.

Kitty Kelly appeared behind her daughter-in-law. 'What on
earth's going on?' she demanded, her wily-eyed gaze sweeping
the scene on the landing.

This time, Hannah clasped Thomas's outstretched palm.
He had a surprisingly firm grip, but his palms were soft. Soon
she was quite gently lifted upright, and gave a muttered,
'Thanks.'

'Hannah's home, Kitty, and she's after giving poor Thomas a terrible fright gadding about in her knickers like so.'

Erm, shouldn't that be the other way round? Hannah bristled, retrieving her jeans and covering herself once more, though why she was bothering now after the display she'd just put on, she didn't know. She and this Thomas might be strangers, but there were no secrets between them now, she thought, face flaming.

'It was bad timing, Nan.' She began to edge backwards once more. 'I didn't know we had a guest staying.'

'If you'd phoned ahead to say you were coming, I'd have told you,' Nora tutted. 'Thomas arrived late yesterday afternoon. Didn't you, Thomas?'

'That's right.'

Thomas was staring up at the ceiling as though Michelangelo had left his mark up there, clearly as embarrassed by the whole debacle as she was. Well, maybe not quite as embarrassed, given he wasn't the one standing here in cotton undies. She reached the safety of her bedroom.

'Just a minute, young lady. Your mam's got a point. Why are you parading about in your underwear? It's winter, in case you didn't realise.'

Jaysus wept! She may as well head down to the pub and do a few laps around the bar while she was at it, giving everyone a good gawp.

Enough was enough. 'I wasn't parading about, as you put it. I'd had a shower and needed a fresh pair of trousers.' She closed the door on them all, shouting, 'I'll be down in a jiffy!' before adding a muttered, 'Now bog off, the lot of you.'

Hannah leaned her head back against the door, tossed the jeans aside and put her hands on either side of her face. You could fry eggs on her cheeks because that was up there with the most humiliating few minutes of her life. The only blessing was none of her sisters had witnessed it. With any luck, she thought, pushing off the door and digging about in her bag for her cords, this Thomas would be checking out before lunch. That way, she could put the whole episode behind her like it had never happened.

Hannah had never been lucky, though.

It was her rumbling stomach that forced her out of her room. She'd happily hide out until Mam knocked to say Thomas had left if it weren't for being starving and knowing there was chicken pot pie in the oven. Her reward for brazening things out when she reached the kitchen was seeing Nan lifting it from the oven.

'Here she is. Emerald Bay's flasher,' Nora announced from where she was standing at the table, pouring a cup of tea. Over the top of her head were Christmas cards draped over the string stretching the width of the kitchen.

Hannah pulled a face while Kitty set the steaming pie – big enough to feed an army – down on the worktop. 'Your pot pie's turned out a treat, Nora.'

'Where were you two earlier?' Hannah asked.

'Nora and I whipped over to Kilticaneel for a spot of Christmas shopping. We're not leaving it until the last minute this year. Young Chloe minds the pub of a Saturday now with your father heading off all rugged up on his rambles come rain or shine. The walking in the fresh air does him good.'

'Never mind all that. What are you doing at home?' Nora demanded.

'I thought I'd surprise you all,' Hannah said.

'And didn't that go well.' Nora held her matronly arms out. 'C'mere to me now, you eejit. If you'd let me know, I'd have made you your favourite dinner.'

This was a Kelly family tradition whenever any of the girls returned home. Although, more often than not, Mam got muddled as to whose favourite was which! Hannah had already decided the pie in the oven was her new favourite as she gratefully sank into her familiar-smelling mammy embrace.

'I didn't want to worry Dad. You know what he's like at the best of times, let alone when the roads are icy.' Then, feeling her mam shaking, she mumbled, 'You better not be laughing at me, Mam.'

'Not at all,' Nora fibbed, releasing her daughter to pick up the cup of tea. 'And your dad will be happy to see you once he's told you off for not letting him know you were on your way. I'm just going to nip upstairs with this cuppa for Thomas. It's for the shock, like.' Her tongue was very much in her cheek.

Hannah watched her go through narrowed eyes. It was her who'd had the shock!

Kitty dropped the oven mitts on the worktop to give her granddaughter a hug.

'This Thomas fella's not leaving any time soon then?' Hannah managed to get out glumly before the air was squeezed out of her.

'No. He's staying for the week.'

'A week!' Hannah shrieked, and in her horror at this revelation, she missed the disapproving set of her nan's mouth. She pulled away from the embrace. What on earth was he doing in Emerald Bay for a week? She decided he must be visiting family because there was no other reason you'd want to park up here that long during winter.

'A week.' Kitty confirmed, looking none too happy.

Odd, Hannah thought. Guests at this time of year were always welcome – or any time of year for that matter. Especially when they were conventionally good-looking. She might not like that he was here, and he definitely wasn't her type, but Tom had the jawbone of someone her nan would have usually cooed over.

She was about to delve deeper into what had Nan lemony-lipped, but her phone pinging in a text made her pause to check it. Her heart began yammering, seeing it was from Dylan, and she opened the message to scan it hungrily, only to see he'd sent her a link. When she clicked on it, the kitchen was suddenly filled with a reggae beat that launched into Bob Marley's 'Get Up, Stand Up' call-to-action song.

'That's very apt, given the circumstances, so it is,' Kitty announced, putting the bag of Brussels down.

Hannah blinked, unsure she was seeing straight as her nan began bopping about the kitchen like she was one of Bob Marley's Wailers.

This was a side to Kitty Kelly she'd never seen before.

6

The only part of Liam Kelly visible beneath all the layers as he stomped in the back door was his face, ruddy from the cold. He stopped dead and stared at his daughter. 'Am I seeing things?'

What would he have had to say if she and Nan were still getting down to Bob Marley? Hannah thought, laughing, her phone in her pocket once more. 'No, Dad. I thought I'd surprise you by coming home early for Christmas.' She didn't want to get into the real reason she was home early until they'd at least had a bite to eat.

Liam made to stride over to Hannah but walked head first into the hanging Christmas cards. 'What the—?'

Hannah was in convulsions, watching him mutter expletives and batting images of peace and goodwill away as though being attacked.

'You're not too old to have your mouth washed out, son. You'd do well to remember that, and muddy boots off!' Kitty Kelly bossed affectionately, going back to her chopping.

Seeing that Nan's winter slaw didn't involve kale had been a relief. She'd gone a little mad with the leafy green superfood after her son's heart attack earlier in the year. He was doing great now, though, and hopefully, she'd found a happy medium with the health food.

'Jaysus wept,' Liam grunted, disentangling himself and yanking the string down before doing as he was told. 'It's not funny. I could have lost an eye.'

'What's happened to my Christmas cards?' Nora, hands on hips, surveyed the dangling string and puddle of seasons greetings piled on the floor after marching back into the kitchen.

'I'm sorry, love, but you can't have those cards hanging across the middle of the kitchen like so. A man can't risk his eyesight every time he ventures in for sustenance now, can he?'

'If you had the good manners to take that hood off when you came inside instead of standing there looking like you're heading down to Antarctica to monitor the icebergs, it wouldn't have been an issue,' Nora said, crossing the kitchen to see if she could give Kitty a hand.

Liam pushed his hood back, pulling a face at his wife behind her back.

'I saw that,' Nora sang out.

Liam and Hannah grinned at each other before she laid the cutlery she'd been holding, ready to set the table, down so she could enjoy a beefy hello cuddle.

He smelled of the outdoors, and Hannah sniffed the familiar scent of her dad, snuggling in. Ozonic and crisp like an apple with a hint of Old Spice.

'You should have told me you were coming, Pearl,' he admonished.

Hannah smiled at the nickname – Pearl, after heath pearlwort. In the warmer months, his rambles extended to amateur botany, and he'd a Connemara wildflower name for each of his daughters.

'I would have, but I knew you'd only worry, and sure, what's the point in that? Besides, it's not as if I can zip around the open roads in Doris. You know yourself, Doris barely reaches the speed limit.'

Liam chuckled, unzipping his jacket. 'Fair point, but I'm just saying there's no need to be pussyfooting around me. At my last check-up, the doctor said I could run a marathon if I'm inclined. Which I'm not, of course.'

'Of course.' Hannah grinned, watching him dislodging himself from his coat and hanging it on the back of the door. Receiving a glance over her shoulder from Nan as she tsked, 'That table's not going to set itself, Hannah,' she set to work while her mam fetched plates.

Liam washed his hands in the sink before his mam and wife could call him a heathen. 'So what is it that's brought you home then, Hannah? Is everything all right over at Bee headquarters?'

'You're not funny.' Hannah pulled a face, saved from having to explain why she'd taken her holidays early by Nora interrupting.

'I just remembered. Hannah, I've news.' Nora's eyes sparkled with the suggestion this was news her daughter would want to hear as she carted the pie over to the table and placed it centre stage. 'I'm telling you now, you won't believe it. I'm only after hearing myself last night.'

'Get on with it, Mam,' Hannah urged, pulling out a chair and sitting down. She wasn't one for gossip, so whatever it was, it had to be good.

Nora placed her hands on the back of a chair, leaning against the table conspiratorially. 'Romance is blossoming in Emerald Bay.'

Hannah's eyebrows raised. 'Between who?'

Her mam was clearly loving this.

'A certain reticent pharmacist and his lovely assistant.'

'No!' This really was breaking news.

'Yes!'

'For feck's sake, woman, spit it out and be done with it,'

Liam grumbled, having joined them at the table while Kitty hovered with the bowl of slaw and jumped in with the punchline.

'Niall Heneghan and Nuala McCarthy,' she announced triumphantly, putting the slaw down next to the pie.

'Thanks a million, Kitty.' Nora sighed. 'That was my line.'

Kitty ignored her. 'It's about time Niall saw what's been right under his nose,' she said, referring to the bay's widowed pharmacist as she fetched the salad servers.

Hannah was smiling because Nuala had been a rock for the pharmacist and his two children these last few years. That she was also head over heels for her boss was plain for all to see except Niall. 'So, what happened for Niall to finally take his blinkers off?' she asked.

'Nobody knows for certain,' Nora replied. 'But the current theory doing the rounds is Niall might have seen Nuala in a new light last St Paddy's Day when he and Nuala dressed up as Danny and Sandy from *Grease* for the parade.'

Kitty's tone was disapproving. 'Yer man would have had to have been blind not to notice Nuala in those spray-on yokes she was after squeezing into.'

'That's true,' Liam added, receiving a sharp look from his wife. 'I mean, it was a miracle she didn't split the arse out of them when she cocked a leg over Niall's motorcycle. Not that I was paying any attention. I was busy, but I heard about it.' He was beginning to waffle under his wife's intense gaze.

Hannah smirked, nudging him with her foot under the table. 'I'd quit while you're ahead, Dad.'

He duly zipped it.

'That's not all that's happened while you've been in Cork. Nora, tell Hannah about the mystery woman,' Kitty urged her daughter-in-law.

'What mystery woman?' Hannah was curious.

'The mystery American woman who's been watching your mam,' Kitty stated, her cheeks pinkened with the drama of it all.

'It's nothing,' Nora said dismissively, busying herself with the lunch things.

'That's not what you said when you burst in through the back door yesterday blathering about how you'd seen her again.' She turned conspiratorially toward Hannah. 'She was in a bit of a state.'

'What's going on, Mam?' Hannah looked first at her mam, then her nan and finally at her dad for an explanation.

Liam and Nora exchanged a look, communicating silently like married couples do. Hannah knew this look well. It meant they weren't sure how much to divulge, but it didn't matter, as Kitty pipped them both to the post once more.

'There's an American woman who's been coming and going to Emerald Bay since last Christmas who seems overly interested in your mam.'

'Like a stalker?' Hannah's eyes widened.

'No,' Nora jumped in. 'Don't talk silly. There's probably nothing to it. I've seen her a handful of times at a distance, that's all. She never lets me get close enough to ask what she's after. I'd have thought I could add hallucinations to the list of hormonal indignities the menopause brings to the party if she hadn't been asking around the village after me. People assumed she was a cousin from across the sea.'

'And no one knows who she is or where she's staying?' Hannah questioned.

A trio of heads shook.

'I'd forgotten all about her until I saw her again the other morning. You're not to be worrying your head now, Hannah. I'm sure she's perfectly harmless.'

'You don't know that. When was the first time you saw this woman?'

'After Ava's wedding last Christmas and only fleetingly.'

'Tell her what you told me, Nora,' Liam said, receiving a look that told him his wife wished he'd kept quiet.

'Mam,' Hannah pressed, not quite believing this was the first she'd heard of this strange woman.

'I've never seen her up close, you understand, but from a distance, something about her put me in mind of my mam when she was younger. It's all a bit strange. And I've probably made something out of nothing. Sure, if I managed to get close to her, I'd probably find she looked nothing like her.'

Hannah's forehead creased. The Kelly girls had never met their maternal nan because she'd cut their mam off when she'd married their dad, deeming him not good enough. It was hard to imagine a mam cutting a child off so coldly, which was why she didn't feel she'd missed out on not having met her. It was too late now, anyhow, given she'd since died. Still, it gave her a chill that, reading between the lines, Mam obviously thought this woman was a relative. Although why she wasn't making herself known was plain weird. She'd mention it to her sisters the first chance she got. Right now, though, she wouldn't get to dwell on it any longer because her mam was clapping her hands together brusquely.

'Enough of all that. Do your sisters know you're here?'

It was a neatly done change of subject.

'No. Well, Imogen does, but only because I bumped into her when I arrived.' Hannah's stomach rumbled audibly, and she wished Thomas would hurry downstairs, but only because she was starving and that pie smelled mouth-wateringly good. She'd give him another ten seconds, after which she'd not be responsible for her actions with the pie. 'I'll give them a call after lunch. I have to say it was strange arriving home and not being greeted by Napoleon.'

Nora and Kitty glanced at one another. 'We miss him too, don't we, Nora?' Kitty said, pulling a chair out.

Nora agreed. 'We got used to having the furry little fella about the place, so we did.'

'Really? Because you did a lot of moaning and telling him off when he was here.' Hannah looked from one to the other sceptically.

'It was banter, is all.' Kitty flapped her hand dismissively.

'Sure, I do an awful lot of the moaning and telling off when you girls are home, but I still miss you when you're not here,' Nora added.

'Thanks, Mam. I think.' Hannah shook her head.

'I miss the conversations we used to have.' Kitty's tone was wistful.

'Nan, he's a cat. He couldn't talk back to you.'

'Ah, but he was a grand little listener.'

'That he was,' Nora lamented.

'He's not dead. He's down the road at Shannon and James's. If you miss having an animal, why don't you get a rescue cat or kitten? They're crying out for a good home.'

'Over my dead body!' Liam thundered. 'It was bad enough with Napoleon and his thieving ways. My poor heart wouldn't be able to take a kitten leaping about the place or an old feral tomcat spraying the furnishings.'

Hannah laughed at the horror on her dad's face. 'I thought the doctor gave you a clean bill of health.'

The conversation was cut off as a shadow filled the doorway. It was Thomas.

7

Hannah watched her mam's face light up upon seeing their guest. Nora Kelly loved a full house, and her longing for a pet appeared to be forgotten at the sight of Thomas's hesitant smile. He loitered with his hands dug into his jeans pockets, waiting to be invited to join them. He'd obviously won her mam over since he'd arrived yesterday, Hannah thought. Unlike herself, and she squirmed on her seat, squashing the memory of what had happened less than forty minutes ago on the upstairs landing.

'Have you ants in your pants, Hannah?' Liam enquired with a raised bushy brow.

Mercifully, Thomas appeared not to have heard this remark. There'd been enough discussion about her underwear for one day.

Nora warmly welcomed him to come and sit down like he was her long-lost son returning home from the Great War, and Hannah took advantage of being able to check him out unde-tected as he sat down at the opposite end of the table to where her dad presided at the head.

Hmm, mid-brown hair, preppy haircut, glasses hiding a set of silvery-grey eyes, clean-shaven and a cute smile. She noticed his mouth quirking a little higher on the right, giving him a cheeky look. He was tall, lanky like a runner and dressed casually but smartly in weekend wear. Beneath his sweater, she could see the muscle definition around his broad shoulders and biceps, further suggesting someone who enjoyed marathons. He'd probably get on great guns with Imo, she thought, finishing her inventory and giving him an 'A' for *attractive* and an 'NMT' for *not my type*. His look screamed conformist, and she decided that this man her mam was fawning over was not a breaker nor a bender of the rules.

'And of course, you've already met Hannah, but let me properly introduce you,' Mam tinkled as Nan served their guest a miserly piece of pie. 'Thomas Flynn, this is my middle daughter, Hannah Kelly. And, Kitty, there's plenty to go around.' She frowned at her mother-in-law.

There was nothing for it but to put what had happened earlier behind her, because while their paths were unlikely to cross during the day, mealtimes were a different story. Her pride did not extend to missing out on Nan and Mam's cooking while she was home. As such, she steeled herself and raised her head to look Thomas square in the eye, only to see mirth glittering back at her. She gritted her teeth. Her tumbling backwards like so wasn't something to laugh about. Sure, what if she'd broken something? Hannah fumed, knowing full well that if the situation had been reversed, she'd have been crying-laughing.

'Nice to meet you again,' she mumbled insincerely, putting her nose in the air and looking away. Mam would undoubtedly be in her ear about being rude to their guest the first chance she got. Well, too bad because it wasn't Mam who'd been caught in flagrante delicto!

Liam was more interested in what Kitty was dishing him up than his daughter's haughty behaviour. 'Don't forget the pastry, like, Mam. You seem to be tunnelling under it with your spoon.

What is it you're hoping to find?' He then adopted a jokey tone, 'There's gold under that there pie!'

Kitty didn't crack a smile. 'No pastry for you, son. It's just the chicken, vegetables and lovely green slaw. It's a new recipe I'm after finding.'

'But, Mam—'

'Don't be but mamming me. 'Tis the way it is, son.'

'Kitty's looking after you,' Nora appeased, but Liam's arms were folded over his chest, and he'd slumped in his seat like a belligerent child about to shout, 'It's not fair!' However, he said, 'I've a word of advice for you, young Thomas.'

'Please, everyone, call me Tom.'

'Well, Tom, don't go having a heart attack. It's not worth the aggravation. I've had nothing but kale, cabbage and anything green grown in the ground since the summer. If it keeps up, I will wake up one morning to find sprouts growing out of my ears.'

'They're superfoods, son,' Kitty soothed.

'They're vegetables, and man can't live on vegetables alone. So don't be getting ideas about Christmas. It's the full monty I'll be having, thanks very much.'

'I don't know what you're complaining about. People are starving in the world, and there's you with plenty of chicken on your plate,' Kitty said, placing it in front of him.

'Nan's got a point, Dad.'

'Don't you be putting your ten pence in and all,' Liam shot across at his daughter.

Hannah grinned then glanced at Tom to see what he made of the bickering banter that was par for the course around the Kelly family table, albeit a diluted version, given her sisters weren't here. A smile twitched at the corners of his mouth.

Silence settled over the table as they all began to hoe in. Nora slipped another slice of pie on his plate as Tom cleared his mean serving up.

'Thanks, Mrs Kelly.'

'If I'm to call you Tom, you'll call me Nora. Fair's fair.'

'And me Liam.'

'I'll stick with Mrs Kelly.' Kitty was tight-lipped.

'Of course, Mrs Kelly,' Tom directed at her politely.

Nan was behaving strangely, and Hannah wondered what her problem was. Nora and Liam were staring at her quizzically, too.

'And thanks, Nora. This is delicious.' Tom smiled across the table.

Ten out of ten for good manners, Hannah thought.

'You're a wonderful cook.'

Good manners bordering on an apple polisher, as Nan would say. Arse licker was more Hannah's terminology.

Nora, however, puffed up like her pastry topping. 'Ah, it's only a simple chicken pot pie, but I'm after making the pastry myself. None of that pre-rolled frozen malarkey.'

'Rub it in, why don't you,' Liam grumbled.

'Home cooking is a real treat.' Tom forked up the remainder of his pie, which proved his point.

He'd just cemented himself in Mam's good books for life, though Nan clearly hadn't taken to him.

Hannah's attention returned to Tom as he explained why he was hard done by on the home-cooking front.

'My recipe repertoire is limited to bangers and mash and spag bol. I tend to order in or eat out mostly. It's easier when you're cooking for one.'

So he lived alone then. Hannah thought that he'd also unwittingly ensured he'd be sent back to wherever it was he'd come from with some frozen meals to pop in his freezer. Then, trying to redeem herself where Mam was concerned, she feigned interest. 'So, where do you call home then, Tom?'

'An apartment in Drumcondra, not far from Croke Park. And yourself?'

'Cork City in a house-share. I work for a non-profit organisation. Feed the World with Bees.'

'Hannah.' Nora Kelly's voice held a warning note. 'Cop yourself on now. Tom's no room for a hive if he's living in an apartment.'

There were a cluster of hives at the bottom of the Shamrock's beer garden thanks to Hannah doing her bit to ensure the world's bee population survived.

'Hive maybe, but have you done your Christmas shopping yet, Tom?'

'Er—'

'Because I've just the thing. I'm your one-stop Christmas shop.'

'You sound like a pushy little elf,' Liam remarked.

'She looks like one, too, with that hair,' Kitty added.

'If she were dressed in green, maybe.' Nora got the final word on the subject in.

Hannah ignored them all and began giving Tom the same spiel she'd given the foot traffic in Cork the other day. To give credit where it was due, his eyes didn't immediately glaze over as she told him about the perfect Christmas gifts still stored in the boot of her car. To her amazement, Tom leaned toward her, head tilted to one side, his body language screaming he was interested in what she had to say! And so she talked. And talked. And when she'd finally run out of things to tell him about on the bee front, her reward was an order for a ten-pack of her seed cards. He flashed her that cute grin as she said, 'The bees of the world thank you.'

Hannah's NMT verdict wavered slightly, and she was curious about him. It wasn't every day she met someone interested in what she had to say. 'So then, Tom, what's brought you to Emerald Bay in the depths of winter?'

'Work, actually.'

She hadn't expected that. Hannah wiped her assumption he

was visiting family. 'Sure, you're very dedicated, working over the weekend.'

'So are you.' Silver glints danced in his eyes.

Touché, Hannah thought, only aware of herself and Tom at the table now. She'd never met a man who suited glasses as well as he did. 'What is it you do then?'

Kitty erupted into a violent coughing fit, and Liam pushed his chair back.

The spell was broken, and Hannah felt like she was coming up for air. She turned her concerned gaze toward her nan, watching as her dad pressed a glass of water into her hand. Kitty took a grateful sip, and the cough subsided to a random hiccup.

'Sorry about that. Something went down the wrong way.' Kitty placed her knife and fork on her plate, half her meal untouched, and rose from her seat. 'I'll put the kettle on, shall I?'

'We've not finished our lunch yet, Kitty, and you've barely touched yours. Are you feeling all right?' Nora asked, concern etched between her eyebrows.

With a look of resignation, Kitty sighed and sank back into her seat. 'I'm grand. I just fancied a cup of tea.'

She didn't sound grand, Hannah thought. She was about to push her nan for more when a gust of frigid air brought her eldest sister, Shannon, and James sailing through the door. Shannon dumped the bag she was carrying and rubbed her hands together, saying something smelled good. James, however, had a bundle wrapped in a colourful sweater in his arms. Hannah could see two pointy ears twitching and not much else. What on earth was it?

For the second time that day, a piercing scream rang out, only this time it was Nora Kelly, not Hannah.

'Get that rat out of here!'

8

'Breathe, would you? In, out, slowly does it. That's it,' Shannon instructed her mam, who'd backed up against the wall.

Those still seated at the table swivelled from James and the unidentified bundle back to Nora, huffing and puffing like she would blow the house down.

'James, you'd better explain,' Shannon said as the colour returned to their mam's cheeks.

'OK, I'm sorry, Nora; we didn't mean to frighten you. It's not a rat we've brought round to meet you but rather a chihuahua.'

Fanning her face with her hand, Nora clarified, 'Definitely not a rat, or even distantly related to the rodent race then?'

'No, very much part of the canine community,' James confirmed.

'You heard the man, Nora. She's the Thumbelina of the doggy world, and there's you making a song and dance.' Liam smirked.

'Don't you dare be laughing at me, Liam Kelly, or it will be the nut roast for you on Christmas Day.'

Hannah sneaked a peek at Tom, who was grinning as he

listened to the banter, and smiled herself. Too late, she realised Shannon had tracked her gaze, and her eyes were gleaming as she registered that Hannah was home and a strange man was sitting at the table, too. From the knowing grin spreading across her face, Hannah guessed her sister was putting two and two together and coming up with five. Before she could explain that Tom was a paying guest, not *her* guest, Shannon introduced herself and James.

'I'm Shannon Kelly, Hannah's big sister, and this is my partner, James. He's not long moved to Ireland from Massachusetts. We live in one of the cottages at the edge of the village.'

'Why don't you give him your personal public service number while you're at it, Shan?' Hannah muttered.

'Pleased to meet you both. I'm Tom Flynn. I'm down from Dublin for work.' His smile from one to the other was warm.

Shannon's face fell upon hearing this, and James covered what would have been an awkward moment by saying, 'And while we're on introductions – everybody, I'd like you to meet Princess Leia. She sees me regularly at the practice to monitor her low blood sugar. It's pretty common in toy breeds.'

Hannah was amused to see Shannon swiftly move on from her disappointment that Hannah and Tom weren't an item. Her sister looked up at James, giving his professional patter about caring for Princess Leia, as though he were walking on water.

'Her owner, Mrs Tansey, telephoned me on my mobile first thing this morning, in a state.'

'What was it had your poor woman blathering?' Nora asked.

'A fall. She's been admitted into hospital with a suspected broken hip.'

'Oh dear! How on earth did that happen?'

'What does it matter how it happened, Nora? She fell,' Liam stated.

Nora shot him a look that suggested he'd just taken a step closer to that nut roast.

'She slipped on the icy pavement,' Shannon informed her mam.

Kitty was making tutting noises about being surprised it didn't happen more often and how you took your life in your hands stepping out the door in Emerald Bay in December.

'She's asked me to take Princess Leia while she's in hospital,' James explained.

Liam asked the obvious. 'Why you and not family?'

'There is no one nearby. Mrs Tansey is a widow, and her daughters both live in England. Princess Leia's her baby, and worrying over what's happening with her won't help while she's in hospital,' James said.

'We can't have her at home, not with Napoleon and Harry. She bit both of them within seconds of us bringing her back to the cottage earlier.' Shannon looked imploringly at her dad, then her mam and finally her nan. 'The poor dote just needs somewhere to stay for a few days.'

Harry, James's placid beagle who'd not long arrived from America, was having a tough time. Hannah recalled Shannon telling her Napoleon had soon made it clear who was boss.

Liam got up from his chair and began backing toward the wall where his wife had taken refuge. Both hands were held up to ward Shannon, James and Princess Leia off.

'Ah, no, you don't. Sure, we've only just got rid of a klepto-maniac knicker-thieving cat. We don't want a nippy little ankle-biter about the place. Do we, Nora? Mam?'

Nora, however, had joined Kitty for a closer look at the little dog. Both women were cooing.

'You're rather sweet, aren't you?' Kitty said, tickling behind Princess Leia's ears.

'Yip-yap.'

Nora looked back over her shoulder at her husband. 'The

poor little love needs fostering, Liam, and you know yourself, we never turn anyone away who needs help.'

'We do dogs, especially chihuahuas,' Liam stated.

'How long roughly do you think she'd be with us?' Kitty was asking James.

'Hopefully no more than a week, but I can't say for sure until I hear from Mrs Tansey what the doctors say.'

'Mam. No,' Liam implored.

'Hush up now, son. You two will be the best of friends before the day's out, mark my words.'

Hannah caught Tom's eye. His hand covered his mouth, but his creased eyes and shaking shoulders gave the game away. It was pretty funny. The odds weren't on Liam's side as the little dog peered over the blankets, and with one look at the glossy, soulful, black eyes looking out, the Kelly women melted.

Liam wasn't giving in without a fight, and he beseeched Tom. 'As our guest, it's only fair that you cast the deciding vote.'

The tips of Tom's ears reddened as he found himself the focus of attention.

'Don't be putting Hannah's poor fella on the spot like so, Dad,' Shannon admonished.

Hannah's face ignited like a gas hob, and both she and Tom spoke simultaneously. 'We're not together!'

'I was just double-checking,' Shannon replied.

'Tom's already said he's in Emerald Bay for business.' Nora said. 'You're an architectural— What's your official title again, Tom?'

If Hannah could have got away with rolling her eyes, she would have – Mam was a sucker for long job titles.

Tom smiled at Nora as he got up from the table, 'An architectural project manager. It's a bit of a mouthful.'

'Did you hear that, Hannah?' Nora looked at her daughter.

What was she supposed to do, give him three cheers? The gift of being subtle wasn't something her mam or any of her family had been blessed with. 'I sure did, Mam. An architectural project manager.' Hannah rolled it off her tongue, not liking its implications. 'What exactly are you architecturally project managing in Emerald Bay then, Tom?'

Tom didn't pick up on the drop in temperature where Hannah was concerned or hear Kitty's muttered, 'Here we go,' as he pushed his chair in and picked up his plate. 'It's a large-scale project for these parts. A garden centre with a cafe, gift shop and Christmas tree farm. It'll be called the Greenhouse and will be a drawcard for Emerald Bay.'

His smile suggested he 100 per cent believed what he'd just said, Hannah thought incredulously, unable to believe she'd been fraternising, bordering on flirting, with the enemy. And he wasn't finished either.

'The proposed site is on a plot of disused land near here, and I'm down to scope it out.' He set his plate on the worktop and advanced on Princess Leia. Then, shooting Liam an apologetic grin, said, 'Sorry, Liam, but she's pretty cute.'

Liam slumped in his chair, a man defeated.

Hannah hadn't moved past Tom's remark that his eyesore project would bring people to the area, and she voiced her thoughts on what he'd said, ice mingling with steel in her tone. 'I would have thought the Atlantic Ocean, castle ruins, blanket bog, picturesque village and general natural beauty of the area would have been all the drawcard necessary for our little corner of the world.'

Liam, Nora, Kitty, Shannon and even James watched Hannah with a wary eye, knowing a storm was brewing, but Tom was oblivious.

'Well, I've got a Zoom meeting in a few minutes. Thanks for a delicious lunch, Nora. Nice to meet you, Shannon, James, and you too, Princess Leia.' After a final scratch behind the chihuahua's ears, Tom excused himself.

'What's up with you, Ms Frosty Knickers?' Shannon asked her sister once Tom was out of earshot.

'This Greenhouse your man's here to project manager.' Hannah jabbed at the ceiling as Tom creaked about overhead. 'It can't go ahead.'

'I don't know what you think you can do about it,' Liam said, eyeing Princess Leia, whose pointy little face was the only thing visible from her swaddles. 'James, lad, sit down. You're making me nervous.'

James passed his doggy bundle to Shannon instead. 'Now we know she's staying, I'll fetch her basket and toys from the car.'

'I'm with Hannah.' Kitty surprised everyone as she emerged from the press, clutching the shortbread tin. 'Not only will it kill our local businesses, but that land's part of our heritage, as is the famine cottage.'

'Well said, Nan.'

'I hadn't thought about it, to be honest. But you make a solid case against it, Nan. What do you think, Mam, Dad?' Shannon asked.

Liam was gazing hopefully at the shortbread tin now being offered to Shannon. 'To be frank with you, Shannon, it's hard to think when you have a hankering for your dear mammy's shortbread. One little piece, g'won. Sure, what harm can it do?'

But with lightning speed, the lid was snapped down.

'Jaysus, Mam, with that reaction time, it's no wonder you're always after winning the bingo. I could have lost my fingers!'

Kitty made a tut-tutting noise. 'It's not your day, is it, son?'

'I don't know why you're both so fired up. Sure, there's not even planning permission for the project,' Nora said. 'And Tom's a lovely lad. He's single, too. I checked. You could do a lot worse for yourself, Hannah.'

'You can nip that idea right in the bud, Mam. It's not happening. He's the enemy as far as I'm concerned.'

'Nora, it's all well and good to say this Greenhouse business isn't even permitted yet, but there's no smoke without fire. The abandoned farm and famine cottage sit on government land, so mark my words, all it will take for the project to get the green light is the greasing of a few palms in the right departments.'

'Nan's right,' Hannah said, knowing that no matter what her mam had to say about Tom being a lovely lad, the next time she saw him, she'd tell him exactly what she thought about his project. Guest of the Shamrock or not, she'd make sure he high-tailed it back to Dublin.

9

Princess Leia was settled in her basket in the kitchen corner, seemingly content with her new surroundings. She lapped up the attention of the Kelly women but bared her gnashers whenever Liam looked her way.

Hannah would have found this funny if she hadn't been so keyed up, itching to head upstairs, tap on Mr Whizz-Bang Project Manager's door and tell him exactly what she thought. However, Mam would have her guts for garters if she were to do so.

Instead, she resolved to duck into the pub and find out which villagers were on her side as soon as Shannon and James headed off. They weren't showing any signs of leaving, though, she thought with annoyance. Shannon was busy texting now, and James was fidgeting in his seat as though there was something he wanted to say.

She wasn't the only one who noticed.

'What's going on with you there, James?' Kitty asked. 'You've ants in your pants, so you have.'

'Enough with all the pants references,' Hannah said, immediately wishing she hadn't spoken when she saw her mam opening her mouth. 'Don't you dare, Mam!'

'I have to. It's too good not to share.' Like James, Nora looked fit to burst.

Bracing for what was coming, Hannah slunk further down in her seat as her mam relayed in painful detail how she'd made a holy show of herself in front of their guest. Shannon was wiping her eyes, and James appeared to momentarily forget whatever had had him behaving like a cat on a hot tin roof as he joined in the laughter.

Liam, however, remained straight-faced. 'Hannah Kelly, it's not a good idea to be getting about the place in your knickers. I hope you don't carry on like that in your house-share. You'll be giving your housemates the wrong idea.'

'Dad, you are such a prude! And you missed the whole point of the story.' Shannon gasped. 'Hannah didn't think anybody was home, let alone a strange man.'

'Well, if she'd let us know her plans beforehand, it wouldn't have been an issue,' Liam replied, echoing what Nora and Kitty had both already said.

'Excuse me, I am still in the room, you know,' Hannah said, eyeballing her sister. Then she added, 'We're even-stevens now.'

'What do you mean?'

Keen to turn the spotlight away from herself, Hannah elaborated, 'Have you forgotten about the time you were parading about behind the bar in front of Father Seamus with your skirt caught up in your holey old tights?'

'And then you showed me upstairs to my room,' James added, grinning from ear to ear at the memory. He received a playful swat from Shannon.

'Low blow, Hannah,' her sister said, but her eyes twinkled.

Hannah felt better now everyone was cackling over Shannon's unfortunate flash. She watched as her sister got up and fetched her laptop from her bag. 'What are you up to?'

'You'll see.' Shannon opened it up on the table. Then she picked up her phone and banged out another text.

'Who're you texting?' Hannah asked, sensing something was afoot.

'Imo. She and Ryan are supposed to be here by now; they're bringing Maeve.'

As though Shannon had magicked them up, the door to the bar opened, bringing a burst of laughter from inside the pub with it. Ryan, followed by Imogen and little Maeve Doolin, James's grandmother, crowded into the kitchen and began unravelling layers.

Imogen spoke up, unwinding her scarf. 'Sorry we're a little late, everyone, but we were collared by Enda and Mr Kenny in the pub. This garden centre and the Christmas tree farm business are a hot topic. There's a lot of people who aren't happy about it.'

Hannah's ears pricked up. She'd message Dylan later and ask whether he thought putting a petition together to present to the architectural project arse sleeping under the Shamrock's roof was a good idea. It was an excuse to contact him, and she wouldn't suffer the wrath of Mam for accosting a guest and berating him about what the hell he thought he was doing in Emerald Bay.

'Proposed garden centre and Christmas tree farm,' Hannah quickly clarified.

Nora held her hand up. 'Don't go there. We've talked enough about that this afternoon; on the bright side, it's brought Hannah home to us early.'

Hannah tucked her thoughts away and got up to greet Ryan.

'For or against?' Ryan asked, zeroing in to give Hannah a burly squeeze.

'What do you think? Against obviously. You?'

Imogen butted in. 'It's tricky. The site will need contractors.' She glanced toward Ryan.

'I can't afford to turn work down,' he confirmed. 'Although I'll be sad to see the old farm carved up. I loved playing there as a kid.'

'We all did,' Hannah said, engulfing Maeve in a fond hello hug before fetching her a chair.

'Don't get me wrong now.' Nora's confusion was evident. 'Imogen and Ryan, this is your home, too, and, Maeve, you know you're part of the family, but I'm beginning to wonder if I've had a menopausal moment.'

'What do you mean, Mam?' Imogen asked as she and Ryan sat themselves down.

'Am I after inviting youse all for afternoon tea? Because if that's the case, I can have a batch of scones on the table in under twenty minutes.'

Imogen laughed. 'No, Mam, you're grand. It was Shannon who asked us to pop round and pick Maeve up on our way.'

Shannon was busy on her laptop.

Suddenly, Imogen's eyes rounded, and her mouth formed an 'O' as she silently pointed at the basket tucked away in the kitchen corner.

'That's Princess Leia, our short-term foster dog,' Liam informed Imogen, Ryan and Maeve none too happily. 'James, would you care to elaborate.'

'Princess Leia,' Maeve spoke up. 'That's Jean Tansey's little dog. Is she all right?'

James explained the situation while Ryan got up to say hello to the little dog, his solid builder's frame crouching down to pet her. There was a growl, and he straightened quickly, an indignant expression on his face as he turned toward the table. 'She bit me.'

'Really? She doesn't exactly look vicious, Ryan.' Imogen was sceptical.

'She's not.' Shannon looked up from the laptop. 'She's a total sweetie.'

'Well, don't expect me to shower you in sympathy if she gives you a nip.' Ryan shook his hand. 'She's sharp little teeth. Like a rat's.'

'Exactly,' Liam replied like a man vindicated.

Imogen warily ventured over to see for herself and received a dainty little lick.

'She likes you,' Shannon said, smiling. 'Maybe it's men she's a thing about. She's not used to being around them because Mrs Tansey lives alone.'

'She was all right with James.'

'But she knows James.'

Then Shannon began waving and smiling into her laptop. 'How're you?'

Grace's voice rang out from the London canal boat she shared with her boyfriend, Chris: 'Is it Hannah we're waiting on?'

'No, she's made a surprise visit home. She's here.'

Hannah got up and moved around the table to peer over Shannon's shoulder. She was surprised to see not only Grace and Chris peering over her shoulder but also Ava and Shane waving out from another box at her. Three other men she didn't recognise pinged into the Zoom screen.

This better not be some sort of Tinder-Zoom dating intervention, Hannah thought, waiting for her sister to greet the newcomers so she could find out what was going on.

'Hi, Alex, how're you, Oliver and Braydon?'

The names rang a bell, and hearing their American twangs as they greeted Shannon, she twigged. They were James's brothers. She moved out of the way so James could squish in beside her.

Nora and Kitty were jostling, trying to get a look in, and Nora, peering over the top of Shannon's head, waved at everybody before tapping her on the shoulder. 'I think you better tell me what this is all about, Shannon.'

'Well,' Shannon said coyly into the screen then twisted to see her mam, dad, nan, Imogen, Ryan and Hannah, who'd all joined the huddle now, 'babysitting Princess Leia is going to be good practice for you all.'

Blank faces stared back at Shannon and James, who were both grinning like idiots. Voices clamoured over the top of one another from the laptop.

It was Kitty who twigged first. 'You're not?'

'I am!' Shannon squealed. 'I'm pregnant. Four months today. God, it's been so hard keeping quiet!' Her smile stretched from ear to ear, as did James's.

Hannah forgot all about what had brought her home early as she soaked in the happy news. She was going to be an aunt!

10

Nora's hands clapped together in delight. 'Our first grandchild! Oh, Liam!' Happy tears rolled down her cheeks while Liam slapped James on the back.

Group hugs were had before questions began firing from the laptop and those in the kitchen.

'Have you felt sick?'

'What's your due date?'

'Do you know what you're having?'

'It's way too early for that, Dad, and we won't be finding out the baby's sex. We don't care one way or the other.'

'No, I don't either, of course, but a little boy would be nice. You know, even up the odds,' Liam said.

Shannon laughed.

'The little bean will be what he, she or they will be, Liam,' Kitty declared.

'That's very modern of you, Nan.'

'I'm up with the play.'

The laughter, love and excitement filled the kitchen from near and as far away as London, New York and Massachusetts.

The celebration didn't take long to spill through to the pub.

Looking around at the familiar faces putting the world to rights over their pints or tipples of choice, Hannah wished the twins and their fellas were here to celebrate the happy news, too. Her eyes settled on James, who had his arm wrapped protectively around Maeve's shoulder while gazing adoringly at Shannon.

What would it be like to have Dylan look at her like that? An unidentifiable quiver shot through her at the very thought.

But then she remembered that James had recently lost his mother, and Maeve her long-lost daughter. They must wish she was still with them to share the happy news, and for a moment, sadness weighed down on her shoulders. The thought that Hazel, with her angel wings, would look down on this happy scene, watching over her birth mother, son, and Shannon, cheered her up.

After congratulating her sister and chatting a bit, Hannah was happy to sit back and soak up the pub's cosy atmosphere. She took it all in, skimming over the fittings and furnishings of the Shamrock Inn to the frames hung haphazardly with photographs of Emerald Bay's villagers, both present and past. The pictures alluded to the strong sense of community that kept its residents here.

The absence of a Christmas tree was noted, as was the lack of festive decorations. It was unlike Mam to leave this so late, but she'd been busier than usual, keeping an eye on Dad. Given the countdown to Christmas was on, Hannah had no doubt she'd be roped into draping tinsel and whatnot and helping her dad fetch the Nordmann fir that would tower precariously in the corner of the Shamrock this year.

The thought of choosing Christmas trees saw her mind turn toward Tom. She prided herself on being a good judge of character. How had she managed to fail so miserably where he was concerned? It was his hand offered to help her up earlier that had thrown her, she decided. It had been a solid, trustworthy grip, of someone who had principles. A comforting hand...

'Hannah, help Chloe behind the bar, would you?' Liam called over, pushing her thoughts about the architectural arse aside as he shattered her intentions to lounge fireside, drink in hand.

Hannah had fancied whiling away the afternoon accepting complimentary beverages and congratulations on the happy news once it was announced there would be a new generation of Kellys and that she would be an aunt. It was an important role, after all. She sighed. Her mam and dad deserved to savour the news alongside Shannon, James and Maeve. She wouldn't make a fuss.

Then, seeing Imogen flop into the seat she'd had her eye on, she hesitated, pulling a face. The only reason Dad had pointed the finger at her to help out was because Imogen was with Ryan. It wasn't fair, she thought with a pang for Dylan. If he was here with her, Imo might have to get off her arse and help out. However, this wasn't the time for foot stamping, and she slid in behind the bar, greeting Chloe, who was pouring Enda Dunne his pint of Guinness.

'How're you, young Hannah?' Enda called over.

'Grand, Enda.' She smiled down the bar to where the retired farmer was perched on his usual barstool. She was the only one of the Kelly sisters whose name he got right. It was down to her hair, she'd decided. 'How's tricks?'

'They'd be better if your father was pulling me a pint. Liam Kelly's a man who knows how to pour a Guinness.' He glowered at Chloe.

But she wasn't in the least fazed as she told him to stop his moaning because, sure, wasn't she taught by the maestro himself, before rolling her eyes at Hannah.

Hannah grinned at the young girl who helped out behind the bar at the Shamrock and began serving the regulars. She'd know her way around the bar with a blindfold, she thought, going through the motions. The Guinness mirror could do with a wipe, and as for the bric-a-brac crowded in between glasses and bottles, she could see Mam handing her a bottle of Brasso and a cloth this week, too. There was no such thing as free lodgings under the Kelly family roof!

Dermot Molloy, the butcher, was chatting with her when a lull in his monologue about the art of sausage-making gave her the chance to bring up the new development. But all she managed to get out was, 'Dermot, it can't go ahead,' before her dad began to ring the bell. Slowly, the general hubbub of chatter filling the pub died away until only the crackle of the logs in the fireplace could be heard.

'Nora and I have an announcement to make on behalf of the Kelly family.'

Clearly, Dad had decided her eldest sister's news was his to share.

Shannon, who was nursing an orange juice, turned pink, and James's chest puffed out as he rested his hand on her shoulder. The proud daddy-to-be.

Nora moved to stand alongside her husband while Kitty nearby couldn't contain her smile. She was fidgeting from foot to foot, fit to burst with the happy news herself.

Liam cleared his throat and received a 'get on with it' elbow in the ribs from Nora. 'The Kelly family has some happy news to share with you all. We've just been given an unexpected and exciting early Christmas gift. Our beautiful eldest daughter Shannon and her, er...'

'Partner,' Nora hissed.

'Partner, James, have just told us that, come summer, we're to be grandparents!'

Excited chatter whipped up like embers being fanned into flame, and someone – Hannah couldn't see who but fancied it was Evan Kennedy – called out, 'Congratulations!'

'There's a free drink at the bar for you to celebrate this happy day with the family and me. And when you've all freshened your glasses, I hope you'll join me in toasting the parents-to-be,' Liam announced, receiving more cheers.

'Not a long-drawn-out one, like, Liam.'

Now that was definitely Evan Kennedy, Hannah thought before adding a silent, 'Thanks a million, Dad.' Then, turning to Chloe, she said, 'Brace yourself. We're about to be run off our feet.'

Chloe barely managed a nod before stools and chairs were scraped back so swiftly some were in danger of toppling over. The sound was thunderous, like the annual buffalo migration in America, as the villagers stampeded for the bar. It was every man, woman and even child for themselves because the free drink must apply to fizz and hopefully a bag of crisps, too!

Some ten minutes later, with the expectant parents toasted, Hannah and Chloe wiped their brows and exchanged a mutual glance of 'thank goodness that's over'. Chloe shot off to the loo, and Hannah began stacking the glass washer. She was aware of someone having appeared at the bar waiting to be served, and after setting the washer to run, she looked up with a smile.

But it faded when she saw who was standing there.

11

‘A pint of Harp, please.’ Tom smiled that lopsided grin Hannah had noticed earlier, but it left her cold this time. Her own smile was fully gone now, as if she'd had a bucket of ice water thrown over her.

Tom was oblivious. Looking about, he said, ‘Everyone seems in good form.’

‘And one on the house for Tom, too, Hannah,’ Liam bellowed.

Hannah refused to make eye contact with Tom as she fetched a glass and curtly explained, ‘Shannon and James announced they're expecting their first baby earlier.’

‘Congratulations! That's a brilliant early Christmas present.’

He didn't know them. He didn't know any of them. Even though his tone sounded warm and genuine, Hannah was irked.

‘It's not me having the baby,’ she retorted snippily, ‘but I'll be sure to pass it on.’

This time, glancing up, she saw bewilderment at her stand-offishness flickering in his grey eyes. Tough, she thought, busying herself pouring his pint. Too bad if he couldn't figure out what her issue was. There was no time to get into what had changed her attitude toward him, not with Isla Mullins, the shops on Main Street closed now, tapping her fingers on the bar, waiting to be served.

'Er, thanks. Cheers then, Hannah.' Tom raised his glass, giving her a searching look, but she gave nothing away. Then, hearing his name being called by Liam, he headed off to join him and Nora.

Hannah rustled up a smile for Isla. 'The same again, is it, Isla?'

'Thanks a million,' Isla confirmed before leaning over the bar like she was about to bestow great words of wisdom. 'Now listen up, Hannah. I've a lovely selection of novelty Babygros in the shop, so I do.'

'Lovely,' Hannah murmured, thinking, *Bully for you, Isla*, as she fetched the bottle to refill the Irish-souvenir-shop owner's stemmed glass.

'So I'll set one aside for you then, shall I?'

'One what?'

'Keep up with the play, Hannah. A Babygro. I think the limited-edition design in green with the Celtic tree of life emblem would go down a treat.'

'It's early days for buying gifts. Shannon's only four months along.'

'Sure, that doesn't matter. Wasn't I just after telling you the Babygro is green? Green's gender neutral, you know.'

Jaysus, the woman did not give up. Thankfully, Eileen Carroll came along to rescue her at that moment. Glad of the distraction, Hannah turned her attention to the knitting shop owner, leaving Isla to mosey off, still muttering about Babygros.

''Tis happy news, Hannah. Shannon's a great girl altogether for putting a smile that wide on your mammy and daddy's faces.'

'It is that, Eileen. A top-up, is it?'

'Grand.' Eileen slid her glass toward Hannah. 'You'll be ever so excited at becoming an aunt for the first time.'

'You're not wrong there.' Hannah refilled her glass, aware she was beaming from ear to ear at the thought.

'Well, I'm an aunt many times over, and take it from the horse's mouth: it's the knitting you'll need to be cracking on with because a baby needs a layette and a wool blanket.'

'I'll stop you right there then. Nan's the knitter. She'll see the baby right.'

'You know yourself knitting is a life skill, Hannah.' This was followed by a derisive sniff. 'I'm surprised your nan isn't after teaching you. We must pass our knowledge on to the generations coming through, or they'll be lost forever.'

Hannah thought that was erring on the dramatic side, adding in defence of her nan, 'Oh, she tried, but it's a little like the parallel parking. I'm afraid I'm a lost cause.' She decided an excuse to exit this conversation was needed, her eyes alighting on a table full of empty glasses. 'Best I crack on and clear some tables – Mam's after shooting me daggers. So, if you'll excuse me.'

But Eileen wasn't to be deterred. 'There's no such thing as a lost cause. It's the right teacher you need, is all. And I know just the woman to teach you.' Her smile was saintly.

Too late, Hannah realised where this conversation was headed.

'I'm after running a two-week evening learn-to-knit class for you young ones, Monday to Friday from seven sharp until nine p.m. in the run-up to Christmas. I'll even give you a discount on account of your happy news. Your little niece or nephew will thank you when they're all snuggled up in their little woolly blanket.' And just like a boat in the wind, Eileen sailed off.

'Why do you have a face like a slapped arse?' Nora

enquired, placing the empty glasses she'd beaten Hannah over to clear down on the bar.

'Eileen Carroll just roped me into knitting classes five nights a week until Christmas,' Hannah groaned because that had not featured in her plans. She had so much to do and only ten working days in which to do it.

'You knitting!' Nora exclaimed incredulously before bursting into laughter.

Her mam's mood was giddy with the news she was to become a nana – either that or the bubbles had gone to her head. Still, the idea of her whipping up a pair of booties wasn't *that* hilarious.

'Sure, I remember that pillowslip you made at school. The seam split the first time I tried to pull it over a pillow. I don't think you'd be a natural at knitting. Oh no, Hannah, it's best you tell Eileen it's not for you. I wouldn't want you making an eejit of yourself now.'

'Eejit' was laying it on a bit thick, Hannah thought, disgruntled. 'Thanks for the vote of confidence. Sure, it's a sad day when your own mammy has no faith in you. Eileen sees potential even if you don't.' She held her hands up. 'You watch this space, Mam. These hands will be whipping up the softest baby vests and cardigans in no time.'

'If you say so,' Nora replied, smirking as she walked off.

'What are you doing?' Imogen demanded, plonking her and Ryan's empty glasses on the bar top and eyeing Hannah. 'Some sort of wrist exercises?'

Hannah, her hands clenched in fists, was twirling her wrists in one direction and then the other. 'I've no choice but to get in shape,' she said.

'What for? The wrist Olympics?'

'Ha ha. Eileen Carroll has roped me into knitting classes now that I'm to be an aunt.'

'You?' Imogen's snort saw several heads turn her way.

'Shut up, Imo. Yes me. I'm starting on Monday evening.'

'*Right*.' Imogen said this in a slow, drawn-out manner that suggested her sister had lost the plot.

'Same again?' Hannah asked tersely. She'd wipe the smirk off her sister's face when she became the favourite aunt thanks to all the cool woollen garments that were going to be coming her niece or nephew's way.

'Thanks.'

Then, as Hannah fetched the drinks, Imogen's voice became sly. 'That Tom, who's in Room 5, has been asking all about you, Han. I think you've got yourself an admirer. It must have been the flash of those sensible, sustainable cotton knickers that did it.'

'Feck off, Imo.' Hannah pulled a face. So Shannon had told her about the incident on the landing earlier. No surprise there. She didn't pause in her pint-pulling as she added, 'And for your information, even if he was the last man in Ireland, I'd not be interested.'

'Why? I think he's cute in a nerdy kind of way. He puts me in mind of Clark Kent. Try picturing him whipping off his glasses and turning into Superman.' Imogen waggled her eyebrows lewdly.

Hannah's mouth didn't so much as twitch. 'I already said your man over there isn't my type.' She looked to where he was laughing at whatever her dad was saying. He was an interloper. Sure, look at him worming his way in over there.

'And what exactly is your type then? Mr Invisible.'

'You're not funny. And my type is someone who values our planet and wants to make it better for the next generation.' Dylan sprang to mind. 'Not an architectural arse who blows into town and destroys local business along with the country-side to build a feck off big garden centre and Christmas tree farm. What do we need a Christmas tree farm on our doorstep for?'

Imogen's eyebrows knitted together. 'So that's why he's staying at the Shamrock? To scope out the work site?'

'Proposed work site, and yep.' Hannah plonked a pint in front of her sister.

'Well, he's only doing his job. You do realise someone's employed him to do it. He's not the bigwig who'll own the complex.'

'He might as well be.' Hannah had made her mind up about Tom Flynn, and her opinion wouldn't be swayed.

'What are you all looking so serious about?' Shannon slotted in alongside Imogen with her empty glass. 'I really shouldn't have another OJ, given how much time I'm spending in the jacks these days, but I'll push the boat out since we're celebrating. Oh, and crisps, please, Hannah. Two packets since I'm officially eating for two.'

Hannah tossed over two different-flavoured bags of crisps. 'No Freya?' She realised she hadn't seen the owner of Mermaids art gallery and bespoke jewellery shop, and Shannon's best friend, at all that afternoon. She'd surely be on her side regarding this Greenhouse project.

'She's scoping out galleries around Kerry this weekend with Oisin.' Shannon's grimace upon mentioning Freya's fickle fella's name spoke volumes.

'Have you told her the news?'

'Of course. She was delighted obviously.'

'You didn't tell her before us, I hope?' Imogen said.

Shannon squirmed.

'But we're your sisters!' Hannah and Imogen chimed in a put-out duet.

'Yes, but you've both also got big blabbermouths, and I didn't want it getting out until I was through the first trimester.'

There wasn't much either sister could say to that. They knew they'd have struggled not to let the happy news slip until Shannon gave them the all-clear.

As Nora breezed past, a radiant grandmother enjoying all the pats on the back as though she'd had a hand in the conception, Hannah remembered the conversation in the kitchen earlier regarding the mysterious woman Mam thought was watching her. She raised the subject with her sisters, wondering if they'd heard mention of it. 'I've only just remembered what happened with your and James's news, Shan, but it's weird, don't you think? Especially the part about her resemblance to Mam's mother.'

'It's weird all right. Mam was after telling me yesterday. Nan's right – she was in a bit of a flap,' Imogen said. 'I feel bad now for forgetting all about it.'

'Me too,' Shannon joined in. 'It went out of my head, what with finally being able to tell you I'm up the duff and sorting out Princess Leia.'

'I wonder who she is?' Hannah mused, wiping a patch of spilled ale on the bar top, aware the hairs on her arm had stood up.

Imogen rubbed the back of her neck. 'I don't suppose we'll find out unless she decides to make herself known to Mam.'

Hannah's musings about the mystery woman following her mam were interrupted when she felt her phone vibrate in her pocket. Pulling it out, she saw she'd missed a call from Dylan, and her hand trembled as she fumbled the phone. He'd already texted her. What was so important he needed to speak to her? Desperate to find out, she said, 'Imo, give Chloe a hand while I take ten, would you?'

'But I was just about to—'

Imogen's protest fell on deaf ears because Hannah had already walked off.

12

'Hi, Dylan.' Hannah hoped she sounded casual and chilled and not like a mouse squeaking.

'Hey. Sorry to bug you on the weekend.' His voice rolled into her ear, sending a quiver through her that would make a girl blush.

Hannah absentmindedly stroked Princess Leia, whom she'd plopped on her lap, as the excitable quivers were replaced by a spasm of shame. He was probably ringing to see if she'd offloaded any Christmas seed cards. Doris's boot was still full of the boxes she'd carted home with her, and she knew she'd missed a prime opportunity to flog them while manning the bar. She could have opened a box on the bar top and run through her bee pitter-patter with every free pint pulled. There was nothing like on-the-house ale to put Emerald Bay's villagers in good humour.

'I've been thinking about what you said yesterday about being up against getting this garden centre thing stopped with Christmas so close, and I want to help.'

Hannah stopped petting Princess Leia. This was music to her ears! Wait until she told Nan! Dylan was a man who didn't back down, and it was his dedication to what he believed in that had initially attracted her to him. That and his devastatingly swarthy good looks. She was only human, after all.

'Hannah, are you still there?'

'Yeah.' She was at a loss for what to say other than, 'Thanks.'

'Have you put anything in motion?'

She didn't want to say no, and Dylan didn't like excuses. It was a straight answer he was looking for. So, knowing he wouldn't want to hear she'd been busy with her family and manning the bar, she told him who they were harbouring at the Shamrock Inn. 'I'm going to tell Tom Flynn what I think of his Greenhouse and where he can put it.'

'I wouldn't.'

That wasn't the response Hannah had expected. 'Why not?'

'You're better to keep your enemies closer. It's how you get information, and information is king.'

'Be friendly with him, you mean?'

'You've more to gain.'

Hannah was shaking her head even though Dylan couldn't see her because it sounded sneaky, and the sneaky gene wasn't in her DNA.

'What else are you going to do?'

She'd not thought about it, but again, this wouldn't do, so she blurted, 'My nan's on board. Together, we'll get as many signatures as possible to take to the Department of Agriculture.' Thanks to Google, Hannah knew the records for the old farm would have passed to the Department of Agriculture when the Land Commission was dissolved in the nineties.

'Good luck with that.'

'What do you mean?'

'If you go down the petition route, the thing will be built by the time any of those paper pushers even glance at it.'

'Well, what do you think we should do?'

'What I told you. Play nice with your man and find out who

the purchaser is behind the land deal. You need a name, Hannah, so we can hit whoever is behind this where it hurts. Look, I've got to go. You get that name, and I'll set things in motion.'

His use of 'we' saw the quivers return, and she sat staring at her phone for a long time after he'd hung up. Dylan's suggestion that she get friendly with Tom wasn't sitting comfortably with her. Still, sometimes, you had to take things further than you were comfortable with, especially for the greater good.

It was no good sitting here, Hannah decided. After plopping a disgruntled Princess Leia back in her basket, she pushed the connecting door open and headed back into the pub.

Hannah saw that Tom was still ingratiating himself with her mam. She ignored Imogen's glare from behind the bar and sidled up to them.

Nora let whatever she'd been saying fall away mid-sentence as she focused on her daughter. 'And where did you disappear to?'

'I just ducked through to the kitchen to return a call.'

'Well, I'm after telling Tom how we spend Christmas, and he's after telling me about this French bistro in Dublin that sounds right up my alley he dined at last Christmas Eve. Your father and I have an anniversary coming up. I might see if I can talk him into whisking me away to the Big Smoke to celebrate in the new year.'

'Mam's a Francophile, but Dad's more of a heathenphile, so I don't fancy her chances,' Hannah explained to Tom, making him laugh. 'So are you a Christmasphile then?'

Tom's smile faded. 'Far from it.'

Hannah picked up on the change in his mood, but Nora was too busy talking to notice.

'Don't pay any attention to her. Liam can be as cultured as the next man when the fancy takes him.'

'Nora Kelly, c'mere t'me now so we can toast your Shannon's happy news,' Clare Sheedy, unusually chipper thanks to the third glass of sherry she was waving about, called out.

Nora excused herself, and Hannah sent a silent thank you to Clare, even though, with Mam gone, she and Tom were left standing alongside one another in awkward silence. Oh, how she wished she was the flirtatious type, but witty tête-à-têtes didn't trip easily off her tongue. So she said the first thing that came to mind. 'What do you like doing in your spare time then, Tom?'

Jesus wept, she thought. *I sounded like I was touting for business on Tinder.*

Tom lowered the pint he'd been about to sup from and replied, 'To be honest, my work doesn't allow for much spare time. Trying to master work-life balance might be a New Year's resolution. What about yourself?'

That threw her. What did she do? 'Erm, I think that might be one of my resolutions, too. I kind of live and breathe my causes.'

'That's admirable, though.'

'Thanks.' It was also lonely. That was something a lot of people didn't understand. How you could be lonely even when you were surrounded by like-minded people. Hannah thought of Dylan. 'Although, I am going to be taking up knitting.'

'Knitting?' Tom raised an eyebrow.

She recounted how she'd been roped into learning the craft by Eileen Carroll.

'It would be quite therapeutic, I'd imagine. What with all that repetitive hand movement.'

'Better than smoking,' Hannah replied, unable to tell if he was being serious or not. 'And it will be that – or incredibly frustrating.' She wasn't a natural-born craftswoman either.

Tom laughed.

Hannah grinned back, thinking he had a nice laugh. She

pressed further. 'It can't be all work and no play in Ireland's fair city, though.'

'Well, I fit the gym in when I can, meet my mates for a drink, the usual stuff, and once a week, I hang out with this great kid, Sean, for a couple of hours. I started volunteering for Foróige as a big brother at the start of the year.'

Hannah forgot about pretending to like Tom as he told her about the relationship he'd established with Sean, a thirteen-year-old whose father had died when he was eleven. 'We both like beachcombing, so I pick him up on Saturday afternoons, and we head out to the beach to look for treasure.'

'Have you found any?' Hannah's eyes were wide as she pictured Tom earnestly hunched over a metal detector with a young lad by his side.

'It depends on how you define treasure. We've found lots of sea glass. Bray in Wicklow's a favourite spot.'

Hannah was intrigued, and found herself leaning closer to him. 'So you're kind of a father figure to Sean?'

'No. I'd say I'm a friend who's a good listener with more life experience than him.'

Hannah nodded slowly and was disappointed when Tom downed his pint, nearly brushing her hand as he popped it on the bar, before glancing at his phone and saying he had to run. 'I'm meeting a client,' he explained.

She watched him go and said softly to herself, 'Well, that didn't exactly go to plan, Hannah.'

It was late by the time Hannah slipped between the cosy sheets of her old bed. The afternoon's hoolie had stretched into the evening with only a fish-and-chip-supper intermission. Her feet ached because Mam and Dad had got their pound of flesh. Once Tom had left, Imogen had collared her, and she'd manned the bar until closing. Still and all, she thought, wiggling her toes and luxuriating in stretching out, it wasn't every day your sister announced she was pregnant.

Who had Tom gone to meet? she wondered, faffing with the pillow until she had it just right. Maybe she'd get to ask him outright in the morning over breakfast. Mam had let her off Mass so long as she cooked Tom the breakfast that was part and parcel of the full board he'd booked into the Shamrock for.

She was tired, but her brain had gone into overtime thinking about how she hadn't expected to like Tom. That wasn't how things were supposed to go. She'd have been completely useless as a femme-fatale spy during wartime or the likes. What Dylan would have to say if she were to tell him she was having trouble separating Tom the person from Tom the architectural arse who was a partner in crime to this Greenhouse project wasn't something she wanted to think about. Instead, her thoughts turned to the strange American woman interested in her mam, and she huffed into the darkness.

It was going to be a long night.

13

Kitty Kelly was sitting alone at the kitchen table, pondering a crossword, when Hannah slid silently into the room. It seemed sleep had also eluded her this evening. The only sound aside from the ticking of the wall clock was Princess Leia's snuffling snores from her basket, so when one of the floorboards let out a particularly loud creak as Hannah approached, Kitty jumped and dropped the pen she'd been twirling thoughtfully around her fingers.

'Jesus, Mary and Joseph! Hannah, what are you playing at sneaking around the house in the dead of night?' Kitty kept her voice low, obviously not wanting to wake those sleeping upstairs.

'Sorry, Nan. I didn't mean to give you a fright. I couldn't sleep either.' Hannah, catching her nan's gaze straying to her hair, half-heartedly smoothed it down. Tossing and turning like she'd been doing for the last hour wasn't conducive to salon style.

'I gathered that. Is it the fish-and-chip supper sitting like a lead balloon in your belly, too? Or are you excited about Christmas? You were always a divil to settle this time of year when you were small.' Kitty's smile was nostalgic.

'It's neither of those. And your man upstairs is taking the shine off the festive season for me. He's a reminder of everything we stand to lose.' Hannah continued to loiter, fiddling with the tie of her dressing gown.

'Well, come sit down and close that door behind you. You weren't born in a tent.' Kitty's bright blue eyes doubled in size, and picking up her pen, she whispered excitedly, 'I've got it. Another word for tent, six down, seven letters. Bivouac!' She hastily jotted it into the squares while Hannah did as she was told.

'Do you want another brew, Nan?' Hannah filled the kettle.

'No. You're grand. I'll only be up and down for the loo all night. Sort yourself out, then come and tell me what's after keeping you from a good night's sleep.'

Hannah opted for hot chocolate, craving sweetness. She helped herself to a big spoonful of Mam's Galaxy Light, added a drop of milk once the water had boiled and joined her nan at the table.

Kitty was eyeing her speculatively, and the magazine with the crossword was now closed. 'You were very friendly with that man supposedly taking the shine off the festive season for you tonight.' There was an accusatory note to her voice. 'Is it him you've got on your mind?'

'Tom?' Hannah blew on her drink, knowing full well who her nan was talking about.

'I didn't see you whiling away the evening with any other young men.'

'It wasn't what it looked like, Nan.'

'Oh?'

'No. I've a conflict of interest where Tom Flynn's concerned, as you know.'

'Then what were you up to hanging off his every word?'

Hannah scalded her mouth on the too-hot drink and scowled into the mug of brown liquid. She'd feel better if she came clean, and she pondered where to start, settling on Dylan.

'Nan, there's this fella at work called Dylan. He's like me, passionate about things.'

'I've heard you mention him, and by passionate, I assume you mean tying himself to trees and the like.'

It wasn't how Hannah would have described it, but she nodded anyway. 'Well, Dylan pointed out the newspaper article about the interest in developing the famine cottage land to me in the first place. He thinks it's wrong, too, and he wants to help us. Nan, the project won't get past first base with him on our side.'

'So this Dylan you work for told you to pretend to be all friendly like with our guest upstairs to find out who's employed him. Is that right?'

Hannah shifted uncomfortably because hearing it said out loud like so didn't make her feel too clever.

Kitty's lips flatlined. 'That's underhanded and not very nice behaviour, Hannah. I'm surprised at you.'

'I know that. It didn't sit well with me either, but sometimes, if you're to make a difference, you've got to do things that make you uncomfortable.'

'Poppycock!' Kitty's teacup rattled in her saucer as she set it down with more force than necessary. 'And are those your words or your Dylan's ones, young lady?'

'Shush, Nan, you'll wake the others, and they're mine.' Hannah had almost convinced herself this was the case. She reached for a piece of the Christmassy shortbread that was always on hand this time of year. Kitty was quicker, however, sliding the ancient Tupperware container out of reach.

'You'll not have a shortbread until you've explained yourself because you were raised better than that, Hannah Kelly.'

'That's not fair.' Hannah meant this in response to not just the shortbread being snatched from her but also her nan's words. 'You're as against this Greenhouse as I am.'

Kitty's expression didn't change, and Hannah sighed. 'It backfired on me anyway because I might strongly disagree with Tom's job here in Emerald Bay, but I liked him. I didn't expect that to happen.'

Kitty remained silent for a few ticks of the clock, and when she finally spoke up, she said, 'I see what you mean regarding a conflict of interest.' The Tupperware slid toward her.

Hannah helped herself. 'Nan, can I ask you something?'

'That depends on what it is.'

'What did you mean when you said the abandoned farm should be left alone with its ghosts?'

Stories about the farm and the old cottage being haunted were folklore in Emerald Bay, or so Hannah had thought. Daring one another to go there and play Ghostbusters was a rite of passage for the village's young people.

'I feel Finbar when I go there, Hannah.' Kitty looked up then with a distant look in her sharp blue eyes.

'I didn't know you went there, Nan.'

Kitty nodded. 'The cottage was our special place. Mine and your grandfather's.'

Surprise registered because this was the first she'd heard of it, but it explained Nan's fervour that the cottage and land not be tampered with.

When nothing else was forthcoming, Hannah asked, 'Would you tell me about you and Granddad, Nan? How did you meet?' It had dawned on Hannah that was a story she'd never been told.

Kitty blinked, the present calling her back, and the faraway light in her eyes dimmed. 'Ah, now it was all a long time ago.'

'But I'd like to hear it.' Hannah had only been young when her granddad passed. 'It would help me know him better.'

'You're a good girl even if you do eejit things at times, but there's none of us born perfect in this world, Hannah.' She got up from the table, carrying her cup to the worktop. 'I think I'd best top up my brew to tell you the tale.'

14

_____

Kitty stared at her mam, who'd her back to her as she diced the vegetables for that night's dinner with a methodical chop, chop, chop. It was such an ordinary, everyday sound echoing around the kitchen. Yet, Kitty's whole world had changed with the uttering of one sentence. 'You're to be leaving school at the end of the month.'

Her younger brothers had run along to school ahead of her, and her eldest brother, John, would be in the cowshed with Da. She could hear the cows' mournful moos and fancied they sympathised with her because it was all arranged. Mam had already notified the school. There was an aching lump in her throat at the unfairness of decisions made around her life without any input from her. Nonetheless, she tried to swallow the lump, knowing her tears wouldn't do her any good. Not when her mam's back was as straight as an ironing board like so. That was a sure sign her mind was made up. She wouldn't be bent on the topic because while Da ran the farm with John's help, keeping food on their table, Mam had the final say in matters pertaining to what went on under their cottage roof.

Kitty wouldn't usually answer back, but she couldn't stop this morning, and the words spilled forth as she said her piece. 'But I don't understand, Mam. Why? Sure, I've only six months until I finish school.' The tremble crept in despite her best efforts not to cry. 'Don't make me finish without my Leaving Certificate, Mam,' she sniffed, half pleading as she brushed hot, angry tears away.

There was so much more bubbling inside her, but Mam wouldn't understand. So far as she was concerned, your lot in life was your lot. She wouldn't understand dreams that were bigger than the small pond God had allocated for you. Kitty swept the breadcrumbs off the table uncaringly onto the floor. How would any of those dreams come true if she were nothing more than a skivvy for a doctor, his wife and their children with no way of bettering herself? Education was the key to bigger things than Emerald Bay or Kilticaneel, where she was being sent. Kitty wanted to go to America. She wanted to see the Statue of Liberty guarding the waters around New York City.

'Sure, the position will have been filled in six months. Think yourself lucky that Doctor Price and his wife agreed to take you on without meeting you. There's many young girls would bite your hand off for such an opportunity.'

'I'd gladly hold out my hand,' Kitty muttered, not feeling lucky or fortunate. What she felt was wretched, and it was Father Barry's fault. The interfering priest had found her the position when Mam went to him worried about how the family would fare during the winter months. He'd known through word of mouth that a new doctor was taking over the neighbouring town of Kilticaneel's practice. The doctor and his young family were moving from Dublin and would need live-in help. She was to help look after the children and keep the house. Kitty, hearing this, had silently raged that housekeepers were old. They weren't seventeen, nearly eighteen years old with their whole lives ahead of them and dreams of going to America!

'I'd rather work in the factory over in Kilticaneel, Mam. At least that way, I wouldn't have to live in.' The large textile printers, known as the cotton factory, had opened two years earlier. If she had no choice but to leave school, at least there, she'd spend her days around girls her own age and could get the bus home each evening.

'And we'd still have an extra mouth to feed at home. This way, you'll receive a full board and earn, Kitty. All this carrying on of yours is nothing short of selfish. Sure, your brothers are growing lads; they need a square meal on an evening table.'

Was it selfish to want a say in your own life? Kitty pondered the question as she stared down at her plaid skirt. She didn't think it was. Sure, things were hard, and the family was doing it tough, thanks to the vulnerabilities of farming. Still, she'd gladly forfeit her share of the meat and live on carrots and potatoes alone if it meant not having to go and live with strangers. Didn't that make her selfless? When she flung this at her mam's back, she shook her head and bossed her to get to school, or she'd be late.

Kitty scraped her chair back from the table in a deliberately annoying manner and got up. She picked up her book bag and moved woodenly toward the door, pausing before tugging it open. She was reluctant to leave the warmth of the familiar kitchen behind and the argument un-won. 'But, Mam, what if they're awful people?'

Still, her mam didn't turn round, carrying on with the chop, chop, chopping.

'Father Barry has assured me the Prices are a fine family, and Doctor Price will have his own practice, won't he?' Her clipped tone implied this was all the qualification needed to be a decent human being. 'And are your ears painted on? Because we've already been through all of this, I don't want to hear another word about the matter. You're giving me a headache, so you are.'

The warning note in her mam's voice registered, but Kitty paid no heed to her frustration, making her want to goad her further. 'I'm nearly eighteen, Mam. You can't make me go.'

That did it. Quick as a flash, her mam banged the knife down on the chopping board and picked up the wooden spoon that was lurking conveniently close by, then spun round. 'Don't think you're too old for this. Not when you live under mine and your da's roof.' She waved the spoon, her face pinkening with irritation, and Kitty's body reflexively tensed. 'Now you listen to me good and proper. We all have to do things we don't want to do sometimes. Do you think your da and John want to be up before light each morning seeing to the cows? Do you think I want to be standing here trying to eke out the meat and vegetables day in, day out?'

Kitty hadn't thought about it. Working on the farm was what Da did, and there'd been no stopping John from leaving school as soon as he was able to join Da. Her brother preferred working with his hands and being outdoors. Sitting at a desk day in and day out with information being shouted at him had been purgatory. As for Mam, well, keeping the family fed was just what she did. For the first time, however, Kitty noticed the weary lines on her mam's face and the grey tinge to her skin. She felt a sliver of shame.

'No. You didn't think, did you? We do what we must in this life, Kitty, and I'd thank you to think about someone other than yourself on your walk to school this morning. Now out that door with you before you feel this on the back of your legs.' She stepped closer, waving the wooden spoon again, and Kitty, not needing to be told twice, headed out the door smartly.

She was only too aware that while she'd had the face eaten off her, at least she'd not felt the sting of that spoon on the back of her legs. Still and all, she'd taken ten or so paces before she relaxed and paid attention to the day that awaited her. The crispness of autumn had arrived, and this morning, it was misty. It would burn off later and, with any luck, leave a blue-sky day in its wake.

Over to her right, she saw her da, an indistinct shape in the haze, as he emerged from the barn and waved. Kitty didn't wave back; she was still seething as she hurried down the path. She needed to put space between her family and the traitorous thoughts of running away. Where she'd go, she didn't know, but right now, she didn't care either.

The route to the school was one Kitty could have followed with her eyes closed. The well-trodden path wound its way past fields and bogs. She possessed a vivid imagination, and on mornings such as this, she enjoyed whiling the walk away by turning the spectral shapes shrouded by the mist into mysterious objects.

In the distance, she could hear whistling and digging. It would have sounded eerie if she hadn't known what it was, and when she rounded the bend, there was no mistaking the team of three transient turf cutters already hard at work. The men had been contracted by Mr Scully, who owned the larger farm adjacent to Kitty's family. Although technically, the land they were working on didn't belong to Mr Scully. It belonged to a poor family who'd succumbed to the Great Hunger and left their farm untended and their cottage empty. They'd literally just walked away, never to be heard from again. Nobody would dare argue the toss with Mr Scully, though. He wielded too much clout in the village, so if he wanted to employ turf cutters on the abandoned farm's land, so be it.

This morning, she could see the lads and the famine cottage with its roof tumbling in on itself behind them clear as day. It was as if someone had come along with a blackboard eraser and rubbed the spaces around the trio and the old cottage clean of the mist. The tall lad in charge of the *slèan* slicing into the earth had caused her heart to flip about like a fish gasping for air, however.

They'd appeared on Monday morning, and he'd leaned on that cutter he was wielding to give her a cheeky hello, a glint of admiration in deep-set blue eyes. Today was Friday, and her heart didn't skip its usual beat at the sight of him. It was too heavy, and she was in no mood for banter. A girl couldn't help but notice how broad his shoulders were beneath his woollen jersey, though. Or how he'd a smile that creased his dirt-encrusted face, making his teeth shine white as he doffed his cap at her appreciatively and called out a greeting. Despite this, she gave no hint of the shy smile she'd sent his way every other morning as she continued to walk. She was too busy imagining herself with a tissue in one hand, wiping someone else's children's snotty noses, duster in the other.

The footfall behind her startled her.

'If I've offended you, then I'm sorry.'

Kitty sighed and slowed, allowing him to catch her up and keep pace. 'It's not you who's upset me.'

'Then who.' He punched the air in front of him, adding with theatrical flair. 'I'll sort them out for you.' The dimple piercing his cheek told her he was joking, and she couldn't help the tremor of a smile.

'Good luck with that. I'd like to see anyone take my mammy on and win, especially when she's got hold of the wooden spoon.'

A sheepish grin flashed. 'I told the lads we're taking a break. I can listen if you can walk and talk at the same time.'

Kitty realised he was in charge as she watched those shoulders on which you could rest the weight of the world shrug with his offer. The need to share the injustice heaped upon her by her mam this morning welled up. So, taking a deep breath, she dumped the whole sorry lot on his shoulders as they followed the path toward the village. When she finished, she felt surprisingly lighter and looked up at him, unsure of what he'd say, if anything.

What he did come back with surprised her. It echoed her mam's words, but hearing him say them made her feel better.

'Sometimes we have to do things we don't want to do. I'm cutting turf at another man's bequest, but it's my own boss I want to be. I will be, too, but not just yet. So for now, I'll keep my chin up and a smile on my face because I'm a firm believer that things usually work out grand in the end.'

The quiet conviction in his words left Kitty with no doubt that things would work out, and her step faltered as it dawned on her. 'I don't even know your name.'

'Nor me yours.'

'Katherine, but everyone calls me Kitty, so you can, too.'

'A pretty name for a beautiful girl. I'm Finbar, but everybody calls me Fin,' he replied with a wink.

By the time Kitty reached the village school, the mist was beginning to melt away. She'd forgotten about the Leaving Cert and fretting about living with a strange family or handing her wages to Mam. The Statue of Liberty and America had even been swept away. Instead, her mind was filled with eyes the colour of the blue marbles she'd always coveted from John's prized collection and a very different future to the one she'd imagined for herself.

≈

Present Day

Kitty's tea was cooling in front of her. 'I knew that morning I'd marry Finbar.'

Hannah's expression was dreamy as she rested her chin on

her steepled hands. Nan had transported her to another time and place. She wasn't finished with her story yet either.

'We'd meet at the cottage. I'd sneak out once everyone was snoring and pick my way down the path to the abandoned farm. He'd bring a blanket to wrap around us, and we'd—'

'Nan!' Hannah wasn't sure she wanted to know what came next.

'What? You young ones all think you invented falling in love, but I'll have you know your granddad was a gentleman. We'd talk for hours inside the old famine cottage. The ghosts inside its four walls were privy to all our hopes and dreams. It was our place, Hannah. Mine and Finbar's; theirs too.'

Nan's conviction that it shouldn't be sold all made sense now, but there was still more Hannah wanted to know. 'Did you work for the doctor and his family?'

'I did, and lovely they were, too. I was happy there, or as happy as I was going to be, until I married your granddad. I'd go home on a Sunday, and by then, Mam and Da knew Finbar's intentions. He'd join us for lunch, and afterwards, we'd walk to our cottage.'

Hannah smiled, but then it faltered. 'How did you come to buy the Shamrock?'

'The publican retired, and your granddad had a little money squirrelled away; he'd an uncle who never married and left him a tidy sum. He was finally his own man.'

'And did you never regret staying?'

'Not for one minute. The grass isn't always greener, and my roots were here in Emerald Bay. I go to the old cottage whenever I want to feel closer to Finbar. It might sound mad, but I still talk to him.'

'It doesn't. I didn't know you did that, Nan,' Hannah repeated her earlier sentiment. Her eyes were smarting as she thought of her nan's shoulders hunched as she made her way to the lonely cottage, sharing her private thoughts with her late husband.

'Nobody does.'

'Does he, er, does he talk back?'

'I might sound mad, Hannah, but I'm not completely around the twist.'

'Sorry.' Hannah was thoughtful for a minute or two before speaking up. 'Thank you for telling me.'

Kitty looked at her granddaughter pensively.

'What are you thinking?'

'You're looking for something, Hannah. You always have been, but sometimes you'll find what you thought was missing is right there under your nose.'

May you have the hindsight to know where
you've been,
The foresight to know where you are going,
And the insight to know when you have gone
too far.

— IRISH BLESSING

15

'Hannah, have I offended you somehow?' Tom asked, taking his glasses off and rubbing them on the sweater that matched his grey-eyed gaze. He was sitting at the kitchen table with the full Irish breakfast Hannah had just set down ungraciously in front of him. 'You didn't have to cook, by the way. Although it looks wonderful, I would have been happy with a bowl of Shredded Wheat, and I could have fetched that myself if it was a lie-in you needed.'

It was a good job Mam wasn't here because Hannah knew she'd eat the face off her if she'd been privy to her clattering about the kitchen frying up bacon, eggs, sausage, black pudding and tomato. Beans and toast were the finishing touches to the heaving plate. Let it not be said she'd let a guest go hungry on her watch. However, as she'd closed cupboards and the fridge with more gusto than necessary, banged the frying pan down on the element and rattled about in the cutlery drawer, she'd wondered whether sitting through Mass might not have been preferable to cooking this morning, given her conflicted emotions.

It certainly would have been a preferable option for Tom,

and for a nanosecond, she felt bad given he was paying to stay here, and you'd have had to have a hide like a rhinoceros not to have picked up on her mood. She'd barely slept a wink after the story Nan had told her, waking up with a woolly head, and it was easier to be angry with Tom than to be mad at herself for liking him despite his commercial intentions for Emerald Bay. However, this was her opportunity to find out who was behind the Greenhouse development.

So, pulling a chair out opposite him, Hannah sat down and poured herself a brew, aware Tom had picked up his knife and fork but had yet to tuck in as he continued to eye her warily.

'Not you personally,' she said as she poured the milk. This was true. Tom had a Boy Scout genuineness to him, and he smelled nice, which was a plus because in the circles Hannah moved, plenty smelled more lentilly than fresh like the sea. 'But what you represent here in Emerald Bay completely offends me.' So much for subterfuge and cosying up to find the answers she needed.

'OK, now you've lost me. What do you mean by what I represent?'

'Corporate greed,' Hannah said rather piously over her teacup.

Tom coughed, signalling disbelief. 'Er, I didn't expect that at ten past ten on a Sunday morning.'

'I expect you didn't, and I'm sorry, but you did ask.'

'That's true, I did, but I'm an architectural project manager, not a business tycoon. And to be fair, Hannah, which I don't think you are being, you don't know me well enough to pass judgment like so.' Then he looked at the food before him. 'This will set me up for the day, by the way. Thanks a million.'

Hannah watched in disbelief as he tucked in. His relaxed, calm manner was infuriating. Her anger flared again, and she quickly retorted, 'I know enough. For instance, I know you've been commissioned to design and oversee an eyesore on the outskirts of my home village that others and I oppose.'

'Ah, now I see. The Greenhouse is one of your causes.'

'Don't say it like that.'

'Like what.'

'How you just said it.'

'Sorry.' Tom shrugged. 'But let me get this straight. In your opinion, my being here makes me the poster boy for corporate greed?'

Was that a twinkle in his eye? Hannah fumed, aware they were getting off course. 'Well, it doesn't make you one of Santa's little helpers, does it?'

Tom wasn't the least ruffled as he began sawing into his sausage like a forestry worker felling trees. 'Personally, I don't see the correlation myself. Or maybe you just enjoy taking the moral high ground.'

That was a zinger. She'd bet he'd been a proper swot at school. He'd probably been head of the debating team. Well, he'd not win this round. 'If I take the moral high ground, as you put it, it's because someone has to when it comes to Emerald Bay's land. So let me lay it out clearly for you, Tom Flynn. This Greenhouse of yours isn't a boon for the bay as you seem to think. It's a blight.' She'd impressed herself with her alliterative response, but Tom looked at her as though she'd spoken gibberish.

'How's that then? You haven't seen my design. It's sympathetic to the landscape, and the Christmas trees will be grown sustainably. So, if you think about it like that, I am one of Santa's little helpers.'

Hannah didn't crack a smile, and her voice rose a notch. Jaysus, he had an answer for everything. 'I'm not just talking visually. That land you want to build and plant on is part of Emerald Bay. It belongs to the village, not the government, and should be left as it is. I used to play there as a child with my sisters, and future generations should have that opportunity, too.'

'What century do you think this is? Nothing stands still, and villages like Emerald Bay need economic growth. The young people leave because there's nothing to keep them here. I mean, look at yourself. Where do you live?'

Hannah desperately sought a comeback, but it wasn't easy given he'd made a valid point. She wanted to tell him what the cottage and its surrounding land meant to her nan, but it wasn't her place to do so. Instead, she found herself blustering like a blowhard politician. 'The so-called jobs you think the Greenhouse will create for locals are a double-edged sword because for the handful of people the garden centre and farm employ, you'll kill nearly all the local businesses on Main Street. Not to mention the environmental concerns – that's blanket bog land, which needs to be protected.' She flopped back hard in her seat, her face heating up how it always did when she spoke about things she felt strongly about.

Tom was silent, appearing to mull over what she'd said as he bit the corner of a triangle of toast. She picked up her tea, sipped it and tried to keep her emotions in check – not one of her strong points. Hannah's shaking hand saw her put the cup back in its saucer. She was pleased Tom, who was making an infuriatingly slow job of his meal, didn't appear to notice her calm facade was an act.

Finally, he swallowed and spoke up. 'The way I see it is this. The land was worked in the past. The Christmas tree farm will see that soil utilised again. If it was environmentally harmful, the project wouldn't have even got this far.'

'And how far is that?'

'The Department of Agriculture is in talks with my benefactor about the project, and it's looking positive that it will get the go-ahead before Christmas because, unlike yourself, they can see the benefit to Emerald Bay.'

'But this benefactor of yours isn't someone connected to the land here. They've no right to come in and destroy part of our heritage, to damage our community and especially not bang on Christmas time!'

'So what you're actually saying is you see me as the man who's going to spoil Christmas?'

'Don't you dare laugh at me, Tom Flynn.'

'I'm not. It's just I've never seen myself in that light before, and to be fair, you don't know my client has no connection to Emerald Bay,' Tom finished quietly.

That brought her up short. What did that mean? She watched his expression shutter as he dipped the remaining toast into his egg. Who exactly was behind the Greenhouse?

Before she could ask her burning question, the question Dylan had tasked her with getting to the bottom of, Tom looked up from his plate.

'I think what you're really saying, Hannah, is you don't like change.'

'No! That's not it at all.' Argh, he made her want to stamp her foot. 'I'm as adaptable as the next person.' That wasn't true, but she wasn't letting on. So she brought the conversation back to where she wanted it and got straight to the point. 'Who's behind the Greenhouse Tom?'

'That, I'm afraid, is confidential.'

It was the first glimmer of unease Hannah had seen. He'd said too much already, she guessed. Well, he could flipping well say more. 'If everything's kosher, why does this person want to hide their identity?'

'There's nothing underhanded going on. My client has asked to remain anonymous for now, and I have to respect that.'

'But I don't.' Hannah had had enough. She pushed her chair back from the table, needing to distance herself from Tom before she grabbed him around the shoulders and gave him a jolly good shake.

'This is really hitting the spot, thanks,' he said, twinkling up at her.

Hannah bit her bottom lip, her grip on the back of the chair white knuckled. He was worse than infuriating. He was, he was...

She was saved from having to come up with a suitable descriptive word by the connecting door to the Shamrock opening. A waft of stale ale floated through after her dad.

'I was just after doing a spot of cleaning up after last night's hoolie. A full Irish, is it, lad?' Liam asked Tom, almost salivating.

'Very nice it is, too.'

'Glad to hear it. You make the most of all that bacon and sausage because before you know it, you'll be my age and having the poached egg with the cholesterol-lowering spread on your toast,' Liam lamented.

His big-hearted beam faltered on seeing Hannah. 'And what's got up your nose this morning then?'

'Nothing,' Hannah muttered through gritted teeth.

'Has my daughter been behaving herself, Tom?'

'I've no complaints. She did me proud with this.' He gestured to his plate. 'I won't need anything to eat for the rest of the day.' Tom's smile didn't give so much of a hint of the conversation that had played out over the breakfast table.

Beyond infuriating Tom might be, but at least he wasn't a tell-tale tit, Hannah thought, flouncing from the kitchen.

16

Hannah was sitting cross-legged on her bed, putting the finishing touches to the petition she'd drawn up because even though Dylan had said she'd be wasting her time, she needed to take action to stop the Greenhouse project. It was personal now. She was doing it for Nan and her granddad. Besides, Dylan was in no position to help. Sonya had texted her not long after she'd stomped upstairs to tell her he'd been arrested at the Climate Guardians rally last night for causing intentional property damage. The group's lawyer was on to it, Sonya had reassured her.

The news had left her feeling unsettled. Smashing windows and the like, which was what had happened when the rally got out of hand, wasn't her style, especially so close to Christmas, the so-called season of peace and goodwill. But rather than dwell on it, she'd decided to get the ball rolling. Nan could take the petition to her craft group during the week – she'd be bound to garner plenty of signatures there.

Her mind flicked to Tom. So far, she'd got nowhere trying to pump him for information, although he might have dropped a clue as to who was behind the Greenhouse when he'd pointed out that she didn't know for sure his client wasn't local. There was no one in the village she could think of who would have the wherewithal to take on a project of that scale, though.

Now she uncrossed her legs and got up, stashing the clipboard with the attached piece of paper she intended to fill with signatures in her satchel before venturing downstairs.

'Is that yer man off to conquer Everest under all those layers or my daughter Hannah?' Nora asked as she dumped the satchel beside the sideboard.

'You missed your calling, Mam,' Hannah said as she took in the cosy scene. 'You should have been a stand-up comedian.'

There was no sign of her dad or nan, but Mam was enjoying a cup of tea with the man who was trying to spoil Christmas.

That wasn't all. Her eyes widened as she spied the best biscuits tin had been opened. This was sacrilege! It was an unwritten but understood rule that the Jacobs biscuits were saved until Christmas!

Turning away, she crouched down to where her dad had dropped the boxes she'd brought home and began stuffing her satchel with Feed the World with Bees envelopes. The sooner she was out of here the better because she needed to put distance between herself and Tom, who was busy making himself at home.

'You missed a lovely Mass, so you did, Hannah. It was very uplifting.' Nora shook the biscuit tin in Tom's direction. 'Will you have another, Tom? Father Seamus was asking after you, but Tom told us you made a grand breakfast in mine and your nan's absence.'

Tom joined in as he leaned back after he'd helped himself to a Mikado, his rangy shoulders settling back into the cushions. 'Best full Irish I've had in I can't remember how long.'

Hannah pulled a face. *'And I'm a big brown-nosing apple polisher, so I am.'* But she said, 'Well, you're certainly looking after him.' It hadn't escaped her notice that Mam hadn't offered her a biscuit.

'Where is it you're off to?' Nora asked, not having picked up on her daughter's sarcasm as she topped up her tea and helped herself to a chocolate teacake.

The woman had no shame, Hannah thought, staring at her mam. Chocolate teacakes were her favourites. There'd be murder when her sisters heard about the best biscuits being snaffled before the twenty-fifth. And hear about it they would.

'I need some fresh air, so I thought I'd also try and sell some of these.' Hannah held up one of the envelopes. She didn't mention the petition.

'Will you be back this afternoon?' Nora asked. 'Because your father's talking about going for a drive to choose the Christmas tree. You might like to go with him, and you'd be very welcome to go along for the ride there, Tom. Perhaps the pair of you might like to decorate the tree later?' There was an interfering twinkle in Nora's eye.

Janey Mack! Mam was after trying to match her with Tom, of all people, and she was about as subtle as a bulldozer.

Hannah was gratified to see Tom had begun to cough. Good – she hoped his Mikado had gone down the wrong way. Nora was up and out of her seat, fetching him a glass of water. He was obviously as uncomfortable about spending time with her after their earlier chat as she was with him.

Once he had his fit under control, he gave his throat one final clear and said, 'Erm, it's very kind of you to include me, Nora, but I've a meeting this afternoon.'

'On a Sunday?' Nora tsked.

'No rest for the wicked.' Hannah's jaw was clenched.

'Is it on-site at the abandoned farm, Tom?' Kitty asked, having appeared seemingly from thin air. 'I couldn't help but overhear. You'll be wanting to wrap up warmly if it is.' She'd her arms full of folded washing and, upon seeing the

Jacobs biscuit tin, set the load down on the table and promptly put the tin back where it had been hidden away for Christmas.

'It is, and I'll be sure to, thanks, Mrs Kelly.'

If he was surprised by her sudden concern for his well-being, he didn't let on.

'Have you seen the news with those hooligans carrying on in Cork? I don't know what the world's coming to,' Kitty tsked, picking up her washing.

Nora joined in the tutting, and Hannah felt sick knowing exactly which hooligans she was referencing.

Tom had stood up and was freeing his wallet from his back jeans pocket. 'That reminds me, Hannah. I owe you some money.'

Hannah was thankful for the diversion from all the tutting and tsking even if she would have liked to have told him where he could stick his money, but given that it was for the bees and not herself personally, she took the wad of notes he pulled out and made a show of counting. Then she handed over ten cards with a stiff thank you on behalf of the non-profit organisation she worked for, refusing to make eye contact with him. She was all fingers and thumbs as she fumbled with the straps on her satchel.

'Why don't you take Princess Leia with you?' Nora suggested, looking over the rim of her teacup at her daughter. 'James said she's to have a half-hour daily walk.'

In response to the 'W' word, Princess Leia was up and out of her basket, all but performing somersaults at the prospect of stretching her little legs.

Nora smiled. 'Ah, bless. You'll find her lead and going-out-and-about sweater on the sideboard.'

It would take someone with a harder heart than hers to leave the chihuahua at home, Hannah thought as she wrestled her into the striped sweater.

'You're a natural at that, so you are,' Nora commented. 'You'll be a grand babysitter for your sister. Won't she, Kitty?'

'Grand,' Kitty agreed, heading toward the stairs.

There was a world of difference between dressing your sweet little baby niece or nephew and putting a sweater on a chihuahua, but Hannah didn't bother voicing this. She could tell her mam had drifted off into a soon-to-be nana daydream.

She realised Tom was smiling at the exchange and busied herself, clipping the lead onto Princess Leia's collar, saying in her sternest voice, 'You'd better behave yourself, young lady. No ankle biting.' Then, straightening and slinging her satchel over her shoulder, she said to no one in particular, 'Right, we're off.'

Without a backwards glance, Hannah opened the back door and left the sanctuary of the warm kitchen behind.

17

The sky was a crisp blue, and the grass was sleeping under a shimmering white eiderdown behind the hedgerow on the other side of the lane. It was a gorgeous winter's morning, and Hannah shook off her fug, inhaling the sharp air and informing Princess Leia, 'Jack Frost's been.' The little dog yipped in her excitement to be out, and once she'd cocked a leg, they set off round the corner to the hub of the little village – Main Street.

Princess Leia trotted alongside Hannah, sniffing at this and that before coming to an obedient halt beside the Christmas tree in the square. Hannah took a lung-filling breath of the energising fresh air. It felt good to be doing something proactive because everywhere she looked, there were reminders that she was up against it. There were red bows attached to the lamp posts, for one, and her eyes flitted to the nearby green post box – even that had tinsel swirling around it. Christmas meant business would grind to a halt in favour of family and friends. She just had to make sure the Greenhouse project ground to a halt, too.

Hannah wondered where she should start as she gazed up

the sleepy street. Given that it was Sunday, the shops, with the exception of the Bus Stop, wouldn't open until midday. So she decided to cross the road and loiter outside the corner shop, which had a steady stream of villagers in need of bread or milk.

Twenty minutes later, Hannah had sold more of her Feed the World with Bees wares than she had in the hours spent flogging them on the freezing city streets of Cork. It was down to Princess Leia. She was her secret canine weapon. She'd also got a good few signatures for her petition. Who knew dogs, especially Thumbelina-sized dogs wearing stripes, were great conversation starters. People were more inclined to listen to what you had to say and open their wallets after a lovely chat about chihuahuas. She'd have to suggest Dylan consider getting a doggy mascot for future Feed the World with Bees fundraisers. Once he was a free man, of course!

'Why don't we try our luck at Mermaids next? Freya will be in the workshop even if the gallery isn't open. We could start at the top of the street and work our way down,' Hannah suggested.

Princess Leia yipped.

Secret weapon aside, Hannah was enjoying the chihuahua's company. It was nice to have someone to chat with, and passing under the Christmas bunting at the top of Main Street, there was a spring in her step. This was partly due to the signatures and sales but mostly due to the yellow orb in the sky overhead. Her good mood faltered as her phone rang, and after fetching it from her dungaree pocket, she flopped down on the nearby bench seat, telling the little dog, 'It's my mam.'

'What was that all about earlier, young lady?' Nora Kelly got straight to the point of her call.

Hannah played dumb. 'What are you talking about?'

'You were rude to Tom. It's not on. You know full well paying guests are part of our bread and butter at the Shamrock.'

Oh, she did. How many times had she and her sisters been told to tiptoe about the place when they were kids if they'd guests staying in Room 5? Too many to count. 'I wasn't rude, Mam. I just wasn't particularly conversational. Unlike yourself.' Hannah couldn't resist adding, 'And while we're on the subject, will you be signing the adoption papers any day soon?'

'What's that supposed to mean?'

'You're behaving like Tom's your favourite child, that's what.'

'Don't be so childish. Tom's a great fella, and if you'd get off your high horse, you'd see that for yourself.'

Hannah recalled her mam's cringeworthy attempts at pairing her and golden boy off earlier. 'As it happens, I've a bone to pick with you, too.'

'Oh yes?'

'Yes. Quit it with the matchmaking.'

'I was doing no such thing.'

Yeah, right, Hannah thought, rolling her eyes. But was there any point arguing her case where Mr Annoying Apple Polisher was concerned? He'd well and truly won Mam over.

Unable to help herself, she fired back, 'Mam, you know how I feel about the Greenhouse. So you can't expect me to be all palsy-walsy with him.' She ignored the little voice in her head saying that was exactly what she'd intended to do.

'Fair play to you. You wear your heart on your sleeve. You always have. But I can expect good manners when you're home under my roof.'

Hannah chewed on her bottom lip. Jaysus, she felt like she was ten years old, getting a smack on the back of the hand.

She'd had enough of the conversation, and Princess Leia was tugging at the lead, wanting to be on the move again. 'Listen, Mam, I can't actually talk. I'm—'

Nora cut her off. 'And your nan's acting peculiarly, too.'

That piqued her interest, especially after what Nan had confided in her last night. 'In what way?'

'She told me she was off round to Reenie Brown's house. You know Reenie's not long back from visiting her son in Canada?' Nora didn't wait for a reply. 'She was after baking an apple cake and had invited Kitty around. Your nan said she was looking forward to a slice of cake and hearing all about how Reenie's son and his family were getting on.'

'There's nothing strange about that. I'd sit through Reenie's holiday snaps for a slice of apple cake, too.'

'Let me finish, Hannah. She'd been gone half an hour or so when who rings?'

'Who?' Hannah felt like she was waiting for a knock-knock joke's punchline as her mam inhaled sharply.

'Only Reenie Brown. She wondered if Kitty fancied calling round for lunch so she could fill her in on her holiday. What's she playing at, all secret squirrel like?'

It was strange, Hannah agreed. Why would Nan fib? She wracked her brains, and the only possible reason she could come up with was that Nan was meeting someone she wasn't ready to share with her family. Someone of the opposite sex. However, the only problem with that theory was Emerald Bay wasn't exactly teeming with eligible bachelors. So who could she possibly have her eye on? And, more to the point, why hadn't she mentioned this Romeo when she'd opened up last night.

Hannah put her thoughts into words. 'You don't think Nan's got some fancy man on the go, do you?'

'I don't know why else she'd be telling fibs. Now, shall I ring your sisters, or will you? Maybe they've an idea as to what's going on?'

As much as she'd have loved to find out whether Imogen or Shannon had the low-down on what Nan was up to, Hannah didn't want to sit on the bench, freezing her arse off any longer.

'You can, Mam, I've got to go. I'm at risk of getting the piles if I sit on this bench any longer.'

'Oh, you don't want that. It can be terribly painful. I've awful memories of the burst haemorrhoid all that pushing you out left me with.'

'Too much information, Mam.' Hannah ended the call grimacing.

It was only as she reached Mermaids that Hannah recalled Shannon saying Freya was away with Oisin for the weekend. Indeed, the closed sign was displayed in the window. She hesitated. Why was there a light on down the back of the studio?

Hannah peered in the window, cupping her hands on either side of her face to see better. There was Freya, bent over her workbench. She may have had a rush order she had to fill and returned early. Her Celtic jewellery designs were sought after, and it wasn't just Emerald Bay where she sold them.

She rapped on the window, making Freya jump. Squinting into the shadowy interior, Hannah hoped Oisin wasn't in there, too. He was one of those men who somehow turned every conversation around to himself. She wanted to talk about the Greenhouse and how it would affect Freya and see if she'd stock some of her Feed the World with Bees cards.

'It's me, Hannah,' she called out. 'If you're busy, tell me to go away.' Stepping back from the window, Hannah rubbed at the patch where her breath had left mist on the glass with her elbow.

Freya didn't reply but got up and made her way toward the door. Hannah heard the key turning in the lock, and her sister's bestie pulled it open.

It was Hannah's turn to be surprised because Freya looked like a bedraggled Mermaid who'd been crying.

Hannah's free hand automatically shot out to touch her on

the forearm. 'Hey, are you OK?' It was a daft question, given her puffy eyes and wet lashes.

'Not really,' Freya sniffed, wiping her nose with a tissue.

So Hannah did what any God-fearing Irish woman did in times of emotional upset. She barrelled on into the gallery and put the kettle on.

18

Freya gratefully accepted the mug of tea Hannah had made her. She was sitting at her workbench, and in front of her was an array of silver paraphernalia needed to twist hunks of precious metal into something beautiful and traditional. How Freya ever located which tool was for what amid that chaos was a mystery, Hannah thought, clutching her own brew. She flapped her hand as the joss stick smouldering away on the bench – presumably to mask the slightly metallic odour – sent smoke spiralling in her direction. She'd probably smell like patchouli for the rest of the day now, she mused, putting the mug to her lips and taking a warming sip.

Princess Leia, who'd enjoyed a bowl of water, was now snuggled onto Freya's lap like she belonged there. Hannah had heard it said that animals always knew who needed them the most, and she shot the little dog a fond glance. Her poor mam laid up in hospital would be missing her, no doubt, but hopefully she was resting assured Princess Leia was being well looked after.

'I thought you were away for the weekend,' Hannah probed. 'Did you decide to come back early?'

'Yeah.' Freya took a few glugs of sweet tea. 'I broke things off with Oisin last night.'

'Were you drunk or sober at the time?' It was essential to ascertain whether it had been a clear-headed, well-thought-through decision or a heat-of-the-moment drunken argument.

'Somewhere in between, I guess.'

That was workable, Hannah thought, hoping all the tears weren't a sign she regretted ending things. She slid the tissue box toward her.

'Thanks.' Plucking a tissue from the box, Freya added, 'The blinkers fell off, and I realised I'd had enough of pretending I was OK with Oisin free-ranging about the country, sponging off anyone who'd have him, including me.'

'You didn't loan him any money or anything, did you?' Hannah asked, envisaging nightmare scenarios of Freya having remortgaged her meagre cottage or taking out additional business loans to further fund Oisin and his art.

'I've been an eejit, but not that much of an eejit, thank God.'

That was something at least. 'How did he take it?'

'I think he thought I was joking initially, but he finally got it. Honestly, I think he was more upset when I told him that, yes, it meant I wouldn't be going ahead with his exhibition.'

'What a complete arse.'

The tentative beginnings of Freya's smile spread a little. 'Do you know something else? And I've never told anyone this.'

Feeling privileged, Hannah leaned toward Freya to hear better what she was about to say.

'I never really thought Oisin was very talented. His work's kind of shite if I'm being truthful.'

Hannah laughed.

'And his ego's bigger than his pecker.'

'Go, girl.'

She didn't need any encouragement. Freya was on a roll.

'The man says things like "Was that good for you, baby?" after the riding.'

'No!'

Freya was laughing now, too. 'He does! He says it in this smooth, velvety voice.'

'Ah no! Not the melting-chocolate voice.' Hannah was crying with laughter now, somehow managing to gasp out, 'And that hair of his. I mean, what does he think he looks like? Jesus?' She was off again, bent double. It took her a few giggles to realise Freya was no longer laughing, and straightening, she wiped her eyes.

'He has the softest hair. I loved running my fingers through it.'

Whoops, she'd put her Doc Martens boot in there.

Hannah held a hand up. 'Don't go there, Freya. Go back to egos and peckers. Think gombeen, eejit and arse.'

Freya sniffed and gave a watery-eyed nod, repeating, 'Oisin is a gombeen with a small pecker. Oisin is an eejit who can't paint. Oisin is an arse who thinks the world revolves around him.' She took a slow, deep inhale as she visibly pulled herself together.

'That's it.'

'Thanks for letting me offload.'

'You're welcome. And for the record, I think you're much better off without him.'

'You think?'

'I know.' Hannah reached out and gave Freya's hand a reassuring squeeze. Then, remembering her satchel, she climbed off the stool to fetch it, placing the clipboard and a bundle of envelopes in front of Freya. 'This is what brought me here,' she said.

Freya's head tilted to one side, and she stroked Princess Leia, listening as Hannah brought her up to speed. She told her about Tom staying at the Shamrock and why he was in Emerald

Bay. By the time she'd finished, Freya had agreed to take a wad
of cards to sit alongside the till and put her name on the petition
to stop the Greenhouse.

As she scrawled her signature beneath the growing list of
other names, she said, 'You can count me in on whatever you
decide to do to stop this thing. A good cause to throw myself
behind is exactly what I need right now.'

'Thanks a million, Freya. I haven't got further than this' –
she pointed to the petition – 'but I'm thinking some sort of
protest.'

That made her think of Dylan.

'You OK?' Freya asked. 'You went a little pale then.'

'Sure, I'm grand.' Hannah didn't want to talk about Dylan's
offer of help because then she'd have to mention him having
been arrested, so she tossed Freya a reassuring smile.

Her eyes strayed to Freya's nod to Christmas in the gallery.
Emerald Bay's Main Street shops were a testament to tinsel
along with their trusty fairy lights and baubles strung around
their front windows year after year. Their ethos seemed to be
the more bling and sparkle, the better. Freya, however, had kept
it simple with an assortment of handcrafted pine-cone reindeer
on display with a bead for a head and their legs, head and
antlers fashioned from pipe cleaners. For someone who didn't
have an arty bone in her body, she could appreciate the
creativity that had gone into making them. However, each time
she thought of how close Christmas was, she'd almost have
palpitations because she only had days to get this Greenhouse
project squashed. Ten business days to be exact.

A mobile's urgent ring cut her thoughts off.

'That's yours, Hannah,' Freya supplied.

Hannah reached for her phone, glancing at the screen. 'It's
Mam *again*. She's been giving out to me for being rude to Tom,
the yuletide saboteur I just told you about.'

'You'd better get it. You never know: it might be important.'

Hannah fleetingly thought of her dad when he'd had his heart attack and Shannon being pregnant and decided Freya was right. You did never know.

'Mam?'

'You'd better get down to the abandoned farm as quick as you can, Hannah.'

'Why?'

'Your nan's after staging a sit-in at the famine cottage, and she'll wind up with hypothermia if she's not careful. I'm hoping you might be able to talk sense into her.'

Hannah's mouth fell open.

'Hannah, are you OK? What did your mam want?' Freya had twisted on her stool to face Hannah, concern replacing her earlier tears.

'It's Nan.'

'Oh God, is she OK?'

'Sorry. Yeah. She's fine, but she's only gone and taken herself down to the abandoned farm to protest the proposed land sale. Kitty Kelly's after staging a one-woman sit-in, and Mam's worried she'll catch her death.'

Freya's jaw dropped this time, but she swiftly recovered. 'Well, good for her, I say. What are we waiting for?' She plopped a disgruntled Princess Leia down on the ground and swung into action, donning her coat and grabbing her car keys in record time. 'I'll drive us there. Sure, it will be quicker than messing about dropping you back at the Shamrock to get your car.'

Hannah was glad to be told what to do. On automatic pilot, she gathered her things, scooped up Princess Leia and was hot on Freya's heels as she headed out the gallery's back door.

'It's open.' Freya inclined her head toward the car that looked like it had bounced off the factory line right behind Doris and then been left to rust in a field for the past twenty years. The only difference was the lack of stickers.

Hannah slid into the passenger seat while Freya locked the back door and pulled the seat belt across herself and Princess Leia. She hoped that, unlike Doris, this car wasn't prone to being temperamental, but it rattled into life as soon as Freya twisted the key in the ignition. She flattened her back into the seat, feeling like she was taking off for the moon in a space shuttle as Freya floored it. At least they didn't have far to go, with the site being a short walk up behind Emerald Bay's park.

As they whizzed past the open green space flanked by trees and the prickly holly bush where the teenagers liked to lurk, Hannah counted only one hardy dad in the small playground area. He was pushing two rugged-up little ones in tandem on the swings. It made her think of the twins when they were small, but she didn't smile. Instead, she chewed her bottom lip as the hurt that Nan hadn't confided her plans set in. Then, turning to stare out the window at the muddy shades of green they were flying past, the American woman who'd unnerved her mam sprang to mind, and she asked Freya if she knew anything about her.

Freya didn't take her eyes off the twisting lane ahead, although she slowed down. 'There was a woman. I'd forgotten all about her, to be honest. I mean, I get a lot of Americans calling in, and it was super busy that day, but she was kind of intense, asking after your parents. Your mam in particular. I probably broke all the privacy laws by chatting with her. Sorry.' She pulled a face.

'You weren't to know.'

'We take people at face value in Emerald Bay. I suppose I assumed she knew Nora and Liam. You don't think it's anything sinister, do you?'

'I don't know.' Hannah ran her hand through her hair, mussing it further. 'I hope not.' The worry about who this woman was was like a little worm burrowing in. Still, there was no time for further debate because the abandoned farm was around the last bend, and as they rounded it, her mouth formed an 'O'.

It was a very different sight from the quiet lane where the only traffic you would likely see was Lorcan McGrath bouncing along on his tractor. Ramblers and adventurous children whose mammy thought they were playing in the park, not ghost hunting at the famine cottage, aside, the place was usually deserted. This afternoon, however, a slew of cars, including Liam Kelly's unmistakable yellow wagon and Sergeant Badger's Gardai vehicle, had pulled over on the verge, rendering the lane virtually impassable, and a quick glimpse past the stone walls surrounding the farm saw Hannah gasp. A small crowd was gathered outside the tumbledown cottage. Word of Kitty's sit-in had spread like measles by the looks of things.

As Freya stilled the engine, the car they'd slotted in behind caught Hannah's attention. It was familiar, and who it belonged to teased the periphery of her mind like a pub quiz question she should know the answer to. She leaned forward, straining against the seat belt to better see the sticker in the back window, and the Rubik's cube slotted into place. *The Galway Gazette.* Hannah clapped a hand to her mouth, causing Princess Leia to quiver. 'Oh no!'

'What?'

'That's Jeremy Jones's car.'

'The reporter who covered Shane's story when he was missing?'

'The *eejit* reporter who covered Shane's story and the same reporter that made sure I got carted off by the guards for trespassing when I was trying to save an oak tree in Galway.' Hannah's eyes glittered. 'I couldn't prove it, but the developer who wanted the tree felled crossed his palm with silver to write a skewed one-eyed piece for the paper. Jeremy Jones is as crooked as they come, and I wouldn't be surprised if someone with a vested interest in this land sale going ahead didn't have him in their back pocket. I bet they gave him a tip-off in the first place.'

'Do you think so?' Freya's eyebrow had raised sceptically.

Hannah, however, was adamant. She'd had experience with this sort of thing and knew how it worked. Money talked. Loudly.

'I guarantee it,' she said, seeing the headline in her mind's eye. 'His angle will be "mad old woman protests progress" or something like that.' She unbuckled her seat belt and flung the car door open. 'We can't let whoever's behind this win.' Tom's face floated to mind. Was it him? Had he called the newspaper? Her eyes narrowed as she climbed out of the car and tucked Princess Leia firmly under her arm before clambering over the low pile of haphazardly stacked stones forming the wall, uncaring as she grazed her ankle.

Freya, not bothering to lock her car, threw a leg over after her and squelched into the field. Shading her eyes with her hand, she didn't move for a second. 'Hannah. Can you see what I see?'

'I can, and whoever's behind this might want to put a Christmas tree farm in alongside their stupid garden centre, but still and all, dragging Father Christmas along for the show is taking things a step too far.'

19

The two women risked life and limb striding over the rutted land, or at least their ankles, as they made their way toward the milling crowd surrounding what was left of the higgledy-piggledy farm cottage.

'What's that noise?' Freya asked as a reedy wailing reached their ears.

'It sounds like an animal in pain,' Hannah replied, but she could make out words as they drew nearer. It was someone singing!

'I know that song,' Freya exclaimed, and Hannah realised she did, too. She'd sung it herself more than once – 'We Shall Not Be Moved'.

'It's Nan.' Hannah's voice came out in a whisper. Despite it stinging that Kitty had taken matters into her own hands, she was awestruck, amazed that her nan even knew the protest hymn. Which she was butchering, though that was neither here nor there. Shannon was the only Kelly family member blessed with the gift of song.

The surprises kept coming because Father Christmas,

looking less than jolly, peeled away from the huddle and approached them with Nora Kelly in tow.

'Hannah.' Nora acknowledged her daughter. 'How're you, Freya? Can you believe this, the pair of you?'

'I can't believe how many people are here.' Freya's gaze swung back and forth like a lighthouse beam over the field.

'We stand by Nan, Mam,' Hannah said. Even if Nan hadn't seen fit to ask her to do so. Then she got to the more pressing point. 'Dad, you're a long way from the North Pole. What are you playing at?'

It might be tradition for Liam Kelly to don the red suit on Christmas Eve to dole out sweets to the children of Emerald Bay during the carolling service, but he was a tad early because Hannah could still count down to Christmas on two hands. Should she be worried he was taking his role too seriously? Princess Leia began growling. She clearly wasn't a fan of Father Christmas.

'Would you tell Cujo there to stand down?' Liam huffed, taking a wary step back from his daughter and acknowledging Freya with a nod.

Somewhere in the surrounding hubbub a child cried out, 'Mammy, Father Christmas is here!'

'Why are you all dressed up like so, Liam?' Freya asked.

'It's Nora's fault I'm parading about a field missing my sleigh and reindeer. And I've not a sweet or balloon on me if that little one decides to head over and tell me how good she's been. Yer man over there's already after snapping a photo without my permission, too.'

Hannah didn't look to where he was gesturing vaguely. She didn't need to. Jeremy Jones was on the prowl. She hoped her dad didn't inadvertently steal the front page and make Nan's protest look ridiculous.

Liam carried on explaining himself. 'I thought I'd try the suit on before I chose the Christmas tree because with all the kale and whatnot, I'm after dropping a few pounds, and it might need taking in. I'd no sooner attached my beard when Nora burst in, telling me my mam was after staging a sit-in at the abandoned farm. I'd no time to change.'

'It was Tom who rang me.' Nora filled in the gaps, reaching out to pet Princess Leia. 'He was supposed to be meeting his client here only it was cancelled due to something having come up at the developer's end. He decided to swing by to scope things out anyway and found your nan sitting cross-legged – at her age! – in the cottage entrance like some sort of guru.'

'That was good of him,' Hannah said through gritted teeth. It was his fault Nan was here in the freezing cold in the first place. His and whoever his partner in crime was. Nan's earlier inquisitiveness about where he was meeting his client as he'd chatted to Mam in the kitchen made sense now. She stood on tiptoes, trying and failing to glimpse Kitty over the huddled pack.

'Well, thank goodness he did, and he was genuinely concerned, Hannah, so that's enough of the snarky remarks.' Nora scanned the faces surrounding the cottage, her brow creased. 'I don't know where he's got to, but he did say he promised to relay to his client how she felt about the Green-house project rather than her sitting out in the cold. Your nan told him she was fine where she was, thanks very much.'

A dart of pride overrode Hannah's bewilderment at her nan's secretive behaviour. It was hard to understand when she'd felt so close to her last night, but a bigger part of her was cheer-ing: good for her!

'What's she playing at? I want to know. Sure, she's like a rebellious reindeer sitting over there with that "Oh Deer it's Christmas" beanie she bought off that online shop she's forever buying useless pieces of tat off. We tried talking some sense into her, but she kept launching into the song like a scratched record. And one in danger of catching pneumonia at that.' Liam tugged his faux beard. 'Would you keep that vicious, fangy-toothed thing away from me?'

Princess Leia might not be a fan of the opposite sex, but she liked Father Christmas even less.

'Nan,' Hannah said, keeping a firm hold of Princess Leia, 'is standing up for what she believes in.'

It was up to Kitty to share what this place meant to her.

'I think you'll find she's sitting down, cross-legged if you recall, Hannah, on one of my good cushions,' Nora fired back. 'Sergeant Badger's after having a quiet word, but she's not breaking any laws, so there's nothing he can do apart from crowd control.'

OK, that was a tad dramatic, given that the number of curious Emerald Bay spectators whose Sunday afternoons had been livened up once word had somehow spread regarding Kitty Kelly's protest was hardly on a scale with the pilgrims flocking to the Holy Mountain.

Speak of the devil, there he was, aviator sunglasses in place in case he should get snapped for the papers, marching about the place like a geriatric Tom Cruise.

'Go and talk to her, Hannah. She might listen to you,' Nora urged.

Hannah was only too eager to do so, wanting to quiz Nan about why she'd left her out. 'I will. Catch you later, Mam, Dad. Come on, Freya.'

They moved away from Nora and Liam and had only taken a few strides toward the cottage when their path was blocked. Hannah coughed as she inhaled acrid smoky fumes and, flapping her hand in distaste, saw the familiar, whippet-like form of Jeremy Jones, cigarette dangling out the corner of his mouth, taking up space in front of her.

'So you're a chip off the old block,' he wheezed.

'Feck off, Jeremy.'

Freya grasped her hand, attempting to tug her away. 'Come on, Hannah.'

'Is this your mascot?' the reporter sneered at Princess Leia, who responded with a yip that meant business.

'I'd get out of my way if I were you,' Hannah warned. She desperately wanted to know who'd tipped him off. Still, she wouldn't give the weaselly-eyed excuse for a reporter the satisfaction.

'I've a few questions for you. I'd like to get your nan's side of the story, but yer Kate Bush wannabe over there's stuck on repeat play, so you're the next best thing.'

'No comment.'

'Hannah, come on,' Freya urged for the second time.

'That's not like you. You're usually only too keen to get your side of the story across.'

'And I've learned the hard way if there's something in it for you, then the "truth" is flexible. So no, I'll not be talking to you.'

'But what's the point in a protest when nobody knows what's being protested?'

Hannah hesitated, and Freya leaned close to her ear, whispering, 'He's got a point.'

He did, and as much as it rankled, Hannah knew she'd have to give him something. 'I'll keep it brief then.'

Jeremy Jones clicked a button on the small tape-recording device he held toward Hannah.

'Kitty Kelly is against selling this land to an out-of-town developer because it belongs to the people of Emerald Bay. She's not the only one either. I've a signed petition in here' – she tapped her satchel – 'that says most of Emerald Bay's residents feel the proposed Greenhouse garden centre and Christmas tree farm planned for this site is sacrilege.' An exaggeration given she'd not yet had the chance to seek out the majority of the villagers for an opinion one way or another. Jeremy didn't need to know that, though. 'The famine cottage and this land is part of our village's history. We don't want that history destroyed in the name of so-called progress, and Freya and I are here to relieve Kitty from her post.'

If Freya was surprised to hear this, she didn't let on, adding to what Hannah had said. 'It's terrible an elderly woman having to put her life at risk by sitting out in freezing conditions like this to be heard.'

Hannah made to move away then, but Jeremy reached out to stop her. 'How do you know who's behind the development? I was told the buyer or buyers wish to remain anonymous.'

The sight of the oily reporter lunging toward her was too much for Princess Leia, who, like a crocodile striking, sank her teeth down on his closest finger as though she'd been offered a tasty bone to gnaw on.

Things seemed to go in slow motion then. The cigarette dropped from Jeremy's mouth to lie smouldering on the damp earth as he raised his bleeding finger and stared at it in disbelief.

Hannah choked back a laugh, seeing the reporter's face blanch white at the tiny trickle of blood running down the inside of his index finger.

'I'm bleeding,' he rasped.

'Sure, it's only a little nip. A plaster will sort that, but I'd be getting a rabies shot if I were you. What do you think, Freya?'

'Oh, definitely. You can't be too careful with wild dogs, like.'

'No, hold that thought. I don't think you need to be bothering the doctor on a Sunday because, sure, you're already rabid. And you're welcome to put that in your paper.'

With that, Hannah and Freya, grinning from ear to ear, linked arms and left the reporter and his bleeding finger to it.

20

'Why didn't you tell me what you had planned, Nan? If I'd known, I could have organised placards and jumped on social media to spread the word. Mam and I thought you were skulking about meeting your fancy man with your fibs about popping around to see Reenie.'

'Fancy man indeed!' Kitty snorted, reaching up to take Princess Leia from her granddaughter and settle her on her lap. 'You'll make a grand little hottie so you will. And I didn't know what I would do until this morning when I overheard Tom saying he had a meeting here. You'd disappeared by the time I'd made my mind up to interrupt his pow-wow and tell whoever's behind it I'm against selling this land by staging a sit-in. You know yourself time isn't on our side with Christmas around the corner.'

Nan's voice had a rawness to it which Hannah suspected was thanks to the cold and the singing.

'Only the developer never showed up for the meeting, and you went ahead with your protest anyway,' Freya said.

Hannah wasn't letting her nan off the hook that easily. 'You still could have called me.'

'I didn't want you to try and talk me out of it.'

'To be honest, Nan, I don't know what I'd have done, but I do know it's too cold for you out here with your chest.'

Freya backed Hannah up. 'She's got a point, Kitty. You were laid up for weeks with the bronchitis not that long ago.'

Kitty flapped her hand dismissively. 'Don't you be telling me what's what and all.' She changed the subject, asking Hannah, 'Where did you get to anyway?'

'Princess Leia and I were canvassing the streets with a petition – well, street at any rate.' She showed Kitty the signatures she'd gathered. 'Mam called me while I was with Freya to say where you were, and we came straight here.'

'So we've both been making our stand.' Kitty looked pleased, and she and Hannah exchanged a smile of solidarity.

'I don't understand how all these people found out what you were up to in the first place, Kitty.' Freya motioned toward the crowd, buzzing about like they were in a fairground. All that was missing was the candyfloss.

'There was no sense in sitting here protesting if nobody knew about it, so I made a few calls.'

The penny dropped, and Hannah caught Freya's eye, silently conveying it was Kitty who'd rung Jeremy Jones. She'd probably rung Eileen Carroll as well. As the village gossip, Eileen could spread the word faster than any text message.

'Well, I'm proud of you, Nan.'

'So am I, Kitty. And I love your beanie, by the way.'

Kitty patted her hat. 'I saw it and I bought it.' She grinned. 'I fell in love with the little reindeer ears myself.'

'They're a lovely touch,' Freya agreed.

'Antlers not ears, Nan, and we'll take over now. Mam and Dad will take you home.' Hannah glanced over to where her parents were waiting expectantly.

'You will not muscle in on my act. This is my protest!'

'But it's for your own good.' Hannah regretted the words as

soon as they slipped from her mouth. They'd only serve to make her nan dig her heels in more.

True to form, Kitty folded her arms over her chest and broke into another round of 'We Shall Not Be Moved'.

'Do you mind if we join you then?' Freya stepped in to ease family tensions.

Kitty patted the hard ground next to her while her throaty voice drifted across the field.

Hannah could see her mam and dad watching the unfolding scene, and she shrugged over at them as if to say, *If you can't beat them, join them*, because just like the song, Nan would not be moved.

The two younger women crowded on either side of Kitty to help keep her warm. Behind them, the door had long since broken free of its hinges and was propped against a wall inside the cottage, the interior of which Hannah imagined was like a cold store preserving memories not of the children who came to play and scare themselves but of the lives lived out within its walls. Mind, if the scuffling she could hear up in the rafters was a clue, she'd say that it was home to a family of mice these days.

Carmel Brady, making her way toward them with a thermos, was a welcome sight, and the takeaway cups she filled with fragrant mulled wine were gratefully received.

'It's very kind of you, Carmel.' Kitty's teeth were chattering despite her being huddled between Hannah and Freya with Princess Leia acting as a hot-water bottle.

Carmel beamed. 'Sure, it's not a bother. When I heard what you were up to, Kitty, I put a pot on the stove to simmer knowing it would be just the ticket. It's that time of the year, after all.' Her eyes flitted to the clipboard on Hannah's lap, and Hannah explained what it was.

'I'll put my name to it, and I dare say you can count on the rest of Main Street's business owners to sign it, too.' She barely paused to draw breath as her attention switched to Freya. 'I must say I was surprised to see you here. I thought you were away for the weekend.'

Not wanting her personal business to be the hot topic of conversation among Carmel, Isla and Eileen for the remainder of the afternoon, Freya mumbled something non-committal, and Hannah rescued her by passing the clipboard up to the older woman.

'Thanks, Carmel.'

'Good on you for being on the front line, like. You've my full support where this is concerned.' She made a sweeping gesture, taking in the land around them and then tapped the clipboard. 'I'll pass it around for you, shall I?'

Carmel was eager to help, and given every signature counted, Hannah thanked her.

The cafe owner's eyes moved over their heads to the cottage behind and she visibly shuddered. 'You can feel them here. The ghosts, I mean.'

Hannah felt a prickling at the back of her neck and wondered if Nan and Freya felt it, too. Was Granddad Finbar here with them now? If so, then she hoped he knew they wouldn't let him down.

21

It was surprising how much colder it was sitting on the ground than when you were milling about, Hannah mused, feeling much-needed heat flood through her veins as she finished her cup of warming wine.

'I need to spend a penny,' Kitty announced.

'I don't see any public toilets, Nan, do you? And there're too many people about for you to drop your drawers behind the cottage. What are you going to do?'

Kitty was clearly in a quandary and, fidgeting, passed Princess Leia to Hannah. 'Here, take her. She's not helping pressing on my bladder like so.'

'Sure, Mam and Dad will give you a lift home, and Princess Leia will want something to eat after her walk earlier,' Hannah said, holding the disgruntled miniature dog.

They all looked to where Liam Kelly, in his Father Christmas suit, was turning his pockets out and making the youngster to whom he was explaining himself cry when no treat was forthcoming. Nora was tapping her foot impatiently, eager for the off, but Hannah knew they'd not be going anywhere without Kitty.

'No. That won't do. They'll kidnap me, so they will. I won't
be taken home against my will. Sure, the park's only round the
corner, and the council does a grand job keeping the toilets
clean. You two will have to hold the fort until I get back, and
don't forget to sing the song.'

Hannah and Freya watched Kitty untangle herself before
she leaned on their shoulders and pulled herself to her feet.
'Here, pass me that lead. I'll see to it your mam and dad take her
home.'

Hannah held the lead up for Kitty, and the chihuahua
nimbly climbed off her lap to stand obediently by Kitty's side.

'I'll be as quick as I can.'

'Mind how you go, Nan,' Hannah warned. 'There's patches
of ice about.'

'You're worse than your mam fussing like so,' Kitty
muttered, plucking her way over to Nora and Liam.

'Good luck to them trying to talk her into going home and
warming herself by the fire,' Hannah said, spying Tom a short
distance away.

She nudged Freya. 'See your man in the tan, posh-looking
belted trench coat on his phone?' She'd bet it was a Burberry
and cost a fortune.

'Uh-huh.'

'That's Tom Flynn, the architectural project manager who's
ruining Christmas that I told you about.'

Freya glanced quizzically from her to him. 'You never
mentioned he was cute.'

'Freya!'

'What? He is.'

'He's only cute if you like the lanky, posh-coat type.'
Hannah shook her head at the very notion of him being fancia-
ble. 'Which I don't. And besides, it's irrelevant.'

Freya's lips twitched. 'You seem to have got his number.

And it's not irrelevant when you're single.' She studied him once more. 'He's definitely cute.'

'Freya, you're not that fickle-hearted, surely? You were crying over Oisin an hour ago!'

'Not for me, you eejit. I need time to lick my wounds.' Freya laid her hand on her chest dramatically. 'I am a man-free zone, but you, well now, you're footloose and fancy free, and they say opposites attract.' Freya waggled her brows.

'Either you're a total lightweight regarding the wine, or you've completely lost the plot.' Hannah's lips formed a prim line.

'Sure, he'd keep you warm wrapped inside his Burberry.' Freya winked.

'Right.' Hannah decided this needed a line drawing under it. 'You know you're an honorary Kelly sister, right?'

'Right.' Freya looked pleased by the notion.

'As such, I'm going to speak to you now as one Kelly sister to another.'

'Fair play.'

'Feck off with you, Freya.'

Laughter pealed. 'Sorry, I asked for that. I'm just trying to take my mind off my desperate love life. And you know yourself when you've been upset and then get all giggly and stupid? It's like an emotional release.'

The only thing Hannah could equate that with was when she'd been at the Feed the World with Bees Christmas drinks last year and had been laughing her head off one minute and crying into her pink gin the next over the state of the world. It was a back-to-front version of what Freya had just said. 'Sort of. But for the record, your man over there represents everything I stand against.'

'Got it.' Freya saluted. 'Although, me thinks she doth protest too much.'

'Freya,' Hannah growled.

'Sorry. I'll say no more.'

'Good, and it's nice to see you smiling, so I'll forgive you. Besides this, here's not how either of us envisaged spending our afternoon, and I am grateful you're here with me, even if you're more of a smart arse than Imo when she gets going.'

That raised another chuckle.

'So there's no one on the scene?'

'Freya!'

'I poured my heart out to you earlier.'

Hannah's hesitancy was all it took.

'Come on – spill the beans.'

'OK, there is someone, but he doesn't know how I feel. So I don't suppose that counts.'

Freya pushed her for more information, and Hannah told her about Dylan. She was surprised at how good it felt to confess her feelings for him.

'I admire his principles and other stuff. I mean, obviously. You can't snog the face off a set of principles.'

Freya smiled at that. 'The heart wants what the heart wants, but can I be honest?'

Hannah would have liked a top-up of the mulled wine for whatever was coming, and as none was forthcoming, her reply was a hesitant, 'OK.'

'It sounds like you've put this Dylan on a pedestal.'

Was Freya saying she hero-worshipped him? If so, she'd got it all wrong. She opened her mouth to correct her, but Freya took hold of her mittened hand and gave it a squeeze.

'Take it from someone who's wasted the last couple of years of her life on a man who wasn't worth it. Move on even if it means looking for a new job.'

It wasn't what she wanted to hear, and Freya had never even met Dylan. He was worth the heartache.

'Look, Kitty's doing a runner.'

Hannah followed the line of Freya's pointing finger. She

watched her nan go, marvelling at her speed as she trotted toward the wall, antlers bobbing, while answering the questions Jeremy Jones, hot on her heels, fired at her.

'She's like the Pied Piper,' Freya announced as others trailed after them, eager to see what Kitty had in store next. 'Only instead of a magic pipe, she's got a reindeer hat, and it's not a cave, she's leading them all to, it's the public loos.'

Hannah would have laughed if she wasn't sidetracked by Tom, who'd finished his call and was hurrying after Kitty.

'I'll give you a lift if you're heading back to the Shamrock, Mrs Kelly!' he called after her.

Then their view was blocked, but there was no mistaking the cry that went up a split second later.

'Somebody help her! She's fallen.'

22

Hannah sprinted to the wall, heart thudding, fearing what she'd find on the other side, then channelled her school gym days, vaulting over the piled-up stones before shouldering through the murmuring huddle like an American footballer desperate to get to the goalpost. The sight of Jeremy Jones with his camera pointed at Nan, lying in a heap on the grass verge, saw a red mist descend. She gave him a hard shove. 'Go away, you ghoul. You're like one of those car accident voyeurs!' Then, barely registering Tom was crouched next to Kitty, she cried, 'Nan!'

Kitty's head snapped up at the sound of her granddaughter's voice. 'I'm fine, Hannah. I caught my shoe on one of those stones and took a tumble, is all.' She beckoned her over, and Hannah squatted next to her. Kitty clutched her arm and whispered. 'I might have had another sort of accident, though.' Her face pinkened.

'Mam!' Father Christmas appeared with Nora by his side, doing her best to hold on to a yapping Princess Leia's leash.

'Janey Mack, there's no show without Punch,' Kitty grumbled. 'I'm all right, Liam. Would you tell this lot here there's nothing to see?'

'Can you stand up?' Tom held his arms out as if to support Kitty. Hannah briefly wondered if being held in his arms would be as comforting as his firm grip, and felt warmth in her cheeks.

Kitty's stony gaze saw him withdraw his offer of help, and hardened Hannah's own heart too.

'You can clear off, too.' Fear had made Hannah snap. 'This is all your fault, Tom Flynn. My nan wouldn't be here if not for you and whoever's pocket you're in.' Her breath was coming in short angry bursts.

Tom's glasses had misted, but she could see the confusion in his eyes as he took them off, gave them a quick rub with the edge of his coat and, taking the hint, got to his feet.

'I'm sorry you feel that way.' He moved away.

Hannah glanced over her shoulder. The curious onlookers had begun to disperse, and, most importantly, Jeremy Flynn had disappeared. She discarded her coat and tugged off the cardigan buttoned over her dungarees. 'Here, Nan – we'll tie this round your waist. No one will know.'

'You're a good girl, Hannah.' Kitty squeezed her grand-daughter's hand.

Hannah deftly knotted the cardigan and beckoned her dad over to help her.

Liam gently pulled his mam to her feet, and Kitty shook herself off tentatively before checking herself over.

Hannah caught her mam's eye, and they exchanged a relieved smile; nothing was broken.

'I'm a bit bruised, is all. It's my ego that's taken the worst of it,' Kitty reassured them.

'Come on, Mam – let's get you home.' Liam took Kitty's arm.

'On one condition,' Kitty said, an immovable rock, even though she was in no position to negotiate. 'Hannah, you and Freya are to stand your ground here. Keep singing the song.'

She might be bruised, her pride dented, but she wasn't beaten. 'Of course,' Hannah reassured her nan.

'Promise me.'

'I promise, Nan.'

Only then did Kitty let her son lead her towards his Hilux.

While the sky had been filled with scudding clouds earlier, the odd patch of blue had still peeked through. Now, though, it hung omnipresent over Hannah and Freya like they'd been draped in a scratchy grey army blanket.

'It won't be long until it starts drizzling,' Freya announced, a prophet of doom taking a break from the song.

Hannah paused to draw breath and gulp down what was left of her third and final mulled wine, given that Carmel had packed up and left ten minutes earlier. Her throat was raw from all the singing, and the spiced wine soothed it.

'For medicinal purposes,' she said, winking at Freya.

She set the empty cup down and then, seeing the handful of villagers who'd stayed the course look heavenward and shake their heads at the leaden sky head off, decided Freya was right. Tom was still there, though. Hannah looked to where he was glued to his phone, nodding at whatever the person on the other end was saying. She remembered Freya's comment about her protesting too much and was telling herself it was rubbish when his gaze suddenly swung toward her. He must have felt her watching him, she thought, realising she'd been staring.

She held her ground. His expression was unreadable, and she was struck by an overwhelmingly childish urge to stick her tongue out at him, given she wouldn't be sitting here freezing her arse off on a gloomy Sunday afternoon if not for him.

Jeremy Jones chose that moment to pop back up again, and Hannah averted her eyes from Tom to focus on him instead. The man was like an annoying wart you couldn't get rid of.

'What do you want now?' Freya asked.

Hannah did her best not to smirk at the sight of his finger wrapped in a child's Disney-themed plaster.

'I need a couple of photos for the road, and then I'll be out of here. If I were you, I'd do the same now the star of the show's gone. The weather forecast isn't good.' Jeremy didn't bother looking up as he fiddled with the lens of his camera before raising it to his eye. 'Say "Cheese".'

It was a magic word because just like that, Hannah was transported back to sitting on the wooden pew in the front row for school photographs, hands clasped in her lap as she automatically beamed for the camera – and immediately wished she hadn't. The protest was a serious business, not a Sunday afternoon picnic, but it was too late now. Jeremy had clicked off a round and was eagerly packing his camera away to return to his car's warmth.

By the time the reporter had reached the stone wall, Freya's forecasted drizzle had bypassed them in favour of steady, icy rain droplets. Tom had gone, and Hannah looked around the nearby deserted field, almost disappointed.

'Shall we sing again?' Freya chirped. 'It might raise our spirits.'

'I don't think there's much point now,' Hannah said, looking around at the empty field. 'Ah no!' She blanched as the wind changed direction, and the rain began to drive toward them, stinging their faces. Then, squinting into the darkening vista, her brow furrowed. 'Who's that?'

A woman sheltering under a red umbrella wearing a matching coat stood beside her car, watching them. From this distance, Hannah could tell she wasn't an Emerald Bay local. Another reporter maybe?

Freya was tracking her gaze, and there was urgency in her tone as she said, 'Hannah, I think that could be her.'

'Who?'

'The American woman you said was freaking Nora out.'

Hannah didn't mess about. She got to her feet and marched purposefully over the damp earth toward the woman. She would get to the bottom of this.

'Hey!' she called out as the woman hurried around to the driver's door of her car. 'Wait!'

Hannah began to run, already knowing it was too late.

Sure enough, the woman got behind the wheel and gunned the engine, and Hannah skidded to a halt, unable to do anything but watch as she drove off in a cloud of exhaust fumes.

23

Nora Kelly was alone at the kitchen table, scanning a recipe book when the back door was unexpectedly flung open. 'Jesus, Mary and Joseph, would you look at the state of you standing there shivering like so.' She shook her head at seeing her daughter backlit by the pouring rain in the doorway. 'You look like that old comic-book monster Swamp Thing emerged from the deep.'

'Charming.' Hannah heard the crunch of gravel as Freya, who'd dropped her home, drove away, and shut the door. They'd decided there was no point hanging about an empty field getting battered by the wind and rain. Once the mystery woman had driven off, no one was left to pay attention to what they were protesting against. Then Mam had texted to say Nan was toasting her toes by the fire and seemed none the worse for having taken a tumble, and Hannah decided she wouldn't mind them clearing out. So they'd picked up their empty cups and sought sanctuary in the car.

As they'd trooped across the sodden field, she'd felt that same prickling on the back of her neck she'd experienced earlier and risked a glance behind her. There was nothing there except for the murky shape of the cottage. Freya didn't seem to have picked up on anything, so she didn't mention the unnerving sensation on the short drive back to the Shamrock, listening to Freya say she couldn't wait to sink into a hot bath. As they pulled up behind the pub, she'd assured Hannah there would be no more tears over Oisin.

Now, running on automatic pilot, Hannah shed her sodden coat, sure she'd never been so cold in all her days. Or hungry, for that matter. What with how her day had unfolded one way and another, there'd been no opportunity for lunch. So, feeling like a poor, frozen waif, she paused to sniff the air hopefully, but there were no tantalising clues as to what dinner was, only the recipe book in front of Mam. It was very disappointing that all she could smell was the faint whiff of bacon from the morning's fry-up. Breakfast felt like a lifetime ago, given everything that had happened since.

After hanging her coat on the back-door hook, she bent down to untie her bootlaces.

'I'll make you an omelette,' Nora said, as if she'd read her daughter's mind. 'Now, get up those stairs and out of those wet things,' she ordered. 'I can hear your teeth chattering from here. An Irish whiskey and an omelette in that order will sort you out.'

Both sounded like pure bliss, Hannah thought, even if it did seem an odd combination. She held back, unsure whether to tell her mam who she'd seen.

'What is it?' Nora studied her daughter's face with a frown.

Worry saw it come out in a big blurt. 'Freya and I saw your mystery American woman. It was after everyone else had gone. Mam, she was watching us from the lane, and when I approached her, she got in her car and drove away. Do you really have no idea who she is?'

'I wish I knew.'

Hannah stood dripping on the kitchen floor, and Nora blinked, registering the state of her daughter. 'But standing there catching your death isn't going to tell us who she is or what she wants. Upstairs. Now.'

Fifteen minutes later, warmed through to her core, smelling sweet and dressed in fresh clothes, Hannah felt like a new woman altogether. Hot water was restorative, and with that thought in mind, she padded back down the stairs. Not much had changed when she'd been gone, but true to her word, Mam had a cup of the special coffee waiting with a tempting blob of whipped cream floating on top and a sprinkle of cinnamon to make it look pretty. Hannah pulled out a chair and sat down. 'This will hit the spot, Mam, thanks.'

'There's a healthy shot of Bushmills finest in there to ward off any chills,' Nora stated, cracking eggs in a bowl.

'Where is everyone?'

'Your dad and nan are through there.' Nora used the fork she was about to whip the eggs with to point to the connecting door to the pub. 'Kitty's rallying up the masses. She's been getting signatures for that petition of yours. She's like a queen holding court, so she is.' Nora hesitated then added, 'Don't tell her about seeing your American woman today, Hannah love. We could be reading something into nothing, and she's had enough excitement for one day.'

Hannah met her mam's stare and could tell she didn't believe they were making a mountain out of a molehill. But fair play – nothing could be gained in winding Nan up over having seen her.

'What about our guest?' Hannah moved the conversation on before taking a pensive sip of her coffee and glancing about as though expecting to find Tom lurking in the corner. Then, as the hot liquid hit the back of her throat, making her cough, she put the cup down with a 'Jaysus, Mam, it's more than a shot you've put in here. My eyes are watering, so they are.'

'It'll put hairs on your chest.'

'Grand. Look forward to it.'

'Tom's gone back to Dublin,' Nora answered her question, fetching the cheese grater.

That surprised Hannah, and she sat up a little straighter. Had their protest sent him back to the Big Smoke with his tail between his legs? The tug of disappointment that victory might have been won so easily, with Tom perhaps talking his client into looking for land elsewhere, surprised her. She'd thought he was made of stronger stuff than that, given the way he'd debated with her in the kitchen that morning.

'He'd an emergency to deal with at home,' Nora continued.

An emergency could mean anything. Still, she'd run with a burst pipe in that swanky apartment of his. It was preferable to worrying about something happening to the young lad he mentored. Tom having hightailed it back to Dublin was a mixed blessing, she decided, unable to stop herself from asking, 'Is he coming back to Emerald Bay?'

'Tuesday lunchtime, although, for your information, that's only because I persuaded him to stay here. After today's protest, he was dead set on checking out and booking elsewhere because he didn't want to make you and Kitty uncomfortable in your own home. But I managed to talk him out of it.'

'Thanks a million, Mam.' So he hadn't folded and got his mystery client to back off.

'Listen, Hannah. You and Kitty might have taken against Tom, but I think he's a lovely fella who's just here to do a job. And even if I agreed with you, which I don't, we need the money. In case you haven't noticed, Christmas is nearly here, and every penny counts.' Nora began grating cheese on top of the egg mix, her back turned to Hannah as she said, 'Still waters run deep with that young man, and you'd do well to soften those black-and-white compartments of yours that you're so determined people slot into. Have a little Christmas spirit, for goodness' sake, Hannah!'

There was a sharp intake of breath as though Nora had more to say but she only banged the grater down on the worktop instead.

'What, Mam?' Hannah demanded. She was ready to bite back because she'd no wish to know what lay beneath Tom's surface after today. Be it still waters or raging rapids. And her mam's words about her seeing things in black and white stung. She didn't have much room for shades of grey in her life, and Christmas spirit, well, that was hard to muster under the circumstances. Mam didn't understand, and silently, huffing, she took a big mouthful of her coffee, which had plenty of spirit in it, not bothering to wipe away the cream moustache left behind.

Nora's tone softened. 'I've sensed Tom's enjoying staying here, mucking in as part of the family, even if a certain someone not too far from where I'm sitting has been determined to make him feel unwelcome. You don't seem to have put him off in the least thankfully. Although to be fair, he's hardly spoiled for choice regarding places to stay in these parts.'

That was true, Hannah thought, her hackles slowly dropping. You'd not get a fry-up like what was on offer at the Shamrock elsewhere in the area, and certainly not at the closest B&B. The tight-fisted woman running that only offered a continental breakfast. There were a few places to choose from in Kiltica-neel, but it was a drive from the abandoned farm and, distance aside, none were as warm and welcoming as the Shamrock Inn, herself and Nan not included. Besides, it was better to keep your enemies close, Hannah thought, suddenly sick to death of talking about Tom Flynn.

She heard the sizzle as her mam poured the omelette mix into the pan and pulled out her phone. Her head hurting from all that had happened and the need to get it off her chest, she tapped out a summons to the Kelly girls' WhatsApp group.

I'm calling an URGENT meeting, sisters, my bedroom ASAP.

24

Fed and watered, Hannah was propped up by pillows on her bed with the laptop open. She'd messaged the twins to tell them she'd FaceTime them when Imogen and Shannon showed their faces but they weren't to worry in the interim. On the screen in front of her was an open Word document, but she'd got no further than heading the letter she planned to write to the Department of Agriculture and typing 'To whom it may concern'. Aware Christmas was breathing down her neck, she would need to email the letter at the opening of business in the morning. There was more chance of it being opened and read if whoever was in charge was at their desk when it pinged in.

Her fingers hovered over the keyboard, but she heard footfall racing up the stairs before she could begin her impassioned plea to accompany the petition. She snapped the laptop shut as a breathless Imogen, followed by Shannon, burst into the bedroom.

'You got my message then?'

'We were hotfooting it round anyway,' Imogen informed her, flopping down at the end of the bed and kicking her shoes off so she could pull her legs up to her chin.

Shannon ordered her to squish up, and Hannah listened as she waffled about having been Christmas shopping. 'We were making up a foursome, and the lads were fed up with the shops, so we headed over to the Galway Market at St Nicholas Church for a wander and a spot of lunch. That's when the call came through from Mam about Nan's protest at the abandoned farm.'

For a moment, Hannah was lost as Shannon lamented, 'It was a terrible waste.'

'What was?'

'The paper plates of food we binned in favour of heading back to Emerald Bay. I was enjoying a lovely curry, so I was, but by the time we reached the farm, the show was well over. The lads are in the pub now, getting the low-down on what happened. Nan's the hero of the hour from what we saw.' She unwrapped her stripy scarf – which put Hannah in mind of Christmas candy canes – and sighed. 'I can't believe we missed it all.'

'Yeah. Me too,' Imogen agreed. Her chin was resting on her knees as she added, 'She's our very own Gloria Steinem – who'd have thought it?'

'I don't know why you're so surprised. Nan's always been strong,' Hannah said.

'That's true enough. I suppose now we know where you get it from.' Imogen grinned.

Hannah was quietly pleased instead of the usual irritation she'd feel when her stubbornness regarding her convictions was mentioned, because to hold firm on what you believed, you had to be stubborn. It was pointing out the obvious.

Picking up her phone, she said, 'Nan was really something. You'd have been proud of her if you'd seen her in action.' Then, swiping the screen of her phone, she added, 'I said I'd FaceTime the twins as soon as you two arrived.'

'Why is your voice all raspy? You sound like you could be

doing a sexy voiceover for a chocolate advert.' Imogen cocked a brow.

Hannah thought of her chat with Freya and her confiding Oisín had a melting-chocolate bedroom voice and inwardly grimaced. 'It's down to the hundred repetitions of Nan's protest song in the freezing cold.'

Both sisters' eyebrows shot up this time as Hannah gave them a throaty abbreviated version of 'We Shall Not Be Moved'. The twins popped onto her phone screen as she finished her verse, and they looked back at her equally incredulous.

'Are you both good to talk?' Hannah got in first.

Ava, a pen tucked behind her ear, informed them she was due a break from the copy-editing work that kept her afloat while she wrote her novel in the city that never slept. Grace, however, was curled up under a rug on the canal boat she shared with Chris, who she informed them was at band practice.

'I was only flicking through a mag, so now,' she told her sisters, 'is a great time to talk. So come on, Hannah – what's with that song and the urgent message?'

If it weren't for their differing backgrounds – i.e., Ava's minuscule New York apartment and Grace's mellow timber-panelled floating home – hairstyles and the tiny birthmark Ava had on her jaw, Hannah wouldn't be able to tell them apart, and that was after sharing a room with them for most of their lives! She rearranged herself so Shannon and Imogen could see the phone she held in front of her. They waved at the twins.

Ava waved back and then frowned. 'I'm with Grace. What's up?'

Hannah thought she detected a slight New York twang in Ava's voice. 'Have you two heard about Nan's protest today?' she asked them.

Their bug-like eyes told her the news had yet to reach the twins, so she updated them on the day's events, starting with her petition, Nan's protest, her tumble and herself and Freya taking over the sit-in outside the cottage.

'But Nan's OK?' Both sisters sought confirmation.

Imogen peered over Hannah's shoulder. 'Nan is lording it over the locals in the pub as we speak.'

Grace looked momentarily relieved, but an expression of annoyance swiftly replaced this. 'I'll be having words with Mam. It's a case of out of sight, out of mind. Why didn't she ring me or Ava and tell us when this was all unfolding?'

'I think it's more a case of her getting sidetracked by everything that was going on, and sure, you know yourself, she can never work out the time difference between Ireland and New York. She wouldn't have wanted to panic Ava if it was the middle of the night or for her to feel left out if she rang you and not her,' Hannah appeased.

Ava, leaning into the screen, had other things on her mind than why Mam hadn't been straight on the phone with her. 'So the protest, with the song and everything, was Nan's idea?'

'Yeah. It was, although I don't know how she came up with it.'

'There's Google, Hannah. She could have looked it up, but I don't understand why Nan feels so strongly about the cottage and the land?' Grace queried, still looking sulky.

'Well, listen to this.' Hannah launched into the story Nan had told her.

All four of her sisters were sniffing when she'd finished relaying it. 'So now you can understand why the cottage and the land around it is special to her. It's her and Granddad's place.'

'I'd no clue,' Shannon said, patting her pockets for a packet of tissues.

'Sign your petition on my behalf,' Ava instructed.

'And mine,' Grace piped up, tears having replaced her earlier churlishness.

Imogen, who'd been on the fence regarding the Greenhouse, blew her nose. 'Shannon and I saw it on the kitchen table. We already signed. The lads will, too.'

Shannon dipped her head in agreement.

'Ryan will always find work, and I figured if it meant that much to you and Nan, then I would have to sign it. Who'd have thought the cottage where we all argued about who got to be Sigourney Weaver wanting the Ghostbusters to come and clear it would mean so much to Nan?'

'From memory, you always got to be Sigourney, or you'd get all mardy and stomp home, threatening to tell Mam where we were after playing. And that cottage's history goes way back, remember? It might have been the setting for our grandparents falling in love, but there's been terrible heartbreak there, too. Don't forget that.'

Hannah softened Shannon's harsh reminder about those who'd suffered during the Great Hunger by swivelling round so she could squeeze Imogen's arm. 'Thanks for signing it, Imo, and you too, Shan.' She paused. 'There's something else I wanted to talk to you about. Which is where the urgent part comes into things.'

Her sisters gave her their full attention as she brought up how she'd seen the mystery American woman watching herself and Freya that afternoon.

'When I called out to her, she couldn't get in her car and drive away fast enough.'

Ava's blue eyes rounded. 'What does she want?'

Hannah suspected her youngest sister's writer's imagination was going wild with possibilities. 'That's the thing, Ava, we don't know. And it's no good guessing. Shannon and Imogen, we need to be vigilant. If we see her about the place, collar her and ask her outright why she's so interested in our mam and what she's doing in Emerald Bay.'

'We'll be home for Christmas soon, too, don't forget. We'll keep an eye out, won't we, Grace?'

Grace had disappeared from the screen, and when she popped back on, her blue eyes were enormous.

'Janey Mack! You won't believe this! My friend Soph just messaged me. She lives on TikTok, and someone using the handle irishisla posted a video of Nan doing her thing today, and it's only after going viral. It's trending under the hashtags protest, Christmas hats, nanas, Ireland and – that's weird – Irish souvenir.'

'What?' Disbelief echoed around the bedroom and from over in New York.

'Check it out for yourselves,' Grace said before disappearing, presumably to find the video. Ava vanished, too.

'Irish Isla?' Hannah questioned while Imogen was searching for the video.

'"Irish souvenir"? It couldn't be anyone else, could it?' Shannon replied.

'Here we go, and yep, it's Emerald Bay's one and only Irish shop owner, Isla Mullins,' Imogen said.

They peered at the screen to see Isla in selfie mode, making sure there was a clear shot of her sweatshirt, which screamed, 'I'm not short, I'm leprechaun size.' A sticker arrow pointed to her top with a text box giving her shop a plug. She was trudging over a field, people milling in the background, talking gravely into the screen about why she was at Emerald Bay's abandoned farm, heading toward the famine cottage.

Hannah wanted to cheer after hearing her say that Kitty Kelly was taking a stand against commercialism and should be applauded. She instantly forgave Isla for her sweatshirt commercialism, saying softly, 'I never saw her there; she must have left by the time Freya and I arrived.'

Her sisters were still engrossed with what was on the screen.

'Look, there's Dad, what an eejit!' Imogen pointed out a conspicuous Father Christmas in the background.

Finally, Isla swung the smartphone toward the cottage, and the screen filled with Nan, her reindeer hat slipping down over one eye, singing her heart out in the doorway of the tumble-down cottage. The video finished with Isla asking for a show of support against bulldozing the ruins and building on a historic site.

Hannah gave a low whistle seeing that the TikTokers had come out in droves as Imogen scrolled through the endless likes and comments from around the world, standing by the Irish nan in her adorable Christmas hat. She also suspected Isla would sell out of sweatshirts.

Hannah rolled off the bed and headed out the door, buoyed by this unexpected boost to the cause. In her letter, she'd reference the viral post and the thousands of comments voicing solidarity that the cottage and farm should be left as they were.

'Where are you going?' Shannon threw after her.

'To kiss Isla Mullins!'

25

Hannah cracked an eye open as her alarm beeped. It felt ridiculously early. How could it be morning already?

Her hand snaked out for her phone, and as she slid the alarm off, she saw it was 7 a.m. Reality dawned because it was Monday morning, and she had things to do – important things, like typing her letter to the Department of Agriculture – but the drilling pain behind her eyeball suggested she'd overdone it with the celebrating last night.

Her lips felt dry and cracked as she grinned despite her tender head at the memory of Isla in top form toasting her newfound TikTok celebrity. At first, Nan had been put-out at having the thunder stolen from her, but then she'd seen the bigger picture and what it meant for the abandoned farm and famine cottage. She'd joined Isla in a round of selfies for their online fans, dragging her and Freya into the fray.

Had Tom seen the TikTok? He didn't strike her as the sort to hang out on that social medium, but she'd no way of knowing until he arrived back in Emerald Bay tomorrow. If he arrived back. Hannah couldn't see how the land sale could, in good conscience, be signed off now, not knowing so many people were against the blatant disregard for their little Irish village's history. Or, at least, whoever was in charge of that side of things at the department would be made aware of this once she'd sent her email.

The thought that Tom may no longer need to return left her with mixed feelings, and annoyance prickled over her traitorous thoughts. That was when it hit her like a rogue wave at the beach. She'd texted Dylan late into the evening. The fear hit as she snatched up her phone.

'Please, please, pretty please, with sugar on top, don't let me have signed off to him with kisses.' She'd felt the love all night, so there was a strong possibility given her exuberant mood as she'd filled him in on the events of Sunday that she'd done just that.

Sitting up, Hannah opened her phone, chewing on her bottom lip, and saw no reply to her text. That wasn't a good sign.

She opened the message she'd sent, wincing as she read over the scrambled, gushing words, then sent a silent thank you to Him upstairs. There were no heart emojis and no kisses lurking at the bottom. Garbling aside, it was a perfectly acceptable text.

At least the fear had taken her mind off her poor head, she thought, galvanising herself. A shower, coffee – because tea wouldn't hit the spot today – and toast would see her fit to rejoin the human race.

Indeed, once she'd been pummelled by hot water and had helped herself to Imogen's forgotten smellies, Hannah felt much improved. It was a bonus to find the kitchen was empty because she'd not have to talk to anyone until after her coffee. She guessed that because of the lateness of the night, Mam, Dad and Nan had opted for a lie-in.

'Good morning,' Hannah greeted Princess Leia, who showed her excitement at seeing her by dancing around her in circles. It was nice to be greeted at this hour with so much enthusiasm with the bonus of not having to make conversation. She totally understood why some people loved their pets more than they loved people.

She tipped the portion size of kibble James had demonstrated into the chihuahua's bowl then set about making her own breakfast. By the time she put her coffee and toast down on the table, Princess Leia was whining at the back door.

'For one so tiny, you've got a good appetite,' Hannah said, smiling as she opened the back door to let the little dog do her business and sniff around the still-dark beer garden, leaving it open a crack so she could come back in. At least yesterday's downpour had eased. Then, mindful of the draft, she sat in Nan's seat to avoid it.

The caffeine was beginning to take effect when her phone pinged. It was Dylan, and adrenaline surged at the anticipation of praise for yesterday's efforts.

It's not enough.

The words jumped out at her, and she barely read the rest of his straight-to-the-point text, clicking on the video he'd attached.

It was like watching a news clip about something happening in a far-off place. The anger of the crowd surging down the street almost throbbed out at her, and there was Dylan, his face twisted into a nearly unrecognisable fury as he lobbed something at a shop window and the sound of splintering glass and screams reverberated back at her.

Hannah felt sick as she watched it a second time. She wasn't naive, having attended protests that had taken an out-of-hand turn, but she'd never felt that blind rage visible on Dylan's face.

Another message pinged through, and Hannah's stomach began churning as she scrolled through it, her hand sweaty and hcr hcart pounding. Dylan wanted to take action in Emerald Bay. He wanted them to do something big that would make those in charge sit up and take notice.

Her hand shook as she put her phone down, frightened at the thought of what he might want her to do, and she closed her eyes as a questioning voice ran through her head. *This was what you wanted, wasn't it? For Dylan to see you the way you see him. A kindred spirit, someone prepared to stand up for what you believe in.*

Not like this, though, she silently replied.

The back door opening made her jump.

'And how are we feeling this morning?' Liam, cheeks ruddy with the cold, was overly chipper for someone who'd not headed to bed until midnight. He stomped his feet on the mat, and Hannah saw he had a small dog tucked under one arm and a newspaper under the other. 'Look who I found? And we might be warming to each other now I've lost the Santa suit, but you can tell your mam and nan from me I'm not cleaning up that poo out there even if it is minuscule.' He set Princess Leia down; she trotted off and began wrestling with her chew toy.

'Grand, Dad,' Hannah croaked, her appetite for her toast having deserted her.

'Are you not eating that?' Liam's eyes moved to her plate.

She shook her head. 'I was greedy,' she fibbed.

'Don't mind if I do then.' He helped himself and then slapped the newspaper down on the table. 'You and your nan are cover girls, so you are.'

'Oh, that's just fecking great, that is.' Hannah's eyes were riveted to the front page of the *Galway Gazette* glaring up at her because there, in colour no less, were two photographs around which paragraphs of text were arranged. The top photo was placed beneath the bold headline 'Protesting's a Family Business'. She bit the inside of her cheek. This didn't bode well for the article because yesterday wasn't about her and Nan personally. And while Freya was as good as family, she wasn't a Kelly, so it wasn't even factual. She should have known Jeremy would find a slant to paint them in a bad light. Had Tom got in his ear? Or did he have a personal vendetta against her? The latter was a real possibility, given no love was lost between her and the reporter.

Her gaze lowered to the photo beneath the headline. Nan looked like what she was – a feisty and opinionated woman with something important to say who was also wearing a reindeer Christmas hat. 'I'd listen to you,' Hannah said softly.

It was the photo of herself and Freya below, however, that made her toes curl to the point of cramping. Well, not Freya. She looked like she always did, with her trademark waterfall of blue hair, her mouth set in a serious line, and her eyeballs pointing at the camera in a 'Don't mess with me' manner.

'I'd listen to what you had to say, too.'

Hannah held the newspaper up for close inspection. 'But as for you, I'd be booking an appointment at the dentist ASAP.' She looked at her dad, who'd sat opposite her, and wailed, 'I look like a woman who's about to lose her teeth and who's just been told she's allowed one more piece of cake before surgery. Could I have smiled any harder?'

Her teeth, on full wattage display, were a gorgeous shade of purple thanks to Carmel's mulled wine. Instead of being inundated with support for keeping Emerald Bay intact, she'd probably find herself the recipient of dental donations, she thought, slapping the paper back down on the table. Jeremy Jones would have been delighted with that freeze-framed moment, and she rubbed her temples, silently running through every expletive she could think of where he was concerned.

'And I don't know why you're grinning away like a Cheshire cat, Dad. It doesn't put you and mam in a good light. People will think you were too miserable to pay for your poor daughter's dental care.'

Hannah steeled herself to read the accompanying article and dipped her head, her lips compressing until they'd almost disappeared as she scanned through it, even though it was pretty much what she'd expected.

Jeremy had painted the three of them as professional moaners with too much time on their hands. There was only a brief mention as to why they'd taken up residence in the old cottage for the day, and that was written in such a way as to make them come across like country bumpkins who should be strumming banjos. What with her teeth added to the mix, it didn't make for good press.

Hannah pushed the paper away angrily. It would have been satisfying to carry it through to the pub and shove it on the fire, but what would be the point? Burning one copy wouldn't change anything. At this very moment, it would be a source of sniggering over the Shredded Wheat at many tables across Galway and the wider district.

The damage was already done.

Hannah would have liked Dylan's input on the letter she'd put together pleading the case for the land sale to be stopped before she sent it, but he'd made his feelings clear; he thought words were a waste of time. She'd used Nan as a second pair of eyes instead, although she'd almost regretted having done so, reluctant to follow her suggestion to delete the paragraph she'd included about the cottage being more than a historical beacon. It was a place for the youth of Emerald Bay to still be kids, to put their phones away and to let their imaginations regarding the ghostly ruin roam free. Given all the fuss around health and safety, Nan argued that mentioning this was a bad idea. In the end, she'd conceded Kitty was right. It would be shooting herself in the foot, so to speak.

Heaving a sigh of relief, Hannah sat back in her chair,

flexing her fingers as she stretched. The email, petition and TikTok video link were sent. All she could do was hope she'd turned the tables on Tom's client and the countdown until Christmas would work in her favour now, with the powers that be at the Department of Agriculture pulling the pin on the land deal, eager for it to go away. The sooner, the better because if the problem disappeared, she'd not have to prove herself to Dylan by participating in something she had no control over.

It would be satisfying to waggle a copy of everything she'd sent under Tom's nose tomorrow evening, assuming he came back because there was always the hope that it would be sufficient to spook his client into backing away.

Hannah decided fresh air was the order of the day now that her work was done – for the time being at any rate. Who knew, maybe she'd come across the American woman and solve that little mystery? And Princess Leia would enjoy a walk, too. So, a short while later, they set off in the soft mist down the back lanes. Unlike Nan, who was chuffed at being a later-in-life cover girl, she wasn't game to show her face on Main Street, not with the *Gazette* photograph so fresh in everyone's mind. Hannah had even caught Nan signing Enda Dunne's copy of the *Gazette* for posterity, giggling like she was a pin-up girl from the fifties.

Needless to say, she'd been quick to veto her dad's suggestion they get the article framed to hang on the Shamrock wall along with all the village's other claims to fame.

26

Hannah's day sped by in a blur of text messages from friends who'd seen the video of Nan and were cheering them on. As for the *Gazette*, she was thankful its readership didn't extend beyond the west country because the ribbing she'd taken from her sisters had been bad enough. She'd told them one by one where to go.

Her phone had been glued to her hand all day, even though common sense told her such a quick response from the Department of Agriculture was as likely as coming across the American woman walking down one of the lanes she and Princess Leia had roamed. Still, she'd checked her emails with religious fervour; other than a standard acknowledgement that her letter had been received and someone would be in touch shortly, there'd been nothing. At least she had breathing space where Dylan was concerned. Whatever he was planning, nothing would happen until next weekend because he wouldn't be able to leave the Feed the World office before then, not when they were short-staffed with her absence.

She'd been sorely tempted to unload all her confused feelings onto someone, namely Freya, given that she was the only person Hannah had confided in about her feelings for Dylan. But in the end, she'd decided Freya had enough on her plate dealing with her post-break-up blues. Anyway, Hannah knew she wouldn't condone Dylan's wilful damage in Cork if she came clean about that, not as a business owner.

That was why, once she'd cleared away the dinner things, Hannah was almost glad to take herself off to the community hall, where Eileen had informed her the learn-to-knit class would be held. The numbers were too high for her woollen shop to host, she'd said self-importantly when she'd poked her head through the connecting door to the pub earlier to let her know where to go and to bring a fiver sub.

Hannah stuffed the crisp new note she'd borrowed off her dad in her pocket as she tugged her coat on. She resented paying Eileen a fee and hoped it meant she'd have at least nipped down to the hall earlier to put the heating on. If not, the cavernous space would be like a mausoleum, and the thought of hunching over a pair of knitting needles in arctic conditions made her shiver. Nan was shouting at the reality television programme she was watching, and Mam and Dad were busy in the pub, but she called out a cheerio anyway.

Outside, a steady drizzle had replaced the day's mist, and Hannah pulled her hood up, pausing to look up at the sky. She could see tiny droplets of water that would otherwise be invisible caught in the sensor light's beam. The accuracy of the forecast and whether they'd be in for snow this Christmas had been a hot topic around the dinner table. If so, it would be the third year in a row they'd been blessed with a white Christmas, Hannah thought, flashing back to Ava's gorgeous wedding. It had been white in more ways than one!

At this time of year, the road snaking past the park to the small stone church with its community-hall appendage was pitch-black. It was only a short walk away, up and around the back of the park, but the risk of twisting an ankle down a pothole was real, so she clambered behind Doris's wheel and crossed her fingers, hoping she'd start.

'You're a grand little car altogether,' Hannah said, grinning into the darkness as Doris obliged, her engine roaring into life, and with the heater blasting, she headed off, arriving at the church in the blink of an eye.

Hannah pulled into the designated parking area off to the side of the hall and nipped in alongside Eileen's car. It wasn't a tight squeeze given hers was the only other vehicle there.

What with Eileen's comments about her shop not being large enough to accommodate everyone who'd booked in for tonight's class, Hannah had expected a few other cars at least and checked her phone, but she was bang on time. Seven sharp, Eileen had said.

Wiping her brow, she vowed to splurge on fixing Doris's heater before returning to Cork after the holidays. Still, for now, it was pointless sitting here sweltering like she'd dressed inappropriately for a day at the beach.

Hannah clambered out of her car and thrust her hand in her pocket to check on the fiver, which was still there. 'Eileen better not hit me up for the shortfall if tonight's class is one-on-one,' she muttered to herself, her feet crunching over shingle as she walked round the corner to the hall's entrance.

The garish yellow glow from the fluorescent tube lights inside momentarily blinded her as she pulled open the door, and the aroma that instantly hit her caused her sense of smell to go into overdrive. *Coffee and sausage rolls*, she thought, blinking against the bobbing light spots on her retinas, *with an underlying hint of egg sambos.*

Her vision cleared enough for her to focus on the group slouching in a semi-circle around Eileen in the middle of the hall.

What the...? Hannah did a double take. This wasn't what she'd expected at all because if it wasn't for Eileen, unmissable in a pink-and-orange polka-dot knit that would make your eyes bleed, she'd have thought she'd got her wires well and truly crossed. She didn't know what she'd expected this evening, but this lot here looked like poster kids for youth delinquency, not a learn-to-knit group, and clearing her throat, she hung back by the entrance. 'Erm, Eileen, hello there. Can I have a word, please?'

'We'll get started in just a minute,' the knitting shop owner told the bored group brightly. Not one of them bothered glancing up from their screens.

Hannah noted that beneath each of their chairs was an unopened kit bag for the evening ahead, and she was relieved Eileen wasn't leaving them holding knitting needles that could be used as weapons. She folded her arms across her chest as Eileen set aside the name roll she'd been busily ticking off and closed the distance between them.

'Why are you and I the only people over sixteen here?' Hannah demanded, keeping her voice low, not wanting the motley crew over yonder to overhear. She wished she could slip on a pair of sunglasses to block out those polka dots. The hall had been pimped up for Christmas by Nan's origami group, too, she noticed, taking in the paper angels hanging from a piece of string along with the truckload of tinsel tossed about the place.

'Ah, well now, Hannah. The thing is, I've not been completely transparent with you regarding my learning-to-knit classes.'

'You don't say.' This didn't bode well. 'Tell me more.'

'You see, it was a role model I was after.'

Hannah wondered if she had water in her ears. Was Eileen saying she was a role model? She'd been called many things over the years, but that was a first. She'd not let the older woman win her over with flattery, though, because role model or not, she'd no wish to spend her evenings attempting to inspire moody teenagers. As such, she edged backwards to the door.

Eileen's eyes narrowed. 'C'mere to me now, Hannah Kelly, and hear me out.'

Hannah exhaled through clenched teeth, knowing she'd no choice but to listen. For one thing, Eileen's hand shot out and was hanging on to her arm like a crab would a toe.

The formidable woman's voice was barely louder than a whisper. 'I'm surprised at you being so judgmental. Those youngsters there are a mixed bag from the bay and Kilticaneel. They're only children, playing at being grown-ups. Your memory's not so bad that you can't remember yourself at the same age. You were forever getting into trouble with your various stunts around Emerald Bay.'

'I never did anything illegal, Eileen; I was only ever trying to be heard.' Eileen's remark about her being judgmental had hit home.

'And you sailed close to the wind doing so. You were a menace at times, so you were. This lot here has been sailing mightily close to the wind, too, and they've a choice of two paths to go down. Unfortunately, Sergeant Badger says they're after taking a few steps down the wrong one, but it's not too late to get them to do a U-turn. It's boredom that causes them to get into bother. Someone has to do something.'

That gave Hannah pause. It wasn't always easy being a teenager in a rural village where throwing yourself on your bed and declaring that there was nothing to do in Emerald Bay was a rite of passage. This wasn't true, of course, but an appreciation for all the area had to offer, including carefree childhood memories – the abandoned farm and famine cottage sprang to mind – didn't come until you'd left it for a while. She could recall how often she'd wished there was somewhere else to hang out over the two-week Christmas break other than freezing her arse off at the park or down at the bay. It was funny how fourteen days could seem interminable when you were young, and Emerald Bay and Kilticaneel sorely lacked safe spaces for its youth.

Realising Eileen was still talking, she tuned back in.

'Sergeant Badger broached the need for constructive activities to be offered at a residents' meeting a few weeks back. Of course, there's no funding in the kitty for a proper youth club like they had in my day – the council cut all of that years back – but I set my mind to coming up with a way of keeping the kids who need to be kept busy off the street. That's when I came up with the idea of giving them something to do with their hands other than vaping.'

'Learning to knit,' Hannah murmured.

'Exactly.'

'It's a noble idea, all right, but how on earth did you get them to agree to come along?' The last thing she'd have been interested in doing at their age was spending her evenings knitting.

'I've Sergeant Badger to thank for that. He was after having a little word about the options they might find themselves left with. Community service in the freezing cold every weekend between now and next Easter or two weeks, Monday to Friday, in the run-up to Christmas, learning to knit in the warmth of the church hall with me.'

Eileen was a force to be reckoned with. Still, Hannah didn't fancy her chances of getting a group of angsty teens to pay attention when they weren't here of their own volition. She kept this to herself, asking instead, 'I don't understand why you've got me pegged as a role model? I wouldn't even know how to cast on.'

'That's what you're here to learn how to do, and why you're here has nothing to do with knitting.'

Hannah stared at her blankly. That didn't make sense.

'It's because of your convictions, Hannah.'

This saw her bristle. Who did Eileen think she was, casting aspersions like that? Hannah was quick to put her right. 'I don't have any convictions, thank you very much, Eileen. At least none that have stuck.'

'Not those sorts of convictions. I'm talking about you wanting to make the world better for future generations and not being frightened to say so. You've got passion. You speak up and make yourself heard. If you could pass on even a tiny amount of that fire to these kids sitting here tonight, you might inspire them to channel their energy into doing right, not wrong.'

Hannah was floored. She'd always assumed most of Emerald Bay's residents thought she was an annoying do-gooder, but that wasn't what Eileen had just said. Eileen saw her as someone with passion, someone inspirational – a role model, no less. How could she turn her back and walk away now?

Then again, would it be hypocritical to stay? Hadn't she been complicit by not speaking up and telling Dylan he'd gone too far with his protest in Cork? Nor had she been courageous enough to ask him to leave Emerald Bay to her because she still desperately wanted his admiration. It frightened her, the uncertainty of how far she'd go. Would Eileen want her here if she knew the truth?

She wasn't role-model material, not at all.

'I need someone here the kids can relate to. I'll keep them in line; you'll keep them onside.'

Eileen wasn't giving up. Hannah, filled with indecision, looked over to where the troops were getting restless. What would it be like to open their eyes to things that were in their power to change to ensure the world didn't just survive but thrived for themselves and future generations? Would the good deed outweigh the bad?

27

Eileen released her grip on Hannah's arm, sensing victory. 'Are you in?'

'I'm in.' Hannah shook her arm and hesitated. 'But what about the knitting?' She'd been looking forward to learning the craft, she realised. 'Will I be learning or sitting here preaching?'

'You're not to carry on like that Greta one, Hannah. And I'll teach you that, all right. These classes are a prime opportunity for knitting Christmas presents, especially for this lot. You'll know yourself money's tight at their age. I meant what I said about that baby of Shannon's needing a layette, but you could start simple with something Christmassy if you like. And sure, there's no harm in having a little chit-chat about things at the same time. Is it the official job title you're after to clarify things, like?' Eileen asked, her mouth twitching.

Hannah was a little disturbed that she had something in common with Isla Mullins besides getting the Greenhouse development squashed. She loved a good title, too: 'Just to clarify things.'

'OK, so. How about youth worker? But you'll not get a name badge.'

'Oh, OK.' Hannah was a little disappointed to hear that, but after gleaning Eileen's assurance that she'd write the role she was officially here for next to her name on the roll-call list, she straightened her spine and followed Eileen over to the group.

Eileen clapped her hands to get their attention. 'For those who don't know her already, this is Hannah Kelly.'

'What did you do?' A spiky-haired blonde with an angry red chin piercing stopped studying her nail and looked at Hannah curiously.

'Nothing recently, but I once tied myself to a tree. Well, more than once, actually.'

That got their attention. She might surprise herself by enjoying this and have a chance to make a real difference.

She headed over to one of the few remaining empty chairs buoyed by this thought and sat down, only to jump straight back up, startled by the whoosh beneath her backside. It was followed by the drawn-out sound of a long, loud and proud fart. Hannah's face went wumph like a gas flame as the kids erupted into fits. Looking around to see what had caused the rude noise, she spied a deflated whoopee cushion on the seat she'd just vacated. What had she let herself in for?

'I beg your pardon,' a bemused voice said as Eileen tried and failed to restore order.

Hannah's eyes flew to the door where Tom Flynn stood, watching.

'What are you doing here?' she demanded, not caring if she sounded rude. Her sense of humour had deserted her the moment she'd seen him standing there, pressing his lips together in an effort not to laugh at her. Being made to look an eejit in front of ten teens was one thing. For it to have happened in front of her nemesis, too... His timing had been impeccable. But what was he doing back in the bay, and what on earth was he doing at Eileen Carroll's learn-to-knit session?

The giggling died down as the rag-tag bunch's mirth was replaced by curiosity about the strange man in their midst.

'It's good to see you again, too, Hannah. I thought the classes sounded fun when you mentioned them, and when I bumped into Eileen, I brought them up.' He shrugged. 'She invited me along, and seeing as I arrived back earlier than expected, I thought I might as well put my time to constructive use and learn a new skill. Starting from tonight.'

'Knitting?' Hannah couldn't keep the incredulous note from creeping into her tone.

'Is that a problem?' Tom eyed her coolly.

'No,' she lied, thinking how different he looked clad in a tracksuit ensemble, having ditched the corporate look. His hair tufted on end for a moment, thanks to the static from his wool beanie as he pulled it off. And what was with this 'Eileen' business? Since when was he on a first-names basis with the proud owner of the Knitter's Nook?

Her eyes narrowed as she looked at Eileen, whose face was giving nothing away, and then back at Tom, trying to figure out what was going on. As for the gathered teenagers, you could have heard a pin drop until one of them piped up with, 'This is better than watching *Fair City*.'

'Ignore Hannah; you're very welcome, Tom.' Eileen was out of her seat, crossing the room in a blaze of polka-dotted glory to take him by the elbow before she steered him over to the remaining empty seat in the circle. 'Everybody, this is Tom Flynn. Tom's down from Dublin on business. He's an— What are you, Tom? I know it's something with a long, important-sounding title?'

'I'm an architectural project manager,' Tom replied as he sat down.

Architectural arse, Hannah thought, scowling, wondering if she should warn these kids that Tom was here to take the shine off Christmas thanks to his part in trying to change the landscape of Emerald Bay. She decided that was erring on dramatic, however.

'That's it,' Eileen said, puffing up proudly at the fancy qualification.

Hannah couldn't believe how easily he was winning the older female generation of Emerald Bay over with his clean-cut good looks. Eileen was supposed to oppose the Greenhouse and Christmas tree farm, yet she was carrying on like he was her favourite nephew.

'What's that then?' a lad clad top to toe in funeral black asked.

'Basically, I'm brought in to manage and orchestrate construction projects.'

'And why are you in Emerald Bay?'

The girl who piped up instantly made Hannah feel ancient. One look at her with her midriff-baring top had her thinking that she shouldn't have been allowed to leave home without putting a vest on. Then, remembering Mam shouting after her many a time when she was around her age, 'You'll catch your death!' told herself to pull her head in. She wasn't that old!

'He's here to scope out the land on which the famine cottage sits for a potential garden centre and Christmas tree farm,' Hannah butted in, her tone making it clear what she thought about that.

'I know where I've seen your face!' the girl with the chin piercing said, leaning forward as Hannah slunk low in her seat. 'You're that girl with the purple teeth. I saw your photograph in my da's morning paper. Gis a look then.'

Hannah bared her teeth and slowly did the rounds to reassure the group she didn't have poor dental hygiene. Remembering she'd been brought in as a role model, she quickly espoused the importance of flossing and brushing twice daily.

Tom was clearly amused, and she could tell by the twinkle in his eyes that he was doing his best not to laugh at her *again*.

Irritation prickled like an annoying rash that he found her such a source of amusement.

'Thank you for sharing that, Hannah.' Eileen steered things back in the direction she wanted them to go by gesturing to Tom. 'Like all of us here this evening, Tom's a culchie originally.'

'I am.'

Aha! So that was Eileen's angle. She was rolling with a country-boy-who-made-good scenario. But this lot wouldn't be taken in by the old 'I used to be like you' malarkey, she thought, settling back into her seat in anticipation of Emerald Bay and Kilticaneel's young rebels without a cause making mincemeat out of him.

Tom smiled winningly at everyone seated in the circle. His toothy grin didn't falter, not even when he met Hannah's steely glare. Maddeningly, he seemed right at home. She watched him lift and cross his leg so his trainer-clad foot rested on his knee. And how come he didn't get the whoopee-cushion treatment? She jotted this down on her list of mental grievances concerning Tom Flynn, directly under the entry of him being offered the best biscuits.

'I grew up in a blink-and-you'd-miss-it village called Ballyfreeman,' he supplied.

'I've never heard of it.' A lad who smelled like he'd sprayed a year's supply of Lynx deodorant before leaving his house eyed him suspiciously.

Tom grinned. 'Exactly. Nobody ever has. It's the arse end of nowhere. Or at least I used to think it was.'

'Like Emerald Bay,' someone piped up.

'Kilticaneel's not much better.' Miss Chin Piercing popped her bubblegum.

'The thing is most of us who grow up here, or in Kilticaneel, or even Ballyfreeman' – Hannah avoided Tom's gaze as she jumped in to defend Emerald Bay – 'feel like that, and it's not until you leave that you realise how lucky you are to have grown up with a strong sense of community.'

This was met with scepticism, but to her surprise, she found an ally in Tom, who agreed. This time, she did catch his smoky-eyed gaze fleetingly before feigning interest in the faded patch on her dungarees.

'What's it like being a jackeen then?' a girl with her arms folded over her bare midriff asked, using the culchies' term for a Dubliner.

'Fierce, I bet.' Mr Lynx Deodorant took his remaining ear pod out. 'I can't wait to get out of home.'

Hannah's head tilted to the side of its own volition as she became engrossed in the story Tom launched into about how he'd gone to university in Dublin and how much of a shock to the system finding himself a small fish in a big pond was, let alone fending for himself in a damp student flat. She was unaware of time passing as he talked about feeling lost and alone, like he had a sign over his head that said, 'I don't belong here'.

'I wanted to quit and go home.'

'Why didn't you?' Mr Lynx Deodorant took the words right out of Hannah's mouth.

'Because there was nothing to go back to. I'd have wound up helping my dad in the pub for the rest of my days.'

There was a melancholy tone to his words, but Hannah couldn't help but burst out at the surprise of the connection between them. 'You didn't tell me your dad's a publican like mine?'

'You never asked.'

They glowered at one another.

'See, better than *Fair City*,' someone piped up.

'But things must have got better because you stayed?' Mr Fluffy Lip and Chin next to Hannah asked.

'Yeah, it did. I joined one of the university societies. I

realised I wasn't owed anything, and people wouldn't come to me. I had to put myself out there.'

'What society did you join?' Hannah queried, expecting him to say rowing or something all-rounded and sporty.

'A Sinn Féin movement for young political activists revolving around republicanism, socialism, feminism, internationalism and environmentalism.'

Hannah openly stared at Tom with her mouth hanging open, surprised because those were all things she believed in wholeheartedly. For Tom to have been part of such a group completely shattered the mould she'd poured him into from the moment she'd met him. 'But if you believe in environmentalism, why did you agree to work on the Greenhouse project?'

'Because everything I work on uses sustainable building techniques.'

Eileen decided to interrupt what promised to be an exciting debate there by clapping her hands. 'Right, time's marching on, so let's crack on with a quick round of introductions before getting on with what you've come here tonight to do, and that's learning to knit.'

Names were reeled off, and Eileen hastily jotted them down on the roll of labels they were to fix to their chests. Once the roll had made its way round and back to Eileen, she retrieved her kit bag, and those who hadn't already delved into theirs followed suit, keen to examine its contents. Next to Hannah, the girl with the chin piercing, named a saintly-sounding Maire, clacked her knitting needles, pretending they were chopsticks.

Hannah ignored her as she examined the green wool balls in her bag. She'd imagined whipping up a dainty pair of booties for her baby niece or nephew and Shannon's delight over her sister having knitted them, but now she was wondering if a Christmas gift for Nan might be a good starting point.

But all the while, she was mulling over what Tom had

divulged. Maybe she hadn't been wrong with her initial feelings about him, and his firm grip when he'd helped her up on the stairs...

She was itching to press him for answers because if he hailed from a small village, he'd understand what the famine cottage and its land meant to the Emerald Bay locals. However, now wasn't the time to drill into his conflicting morals. Eileen was introducing the art of casting on, and Hannah knew it would require her full attention.

28

It was funny, but Hannah was reluctant to put her needles down when Eileen interrupted the banter and chat infusing the hall to say it was time to pack up. The two hours since she'd dragged her heels over to the group had whizzed by, and the strangest thing had happened. She'd enjoyed herself. Tom and herself had even locked horns in a healthy for and against discussion over the development he'd been brought to Emerald Bay for. The teenagers had joined in, with Eileen moderating when things got heated between demonstrating a basic knit stitch to get them underway.

As Hannah stashed her needles and the rows she'd managed back into her kit bag, she looked at the faces of the kids around her. Their cheeks were flushed with the shared conversations and the warmth of the hall. Their eyes were bright, too, she noticed because they were a clued-up bunch, and it was nice to see the surly expressions had vanished. Hannah smiled when Maire said she planned on knitting her nan a tea cosy for Christmas. Eileen was right, she realised, because beneath all the anti-social affectation lurked kids with good hearts.

Hannah caught Tom's eye, and his smile conveyed that his thoughts were identical to hers.

Eileen Carroll's first learn-to-knit class had been a resounding success, and she was about to offer her services to help Eileen pack up, but Tom beat her to it. She didn't fancy staying and hashing over how the evening had gone as they stacked chairs, so she called out a goodnight, fished her keys out of her pocket and stepped outside.

Car lights sluiced in and out of the parking area as parents or older siblings picked the kids up, and she shielded her eyes as she picked her way round to her car. Tom's hire car was cosying up to Doris, so she'd be sure to mention spatial awareness when parking with him later. She'd have to be a contortionist to get into the driving seat.

It was a good job she was flexible.

But Hannah's success was short lived because Doris refused to tick over. The slew of parents who'd rolled up to collect their offspring had all driven away, meaning the only witness to Doris's backfiring as she began bunny-hopping toward the road was Tom, who happened to be exiting the hall.

Hannah slapped her steering wheel. 'Janey Mack, Doris! What do you think you're playing at? Showing me up like so.' It was a rare outburst, and she immediately apologised. 'Sorry. It's just you really know how to pick your moments.'

With each belch of black smoke from her car's exhaust, she was reminded of the whoopee-cushion incident. This wasn't her finest environmentally friendly moment, and she'd be messaging Elon on X about the freebie Tesla again as soon as she got home. If she got home.

There was nothing else for it but to pull over because she might do irreparable damage to Doris's engine driving back to the Shamrock, and the car would be fine overnighting in the church hall parking area. Dad would come down and look at Doris in the light of day, and fingers crossed, he'd work his magic and get her ticking over properly. The only thing was she'd have to cadge a lift from Tom as he was heading back to the pub anyway.

Sighing, she manoeuvred away from the exit and stilled the protesting engine, clambering out and locking Doris up.

Tom moseyed over. 'I see you're having a spot of bother.'

'You noticed then,' Hannah glumly muttered. 'Can I get a ride home with you?'

Tom inclined his head toward his car. 'Come on.'

She tossed a glance at the hall. Eileen had yet to turn the lights out. 'Give me two ticks. I'd better let Eileen know I'm leaving the car here, or she'll think I've been abducted and raise the alarm. You heard her say she's a true crime aficionado.'

Hannah hadn't known that about Eileen Carroll until this evening when she'd suggested they share something that wasn't common knowledge about themselves as an icebreaker. As for Tom, she'd turned her curious gaze on him, surprised to hear him confess to an addiction to Rolos with the same gravity he might have announced he was an alcoholic.

When Hannah opened the door to inform her of the situation, Eileen switched the lights off and quickly replied, 'Well, you can hold your horses and see me to my car. A girl can't be too careful.'

'Girl' was a stretch, Hannah thought, hanging about while Eileen locked up. But given her choice of television viewing, it wasn't surprising she wanted an escort to her car.

'Good night,' Hannah said, waving, once the older woman had arranged herself in the driving seat. Then she hurried over to where Tom had his car idling and jumped in. 'Sorry about that.'

'Don't be daft. I'll be sure to wait for Eileen to lock up tomorrow night. I never thought, given what a sleepy place Emerald Bay is. It was bad manners on my part.'

'I didn't think either.' Hannah pulled her seat belt across

and buckled in. 'I wouldn't fancy anyone's chance of accosting Eileen, though. She'd take them out with her knitting needles.'

Tom laughed. 'I can imagine.'

She spied the half-eaten tube of Rolos and a takeaway coffee cup in the beverage holders. So, he hadn't been making up his chocolate habit. 'You're a sweet tooth then?'

'What? Ah, the Rolos. You know all my secrets now. Well, almost.' Tom flashed a grin. 'Help yourself.'

Hannah wondered what other secrets he had as she unwrapped the paper and held the tube out.

He took one and popped it in his mouth, talking with his mouth full. 'Thanks. They're my new vice. I swapped vaping for Rolos. I didn't get on with the whole chewing gum instead, and I needed something to do when I'm driving distances.'

'I wouldn't have had you down for being a vaper. But fair play to you for giving it up.'

'Why not? What does a vaper look like?'

Hannah's brow puckered; there was no point in beating about the bush. 'You look like too much of a goodie two shoes for that.'

She took Tom's laughter to mean he hadn't taken offence.

'You don't hold back, do you?'

'Mam says I've foot-in-mouth disease. Sorry, but I've always been a blurter. Things pop out of my mouth before I can stop them.'

'Well, to give you a taste of your own medicine, I'd have said that from how you present yourself, you wouldn't be the sort to pass judgment on others.'

Hannah took offence because this wasn't the first time he'd alluded to her being judgmental. Hadn't Eileen also told her off this evening for the same reason? She spluttered her defence. 'I'm not. I don't!' Then she hesitated. 'Do I?' He'd made a valid point because she'd stuffed him in a box and labelled it the minute she'd met him, and yet he kept proving her theories about him wrong.

He was eyeing her as they bounced down the dark road. 'An honest answer?'

She gave a meek nod.

'I can't speak for anyone else, but yeah, where I'm concerned, you did.'

Hannah mumbled an apology. She knew Tom's eyes were still on her and wanted to escape this uncomfortable subject. 'Why are you driving so slow?'

'In case livestock wanders out on the road.'

'Oh, you mean the herd of cows and flock of sheep grazing in the park there,' Hannah said.

'Exactly. You never know when a sheep or cow will take it upon itself to cross the road.' He flicked her a look, eyes crinkling, and the humour broke the tension.

'Did you see the change come over the kids when they left the hall tonight?' he asked, turning off the road to where the Shamrock stood like a lighthouse beacon.

'I did. The armour went straight back on when they saw their parents waiting outside for them.'

'Yeah, but for two whole hours, it slipped.'

Tom nosed the car between her mam and dad's, and Hannah risked a peek at his profile. He was right; it had, and so had theirs. Unwilling to examine that thought further, she concentrated on how the kids had stopped being angry and become engaged.

'Will you walk me in?' Tom asked, unbuckling.

'Why do you need an escort?' The sensor light had automatically gone on, and Hannah already had one leg out of the car.

'For protection against Princess Leia.'

Hannah twisted round to stare at him for a minute, unsure whether he was having her on or not. Seeing that he looked about ten years old, she laughed. 'You want me to protect you from a chihuahua?'

'It's not funny. It's all right for you. Princess Leia doesn't bare her pointy little needle teeth your way. They could do some damage if she decided to latch on to my ankle. And I heard she bit that reporter fella yesterday.'

This time, Hannah saw a flicker in the corner of his mouth.

'He deserved it. Come on then – Chihuahua Protection Services at your, erm, service.'

She was pleased to find the back door unlocked as she'd left it. This meant they didn't have to troop through the pub and answer twenty questions about how the knitting lesson had gone. She didn't trust her mam not to ask whether Hannah had moved on from her gripe where Tom was concerned and managed to separate business from pleasure either. It was a question she didn't want to be asked because, throughout the evening, there'd been a shift in her feelings toward him, but the jury was still out. Accordingly, she was relieved to enter an empty, dog-free kitchen. 'Clear,' she called over her shoulder to Tom like an FBI agent storming a building.

He followed her inside, shutting the door behind him, and cast a wary glance at the basket to double-check it was empty.

'Princess Leia will be in the family room with Nan watching a spot of tele. Do you fancy a brew? I'm gasping.'

'Me too, thanks. Where is everyone else?' Tom pulled a chair out and sat down at the table.

He looked right at home, Hannah noticed. Mam would be pleased because hospitality was close to godliness in her book. She went through the tea-making motions. 'Let me see. Mam will be in the Shamrock. She hosts her Menopausal and Hot weekly meeting on a Monday night. It's a thin guise for drinking wine and having a good old moan about being unable to shift the poundage around their middles with her pals.'

Tom laughed, and she warmed to the sound.

'Dad will be manning the bar but mostly putting the world to rights with Enda Dunne and Mr Kenny of motorised scooter infamy because, the Menopausal and Hot group aside, Monday night is quiet in the Shamrock.'

As she set the mugs on the table, Hannah remembered the email she'd tapped out for the Department of Agriculture and fetched her laptop before sitting down. Who knew? The defrosting between them this evening might mean he'd see things from her, Nan's and most of Emerald Bay's residents' perspectives. Perhaps he'd even swap sides, she thought, getting carried away as she opened her device.

'Work?' Tom asked.

'More like a labour of love. I've written a letter to the Department of Agriculture and included all the signatures I've got so far on the petition to prevent the land from being sold to your benefactor. And there's the matter of the viral TikTok.'

'I heard about that tonight. Maire showed me the clip when you went to the bathroom. Your nan's an impressive lady.'

Hannah nodded her agreement, unsure if she was picking up on caginess or not as she slid the laptop over to him and sat down to drink her tea while he read through it.

Her leg bobbed up and down under the table. This was worse than waiting for a teacher's verdict on an essay you'd just handed in, she thought, trying and failing to read his expression as his eyes flicked back and forth over the text because Tom Flynn was giving nothing away.

29

Hannah was halfway through her tea when Tom finally looked up, the light glinting off his glasses as he pushed the laptop back toward her. She bit her bottom lip, closing it down and waiting for him to say something, but frustratingly, he just picked up his tea and sipped it. Patience had never been one of her virtues. She tapped the side of her mug, wishing for Imogen's fingernails because it was nowhere near as satisfying when hers didn't make the tip-tap sound.

Kitty's sudden throat-clearing appearance saw them both glance toward the door.

'Hello there.' Princess Leia was at her feet, her molten eyes firmly on Tom, her lip beginning to peel back.

Hannah was aware of a pair of trainer-clad feet thudding onto the seat next to her as Tom raised his legs to ensure his ankles were out of reach of the little dog. Oh, to be so small and mighty! she thought, amused as Princess Leia was told off by Kitty for snarling.

'There'll be no treat if you don't cut that out,' she admonished the chihuahua.

Hannah grinned as the little dog immediately sat back on her haunches, blinking up at Kitty angelically.

As Kitty fetched the little bag of doggy treats, she remarked, 'You two looked very shifty just now.'

'We're not up to anything shifty, are we, Tom?' Hannah was indignant, flashing back to being busted having had a sly cigarette down the back of the park or a sneaky sip from the top shelf behind the bar in the wayward youth she'd conveniently forgotten about earlier.

'Not at all. Sure, we're just enjoying a cup of tea, is all, and Hannah asked me to read the letter she sent to the Department of Agriculture. It's well written.' He looked at Hannah with an acknowledging nod.

'Thanks.'

'I thought so, too,' Kitty said, not looking convinced.

This would be Nan's opportunity to tell Tom why the land and famine cottage meant so much to her personally, but when she didn't say anything further, Hannah decided not to keep nudging the topic along. Tom had read her letter, so it was best to let him digest it without pushing things too far, as she was prone to doing.

Kitty didn't feel the same way. 'So, what will you do about it, Tom?' she demanded.

Tom cleared his throat. 'My client's aware of the strength of feeling in the community.'

'Nan—' Hannah began, but Kitty abruptly changed the subject.

'How did the knitting class go?' she asked, stooping down to give Princess Leia the promised treats from the palm of her hand.

'Surprisingly well.' Hannah glanced to Tom, who reiterated that it had but left her to explain the details. 'Eileen thought the classes would be a good distraction for local, wayward teens and give them something to do in the evening between now and

Christmas. It's a sort of community-service arrangement she came to with Sergeant Badger.'

'Good for Eileen doing her bit. I always say there's no such thing as a bad child, only a lost child.' Kitty straightened, and her brow furrowed. 'So why did Eileen invite you along? I don't recall you ever expressing a strong desire to learn to knit. I can't speak for yourself, of course, Tom. Aren't you both a little long in the tooth for mixing with teenagers?'

'Well' – Hannah sat up straighter, determined to seize her moment to shine – 'Eileen says I'm a role model because of the strength of my convictions.'

Kitty's reading glasses, used predominantly for recipe reading and watching the television, slid down her nose upon hearing that. 'I'd have said that was stubbornness.'

Hannah chose to pretend she hadn't heard. 'With Tom, I think Eileen thought his country-boy-made-good vibe would resonate with the kids.'

This time, Tom's glasses needed to be pushed back up his nose. 'Jaysus, Hannah. You make me sound like Garth Brooks without the cowboy hat. Is that what you thought her angle was?'

'Well, yeah, she made it pretty clear getting you to drop in where you were from and what it was like moving to Dublin as a culchie.'

'You don't think there might be more to me than someone who moved to Dublin and did OK for themselves?' Tom rubbed his temples. 'You really do judge a book by its cover.'

'I wish you'd stop saying that. I'm just pointing out why Eileen invited you tonight.'

Kitty, whose head was moving like a ping pong ball being lobbed across a table, butted in, effectively ending that line of conversation. 'And what is it you're after wanting to knit then?' She swung her gaze to Hannah first.

The first few green rows she'd got underway this evening

floated forth in her mind, and Hannah regrouped. 'I planned on making booties for Shannon and James's baby, but with Christmas so close, I'm making a surprise present for someone, and I'll say no more than that.'

'Grand.' Kitty's blue eyes registered surprise. 'I never thought I'd see the day when you were enthusiastic about knitting.'

'I haven't actually started on the present yet, Nan. Eileen had us knitting squares to get the hang of the basics first. She did say I was a natural, though, and how all it took sometimes for hidden talents to be uncovered was a good teacher.'

'Did she now?' Kitty's expression darkened momentarily, but then she brightened, turning to Tom. 'And what about yourself? What do you plan on graduating to after the squares? A hair shirt perhaps.'

'Nan!' Hannah admonished, unused to this prickly side of Kitty.

Tom brushed the remark aside with a good-natured, 'I suppose wool is sheep hair in a roundabout way. It's not a shirt I've got in mind, though, and this might sound a little large-scale for a beginner, but I like to push myself. I'm a quick learner, too, so I'd like to try knitting a Christmas jumper. I've always wanted one.'

Hannah's eyes rounded. 'What? Like the reindeer sweater Mark Darcy wears in the first Bridget Jones movie?'

'I can tell you hand on heart I've never seen those films.'

'Really? Shannon binges them, doesn't she, Nan?'

'She does,' Kitty agreed. 'Well, not so much now she's got James, but they were her go-to films when things were rocky with that French fella who gave her the runaround.'

Hannah was already conducting a Google search on her phone for Mark Darcy's Christmas sweater and, not looking up, said, 'You won't be in Emerald Bay long enough to finish your square, let alone a sweater.'

'Who says I won't?'

What did he mean by that? Hannah didn't get a chance to ask.

'Eileen will get me underway with the basics. I'll muddle my way through from there.'

'Still and all, Christmas is just under two weeks away. I can't see you wearing your sweater this year.'

'There's always next Christmas.' Then, addressing Kitty, Tom said, 'I'm also a realist, so I thought I'd compromise and settle on a Christmas pullover vest or maybe a gilet for my first attempt. What do you think?'

Before her very eyes, Hannah saw Nan soften as she forgot she viewed Tom as the enemy. Was it the mention of a gilet that had done it? What even was that?

'I think that's a grand idea, and I'm erring toward a gilet myself.'

Bingo! Hannah rolled her eyes. 'Of course a man who wears a tan Burberry coat would want a gilet.'

'There you go again judging.'

'I'm not! And that's getting old. I'm merely stating a fact.'

'For your information, the Burberry is vintage. You're not the only one who believes in sustainability.'

Hannah's surprise saw her suffer lockjaw. Was she going to have to apologise to him for the second time in one evening? And, more to the point, what was a gilet?

'Oh yes, definitely a gilet. A vest with a zip is very sensible.' Kitty was clearly enamoured with the idea.

'And will your gilet have a reindeer on the front? I suppose you could have one set of antlers on either side of the zip.' Hannah's mouth was trembling as she tried to contain her laughter. She held out her phone and showed Nan the Colin Firth snap she'd unearthed.

Tom took the phone and examined the picture. 'That could work.'

The upward tilt of his top lip told Hannah he, too, was desperately trying to keep a straight face.

Kitty interrupted the exchange. 'I might not like what you stand for by being here in Emerald Bay, Tom, but I applaud you for aiming high. And while I'd love to chat with you all evening about your respective knitting projects, I'm missing my programme, so I shall get what I came through for.' She fetched down the best biscuit tin. 'There's no point saving these now. They're already half gone.'

To Hannah's gratification, she was offered first pick.

'I don't know why I bother with that *Love Me, Love Me Not* rubbish on the idiot box, though,' Kitty muttered once Tom had chosen his biscuit. She took the last of the chocolate-covered ones, half talking to herself as she put the lid back on the tin. 'I think it's your Casey and Carl's teeth. I can't look away from the screen.'

Hannah tried not to spit biscuit crumbs. 'What do you mean, Nan?'

Tom's silvery eyes were crinkling, Hannah noticed as Kitty explained the hypnotic effects of the on-again, off-again reality TV couple's teeth.

'They're enormous, so they are. Sure, it's like watching camels with neon-white gnashers perform a long and dramatic courting ritual. I'm getting fed up with them, to be honest. And it's unnatural seeing young ones cavorting about in their swim-suits in the sunshine when the rest of us are counting down to Christmas in the cold. I might have to tune in to the *Big Brother Reindeer Games* special rerun instead.'

'The teeth are veneers, Nan. Turkey teeth they're called,' Hannah supplied.

'Turkeys don't have teeth, Hannah. Did they not teach you anything at that school you went to? Besides, I said camels, not turkeys.' Kitty put the tin away. 'Come on, Princess Leia – let's see what that eejit Carl gets up to on his boys' weekend in Menorca.'

With that, Kitty left Tom and Hannah snickering into their tea.

Once Kitty was settled back in front of the TV and the risk of a chihuahua attack was over, Tom said, 'I'll talk to my client.'

Hannah's head snapped up. 'You will?'

'I can't promise anything, but I'll ask her to look at other sites.'

That he'd said 'her' barely registered. Hannah was taken aback that he'd agreed to stick his neck out for her and Nan. 'Thank you.'

'You understand I don't make the final calls?'

'I get that.' She did, but she could still hope.

Hannah was beginning to think she'd been very wrong about Tom Flynn, and the words, 'What are you doing tomorrow?' spurted forth.

'Are you asking me out?'

'No!'

'Relax. I was teasing you.'

'I knew that.' Her face flamed.

Would going on a date with Tom be so unpleasant, though? If she'd been asked yesterday, she'd have found it abhorrent. Now it wasn't at all unappealing, and stealing a glance at him, she felt a frisson of something that, unlike swimsuits in December, was completely natural. Attraction.

She quickly averted her gaze, picking up the empty mugs and moving to the sink so her back was to him. 'I want to take you to the famine cottage tomorrow because there's another story I need to tell you. One I didn't write in my email.'

'OK.'

Hannah had decided to tell him about her nan and granddad so he'd understand that, politics aside, the cottage couldn't be sold.

30

Hannah had dreamed of Mark Darcy, reindeer gilets and Tom. However, the dream had taken a darker turn when Dylan had appeared, rampaging down Main Street, throwing rocks through shop windows. It had been a relief when her alarm went off.

When she went downstairs for breakfast, there was no sign of Tom, and Mam told her he'd headed out early for a meeting. She shook off the last vestiges of the unsettling dream, and her spirits lifted. Tom had kept his word because he must have gone to meet his client! Things were looking up!

As soon as she'd finished her breakfast, she forwarded Dylan her letter to the Department of Agriculture and told him the tide seemed to be turning in her and Nan's favour. She wanted him to know her way was working and to ensure he wasn't planning to come to Emerald Bay this weekend.

An hour later, she was draping tinsel and various sparkly decorations about the bar with the assistance of Enda Dunne and Ned Kenny perched on their barstools. The pair of them were like annoying back-seat drivers.

Mam had roped her into helping with the Christmas decorations in the pub, given her refusal to go with Liam to pick the Christmas tree. He'd looked crestfallen, but Christmas tree farms, even ones a good hour's drive away, were too close to home. She was betting she'd be expected to do the decorating honours when he returned with the biggest tree he could squeeze through the doors of the Shamrock in a little while.

That Tom, who'd returned from meeting his client as Liam had been about to set off, had eagerly agreed to keep him company and provide a set of strong arms for the carting of the tree had surprised her. It was disappointing to see him disappear again no sooner than he'd returned because she was desperate to know whether he'd spoken to his client as promised. It would have to wait, though, and she'd gladly left the two men to their mission, but not before asking if they could get Doris going on their way back.

Mam had insisted on draping purple tinsel around her neck like a glitzy scarf, and Hannah had laughed at the ridiculous headband with bobbing bells she'd donned. She wished she'd stop singing 'Jingle Bells', but the alternative would no doubt be her putting on Michael Bublé's Christmas album, and she drew the line at that. Michael would get enough airtime on Christmas Day.

Dylan's response to her message pinged in as Hannah inspected the tin Father Christmas that had stood sentry by the fire this time of year for as long as she could remember. She set him down on the hearth to read it.

His response to everything she'd told him about Tom being on their side and the letter she'd laboured over – the letter Tom had said was well written – saw her heart sink. He held firm to his talk-being-cheap ethos and was sceptical that the developer would roll over so easily. Her certainty that Tom would have talked his client into moving the project elsewhere wavered as she shoved her phone back in her pocket. If he'd had good news, surely he would have relayed it before going tree picking?

Kitty pulled her out of her thoughts then, or rather, the plate of mince pies she was wafting under her nose did. They were fresh from the oven and dusted in icing sugar, rapidly melting into the pastry. Hannah couldn't resist. Perhaps this was the taste of Christmas she needed to put her back in the spirit of things. 'Thanks, Nan.'

A voice drifted over from the bar. 'Kitty Kelly, you're a wonder in that kitchen, so you are.'

Hannah had to be careful that the minced fruit pastry she was about to swallow didn't go down the wrong way as she witnessed the unseeable: Enda Dunne giving Kitty a 'come hither' look.

'You've an icing-sugar moustache, you eejit.' Kitty slid him a serviette and marched back to the kitchen.

Nan was strong, Hannah thought, watching her go. She took no nonsense off anyone. Right then, she wished she were more like her and had the guts to text Dylan back and say, *You're wrong – watch this space.*

Hannah thought it was questionable whether the huge tree Tom and Liam had chosen would even make it through the door of the Shamrock. It was certainly entertaining watching them try, though! She only had her dad's word that Tom was with him because all that was visible in the doorway was the tree. The poor fella would be freezing his arse off outside as he played push me, pull me with Liam and the world's largest Christmas tree. She shook her head, and her mam, standing beside her, did the same. The only difference between them was Nora's merrily jingling bells.

'Liam, you've outdone yourself this year. Why did you have to go so big?' Nora was perplexed. 'Sure, that thing will take up half the pub. We'll be fighting our way through the forest to clear the tables.'

Hannah leaned into her mam's ear and whispered, 'You know what they say about men who buy big toys, don't you, Mam?'

Nora's bells tinkled away once more as she shook her head, puzzled. 'I haven't a clue.'

Was she having her on? 'You know, Mam.'

'I do not.'

'Think the opposite of what they say about men with big feet.' Hannah waggled her eyebrows suggestively.

'That they've very good balance?' Nora eyed her daughter. 'And why are you doing that thing with your eyebrows?'

'Give me strength, Mam!'

'Are you two going to stand there watching us struggle or get over here and give us a hand?' Liam shot in their direction as if it was their fault he'd bought a tree so big he couldn't get it in the door.

Nora, sighing over the ridiculousness of the situation, moved toward her husband to help, wrapping her arms around his waist. 'You come and hold on to me, Hannah,' she ordered.

Hannah attached herself to her mam.

'Are you two even pulling?' Liam bellowed.

'Don't shout at me, Liam Kelly, or I won't help you,' Nora bellowed back.

'Shouting isn't helping anyone,' Hannah shouted at them both.

Tom's muffled voice floated through the foliage as he enquired what was going on. 'You do realise it's minus something degrees out here!'

'Sure, it's like that children's story about the enormous turnip where all the villagers get in on the act to try and pull it out of the ground,' Ned Kenny said, chortling.

Enda was wiping his eyes, muttering about this being better than a day out at the gee-gees.

'If you're not going to help, pipe down, the pair of you,' Nora flung at the two regulars propping up the bar. 'Count of three we pull, OK?'

Liam, who saw himself as being in charge where the tree was concerned, got in before her. 'One, two, three, heave!'

They all staggered backwards as the tree finally gave way with a splintering of branches and applause from Enda and Ned.

'Hi there,' Hannah greeted Tom, who looked dazed at finally finding himself inside the pub. He was still holding up the business end of the tree.

'That was touch and go,' he said. 'I thought I'd have hypothermia by the time I got inside.'

Hannah decided she'd give him a minute to warm up before hitting him up about his client's response to her email and putting her mind at ease where Dylan was concerned.

There were a few false starts, but the tree was finally positioned in pride of place. Liam performed a triumphant fist pump as he gazed up to where the tips of its dark needles grazed the timbered ceiling. 'I'll have to get you a footstool if you're to decorate those,' he said, half to himself and half to Hannah.

Yep, it was as she'd thought. She'd been given tree-decorating duty. Hannah crossed her arms over her chest. It would take her the best part of the day to festoon that monstrosity. If she were to take Tom to the famine cottage, she'd need to call in reinforcements.

'Mam, will we make a start?' Hannah gestured to the tree.

'I said I'd help your nan with the baking she's doing for the Christmas party her craft group is having this afternoon.'

'Oh, right.' Looking at the tree, the thought of the hours of decorating ahead was overwhelming.

'I'll help,' Tom offered. 'I can decorate the top half. You can do the bottom.'

'Grand. That's sorted then,' Nora said, and Hannah was certain her mam had a smile of satisfaction on her face as she left them both to it.

31

'You can't beat the smell of a real tree,' Tom said, placing the box of decorations down and breathing in the tree's scent like a hungry man smelling a much-anticipated meal before digging in.

Hannah had to agree with him as the rich camphor fragrance of Christmas washed over her.

'I suppose you want to know how I got on this morning?' Tom asked, reading Hannah's mind as he opened the box and looked up at her.

'I figured you'd have already let me know if you'd anything worth telling me.'

'I didn't have you pegged as a Debbie Downer.'

Hannah bit the inside of her cheek, picking up a shiny red bauble from amongst the decorating treasures before shrugging.

'That's not the right attitude. Try being a Positive Pauline.'

Hannah snorted, startling them both, but was unapologetic. 'I've never heard that before, and I'm not in the mood to be a Positive Pauline.' She remembered her plan to head to the famine cottage with Tom to tell him Nan's story, but now it seemed pointless.

'Have you not?'

'No. I think you made it up.'

Tom grinned, giving nothing away, but something in his smile said he knew something she didn't, and Hannah felt a glimmer of optimism.

'OK, if I try to be a Positive Pauline, will you tell me how you got on and stop grinning like an eejit?'

'Maybe.'

'Tell me!' Hannah demanded. 'Or I'll hit you with this bauble!' She swung it menacingly.

Tom raised his hands in mock defence. 'All right, all right. I think I sowed the seed that it would be prudent to look for another site.'

Hannah gasped, not quite believing what she'd heard. 'How?'

'By telling a little porky about having struck animosity like this over a project I was overseeing in a small community once before, which turned into a nightmare. I said roadblocks had got in the way from start to finish, which saw costs balloon, and that it was a miracle it was ever completed.'

Hannah gaped at Tom.

'Come on then – say it.'

'Thank you! That's amazing. Oh my God, wait until I tell Dylan.' Hannah's despondency vanished.

'Who's Dylan?'

'Oh, I, erm, I work with him. He knows what it means to me to stop the sale of the land and famine cottage. He wanted to help, actually.'

'Right.' A shadow crossed Tom's face, and his tone lost its jokiness. 'Remember I said I'd sown the seed. It's not a done deal yet. Maybe hold off on saying anything to your nan, too. I'd hate for her to be disappointed if I'm wrong.'

'OK.' It would be hard to keep quiet, but she'd no wish to get Kitty's hopes up only to have to crush them.

'And that's not what I wanted you to say. I want to hear you admit you misjudged me.'

Hannah squirmed because he was right, and she felt her cheeks pinken as she apologised. 'I'm sorry, Tom. You're right.'

'I'm right! Can I get that in writing?' The jokiness was back.

'Don't push it.'

They grinned at each other.

'That tree won't decorate itself,' Liam called over as he pulled a pint, breaking the spell.

'He's got a point,' Tom said.

'I'd still like to tell you that story about the cottage,' Hannah said before they got stuck in. It was even more critical to tell him of her nan's connection with it now. She wanted Tom to understand how much his stepping up for them meant.

'And I'd like to hear it. We could go there once we've finished the tree?'

'Grand.'

'Is there a theme you like to go for?' Tom turned his attention back to the fir. 'I saw a tree in a shop window decorated with only silver ornaments. It looked really effective.'

'We don't subscribe to themes at the Shamrock. The rule of thumb is to hang as much bling as possible.'

'I like that rule of thumb.' Tom pushed up the sleeves of his sweater.

Hannah was tickled watching him delve into the decorations with the excitement of a child being told he was off to Disneyland. He had enough Christmas spirit for both of them.

Tom caught her smiling at him and looked a little sheepish. 'I know I'm behaving like a big kid. It's just I've never decorated a Christmas tree before.'

'What, never?'

Tom rubbed his chin. 'Maybe that was why I was keen to work on the Greenhouse project, because of the Christmas tree farm.' He gave her a rueful half-smile. 'My dad and I didn't really do Christmas, and I never saw the point when I moved into my flat. It's only me. I bought a miniature sparkly Argos tree before they closed in Ireland. I put it on the coffee table, but that's as far as I go.'

"How come?' It was incomprehensible in Hannah's world not to 'do' Christmas, and her face must have mirrored her thoughts. Even her divey house-share in Cork had a tree. Well, it was more a spindly, twiggy thing one of her housemates had dragged home and another had decorated with empty cans. Still and all, it was a nod to Christmas.

'My mam was killed in a car accident three days before Christmas when I was small.'

Hannah's jaw went slack. She hadn't seen that coming. 'I'm sorry, Tom.' It was the second time in under ten minutes she'd said those two words to him, but this time, they were laced with sadness for the motherless boy he'd been. She wanted to reach out to him.

His eyes were fixed on the tree. 'I don't remember her, and what does feel familiar is probably down to photographs. You know how sometimes you can't be sure if something is an actual memory or something you've been told or seen in a picture?'

Hannah nodded.

'Besides, I didn't know anything different. It was only ever my dad and I, and he didn't see that there was much to celebrate at that time of the year. He never moved on from what happened.' He rocked on his heels. 'I don't mean forget. You don't forget, but he got stuck in his grief. I always got packed off to my gran's on Christmas Eve, came home on Boxing Day, leaving him to drink himself silly.' Tom's gaze was blank. 'He was in the right profession.'

Hannah recalled him saying his father was a publican, and she didn't know what to say, not wanting to echo her apology. On occasion, she took her family, with their bickering and banter but mostly love, for granted. However, right then, the feeling of being fortunate to be a Kelly was overpowering. She was lucky, and she knew it. Without thinking, Hannah acted on her earlier instinct, reaching out and gently touching Tom's face.

Time stood still, and then, realising what she was doing, Hannah let her hand drop to her side. She'd overstepped big time, and stooping down to hide her flushed face, she began rifling through the various curios in the box as though she'd never seen any of them before.

Tom immediately busied himself, too, attaching a miniature elf to the tree. After a full second, he said, 'It sounds more Dickensian than it was. Gran made sure to give me a good day, but the tree was always up when I came to stay.'

Hannah settled on a gingerbread man with a red Santa hat and straightened, looping it over a spiky bough while avoiding eye contact. Then, realising the tinsel was still wrapped around her neck, she unwound it to drape a purple shimmer around the tree. 'Do you still go to your gran's for Christmas?'

'She died a few years ago now, and my dad's a lost cause.'

He didn't elaborate on how he'd spent the Christmases since his grandmother had been gone. Hannah's picture of him sitting alone in his Dublin apartment eating a microwaved dinner in front of the TV with a paper crown on was filled with sadness.

'I usually go to a mate's. His mam puts on a feast.'

The illusion was shattered, but Hannah's words – 'Why don't you spend Christmas with us this year?' – were already blurting forth, leaving them both blinking at one another in surprise.

'What about your mam and dad?'

'They're firm believers in the more the merrier.' It was out there now; she'd invited him. There was no retracting it. 'They' – she cleared her throat – 'what I mean is, we'd love to have you.'

'Your nan, too?'

When Kitty heard what Tom had done for them, she'd be grand, and Hannah nodded. She desperately wanted him to accept.

'I'd like that. If you're sure.'

'I'm sure.'

32

When Tom and Hannah stood back to admire their handiwork, the Christmas tree was resplendent with glittering knick-knacks, and Tom was rubbing his hands together in satisfaction of a job well done. Hannah looked on, pleased because after hearing about Tom's childhood, she'd thrown herself into beautifying the tree, determined not to dampen his enthusiasm for the task.

'I think the smell of a real tree is good for the soul,' Tom said.

'I think you're right.'

He raised his eyebrow at that.

'I mean, I agree,' Hannah modified, making him grin. Her stomach killed the moment by protesting loudly that lunch had yet to be served, and she wrapped her hands around her tummy. 'Sorry. It's a law unto itself, my tummy, and it's telling me it's starving.'

'Mine agrees with yours.'

Nora had ducked in over half an hour ago to let them know there was a pot of home-made soup left on the stove that needed warming. Nan had gone off to her Christmas party.

'Come on then.'

Tom didn't need to be asked twice. He picked up the box of decorations and glanced over to where Liam was entertaining Americans at the bar with a Guinness-pouring demonstration. Nora, baking done, was teaching another tour-group member how to order a pint in Irish.

Tom picked up his pace, seeing Hannah holding the connecting door to the kitchen open for him. 'Liam and Nora are natural hosts. My dad could learn a thing or two from them.'

'They love it. I don't think either of them could imagine a different life,' Hannah replied, directing Tom to the storage cupboard where the box could live until it was time to take the tree down. She was rolling her sleeves up, having fetched a couple of bowls, when he returned empty-handed a moment later. But instead of sitting at the table waiting for his lunch like the paying guest he was, Tom automatically went to the stove to begin heating the soup.

He belonged here.

The rogue thought made Hannah freeze.

'OK?' Tom glanced at her statue-like form.

'Grand, just looking for the bread knife.' Hannah made a show of looking for the knife. She located it in the sink, telling herself, *You are being ridiculous, Hannah Kelly*, then wiped it and began slicing into the remaining hunk of her nan's soda bread. Thank goodness Tom couldn't read her mind!

They set about putting their meal together in silence, and before long, they were sitting down to enjoy the fruits of their labour. If you could call reheating soup and buttering bread labour, Hannah thought as she dipped her spoon into the creamy blend of leek and potatoes, determined not to slurp like she usually did with soup. She was soon wiping her bowl clean with the last chunk of bread, and when she glanced at Tom, she saw he was smirking. 'What's so funny?'

He tapped his chin. 'Soup.'

Hannah swiped her chin with the back of her hand. 'Gone?'

'Not quite.'

He reached over and wiped the remnants away with his thumb, and Hannah could feel the imprint of his touch long after he'd lowered his hand. She set about collecting up the dishes, glad of something to do.

What was going on with her? Why was he having this effect on her?

'I'll wash – you dry,' Tom stated, following her over to the worktop.

Hannah was puzzled over how she could have done an emotional U-turn where the Shamrock's guest was concerned in just a few short hours. Come to that, her feelings had done a complete 360 degrees, not just a U-turn. 'Fine by me.' She picked up a tea towel, waiting while he filled the sink.

'Are we still on for heading to the abandoned farm?' she asked.

'Of course.'

'We could walk lunch off.' A blast of fresh air would sort her out, Hannah decided.

Tom turned the taps off and glanced over at her. 'I'm up for it if you are?'

For some reason, his response to the straightforward suggestion felt loaded, and Hannah brooded as he set about scrubbing the bowls. What was he up for exactly? And more to the point, what was she up for?

By the time they rugged up to venture out, the kitchen was tidier than when they'd found it. A briny wind blowing straight in from the Atlantic cut through them as they hunkered down and followed the road past the deserted park.

'Have you always worked for non-profit organisations like Feed the World with Bees?' Tom asked as, from the park, the sound of the swings' forlorn squeaking as they were blown back and forth reached their ears.

'Pretty much straight from college.' Hannah relayed the infamous Christmas tree story where it had all begun then gave him a brief rundown of her work history, opening up about how things weren't working out like she'd thought they would.

'I don't feel like I've found where or what I'm supposed to be. When I left college, I saw myself heading abroad to work on the front lines for different organisations where I could make a difference. But when it came to it, I was frightened. I don't think I'm strong enough to cope with the reality of it.'

Hannah swallowed. She'd never told anyone this before, but she had nothing to lose. If the Greenhouse project didn't go ahead, then in all likelihood, she'd never see Tom again once he left Emerald Bay. The thought made her sad, and she felt small inside her coat as she said, 'All I ever wanted to do was something that contributes or helps people or the planet in some way, but I'm a glorified paper pusher with a big mouth.'

'There she goes again: Debbie Downer, and you are helping. The work you do is important.'

'Maybe. I wonder sometimes. And I don't know if I want to pass out flyers and flog seed cards for the rest of my life.' She didn't know if she belonged in Dylan's world either. 'Mam talked to me about following in Shannon's shoes and going into nursing once, but I don't have the right temperament.'

'No?'

Hannah side-eyed him. His mouth was trembling, and she gave him a playful shove, seeing the funny side of it. 'Are you questioning my bedside manner?'

'I wouldn't dare.' His expression softened. 'You're forthright, is all. You say what's in your heart.'

'And sometimes there's a time and place for that, which I don't always pick up on.'

Tom's hands were thrust deep into the pockets of his Burberry, and he was quiet for a few steps. Hannah was unsure whether she'd talked too much about herself. She was about to ask him about the route he'd taken to architectural project management, feeling bad about all the times she'd silently called him an architectural arse, when he spoke up.

'You were great with the kids last night.'

'Do you think?' Hannah's eyes lit up at the praise.

'Yeah. I do.'

'It was surprisingly fun.'

'Yeah, it was. Have you ever thought about work that involves youth mentoring?'

Youth mentoring? What did that even entail? Hannah wondered, her step faltering. Her response was automatic. 'Sure, I'd be hopeless at it.'

'Why do you think that?'

'That type of work's for people who have their lives sorted, and mine's a long way from that.'

'I disagree. You know your own mind, and that's admirable.'

Hannah wished that was true. 'What about what you do? Is it your passion?'

'Yeah. It is. The only word I can think of that explains how it feels to see something step out of your head and take physical form is magic. I like overseeing the whole process.'

Hannah listened as Tom explained his work, seeing how animated his features became when he talked about it. There was so much more to his job title than she'd thought. It embarrassed her to think how easily she'd pigeonholed him, and she vowed to work on that whole judgemental thing.

They were closing in on the abandoned farm now, the lane devoid of the vehicles that had blocked it on Sunday.

'Here we are,' Tom said, gesturing to the cottage. He climbed over the stone wall, holding his hand out to Hannah, and she took it even though she'd no need of help. Today, the field was eerily empty, but muddied footprints were still visible in the soft soil where spectators had loitered less than forty-eight hours ago.

'The cottage will act as a windbreak,' Hannah said, swiftly approaching the ruin, which sat at a haphazard angle, like it was sinking into the soil in the middle of the field. She didn't want Tom to see the colour in her cheeks from holding his hand.

A crow, startled by their presence, flew off its rooftop perch, cawing. It was a bird cry that always made her feel lonely. She looked over her shoulder to ensure Tom was still there because today, the prickling sensation at the back of her neck was an intense reminder of the ghosts that haunted this place.

Hannah stooped at the entrance to the cottage – the gaping rectangular frame where she'd sat huddled with Nan and Freya – and once inside, she straightened. The earthy smell was over-whelming, and she fancied that if memories had a scent, this would be it. The two windows were like empty eye sockets letting in the bare minimum of light, and overhead, through the rafters, were glimmers of the sky above.

When Tom blocked the doorway, Hannah had to strain to see. 'Don't bang your head on the frame,' she warned.

Accordingly, he hunched over then stepped onto the mix of chipped flagstones and compacted dirt, giving his eyes a moment to adjust like Hannah had before taking in their surroundings. Then he moved to the interior door to check out the adjoining room.

Meanwhile, Hannah took a few steps, touching the dank bricks where the wattle and daub covering the walls had begun to crumble. They were slick, and she thought it was probably colder in here than outside. Her eyes swept over the chimney, which was now in a state of collapse. Once upon a time, a blazing fire in the hearth would have had a pot hanging over it. The soupy smell of stretching out food would have filled this space, growing more watery each day, until there was nothing left to put in the pot, and the people who'd lived here had to go.

A bottle clinked as it rolled on the ground in the room into which Tom had disappeared. Hannah closed her eyes, trying to imagine the previous occupants' lives. For a second, she thought she could hear better times, when the clucking of hens had scratched in the dirt outside the cottage, but as Tom re-entered the space in which she stood, Hannah blinked the echoes away.

'You can feel them, can't you?' Hannah shivered. 'Those who came before.' She might have played ghost hunting with her sisters and their friends when they were kids, but today was the first time she'd known in her heart they were here.

Tom's eyes had widened to deal with the gloom, and she could tell by the glint she saw there that he could.

It was time to tell him the story that had brought them there.

'When my nan and granddad first met, this was where they used to come. They planned their life together inside these walls.' Hannah spoke with reverence. 'I didn't know, but Nan still comes here occasionally. To remember and to feel close to Granddad. That connection can't be taken from her, Tom.'

'Tell me how they met,' Tom said quietly, and Hannah relayed the story still so fresh in her mind. And when she'd finished, she could feel the tug of the past keenly, gradually becoming aware of Tom's eyes on her.

'Now I understand,' was all he said.

33

Tom pulled in behind the Shamrock, still laughing with Hannah over the knitted Christmas stocking Eileen had brought to the hall tonight for inspiration. She'd stuffed it with old socks to demonstrate how much it could hold, resulting in a decidedly phallic stocking. Hannah and Tom, who'd laughed the loudest, had been taken aside by Eileen for a stern talk about setting examples and not behaving like children. It had almost been as funny as the stocking.

The second class had been gas, and Hannah had felt connections forming with the disgruntled teens, seeing glimpses of the kids they still were as they tackled their projects. She thought she could sense a connection forming between her and Tom, too, and felt like a teenager herself as they walked toward the back door. If only there were mistletoe hanging over it! No such luck, though, she thought, stepping inside the kitchen.

Hannah was eager to sit down and unpick the rest of the evening with Tom over a hot chocolate and was about to suggest just that when Nan appeared in the doorway. Voices from the television echoed behind her. 'You missed a grand session in the pub tonight. Your dad and the lads decided to entertain the American tour group.'

'Dad plays the tin whistle, and his pals Dermot and Ollie are on uillean pipes and the fiddle,' Hannah explained to Tom.

Kitty gauged their cheery demeanours. 'You two had a good evening, I take it?'

'We did.' Hannah, still giggly, was about to fill her nan in on the craic over the stocking when she cut her off.

'You've got a lad waiting to see you in the pub, Hannah. He arrived an hour or so ago, and your mam's been looking after him with the ale while he waited for you to get back.'

Hannah looked to Tom as though he'd know who it would be. However, he was taking his coat off and had his back to her.

'He's a colleague of yours from Cork,' Kitty continued.

Hannah stared at her nan, suddenly light-headed, because it couldn't be, could it? 'Dylan?' she exhaled, feeling winded.

'That's right. Dylan something from Feed the World with Bees.'

'I'll leave you to it,' Tom said, his relaxed demeanour stiffening as he slung his coat over his arm and moved to bypass Kitty.

'Will you not stay and have a brew with me, Tom?' Kitty asked, blocking his path.

If Hannah hadn't been thrown into such a spin over Dylan's arrival, she'd have been pleased that, like her, Nan seemed to be warming to Tom, and she didn't even know what he'd done for them yet.

'No. Thanks anyway, Mrs Kelly. I've work I need to be cracking on with.'

Kitty stepped aside.

'Tom,' Hannah called ineffectually after him, unsure what she wanted to say, but he was already taking the stairs two at a time.

She hovered in the kitchen, anxiousness bubbling, knowing Dylan was on the other side of the wall.

'What's going on? You could have cut the air with a knife then.' Kitty rested green-veined hands on the back of the chair and fixed her gaze on her granddaughter.

'Nothing, Nan.'

Those all-seeing blue eyes didn't budge from hers, and Hannah crumpled under their scrutiny. 'Everything,' she whispered, tears threatening, still grasping the fact Dylan had shown up at the Shamrock.

'Your man's sitting by the fire with a pint and a bag of crisps. He's waited this long. Another few minutes won't make any difference. So sit yourself down and tell me what's going on.'

Hannah sank into the chair opposite her nan, clasping her hands in front of her tightly. Kitty waited with an air of expectancy, and after a moment's hesitation, Hannah began talking. She started at the beginning with her crush on Dylan, telling her nan she'd thought he was the one for her, given everything they had in common, but he'd shown no sign of picking up on her feelings. Or reciprocating. She wasn't game to let him know how she felt either and risk ruining a good working relationship. Hannah paused, embarrassed.

Kitty had her head tilted to one side, listening. Then she reached out and patted her granddaughter's hand, encouraging her to continue.

She'd come this far, so there was no point in not unloading everything now. Her fingertips were pressing into her knuckles as she fessed up about Dylan's part in the rally in Cork, confiding how uncomfortable his actions made her feel and how it had left her wondering exactly how far he'd go to be heard and how far she'd go if he asked her to join him. 'I wanted him to respect and admire me like I did him, Nan. I thought he might finally see me in a different light if I did.'

Kitty's eyebrow lifted. She'd clearly picked up on Hannah's use of the past tense.

'He's told me he doesn't think our efforts to stop the Greenhouse from going ahead have been enough. Money talks, he says, and I don't know if he's right or wrong in this case, but I'm hoping it's the latter. Surely, people's consciences have a part to play, too. Otherwise, there's no hope.' She was venturing into Debbie Downer territory again.

'I think we must believe most people are fundamentally good, Hannah.'

'But what's he got planned? I'm sure he's not driven from Cork to confess his undying love for me.'

'And if he had?'

'He won't have, but Tom's muddied everything. And that's another thing. How can I have all these big feelings for him when I've just met him?'

'Sure, wasn't I after telling you I knew I'd marry your granddad within a week of laying eyes on him?'

'Steady on, Nan – who's talking marriage?' Hannah raised a watery smile. 'How can I be so fickle, though? One minute, I'm mooning after Dylan, convinced Tom's the devil incarnate; the next, I'm convinced he's the best thing since sliced bread.'

Kitty laughed. 'You've a way with words, Hannah Kelly, I'll give you that.'

'It's not funny. I'm all over the show.'

'There's no right or wrong way to fall in love. Remember that. You need to look inside yourself and listen to what your heart tells you to do. It's no good hiding away in here.'

Nan was right, and Hannah pushed her chair back. Knowing Dylan was sitting in the pub waiting for her would have turned her into a giddy, weak-at-the-knees mess a few days ago. Now she felt she was heading for the gallows as she grabbed the money from the sale of the seed cards and pushed through to the pub.

Liam was behind the bar, and Nora was busy clearing tables full of glasses left by their American guests. Hannah caught her mam's eye, and Nora beamed a greeting before pointing to where a familiar dark head was bent over his phone. Dylan had his back to her, his thrift-store great coat draped over the back of the chair, facing the fire. A half-drunk pint sat on the table alongside him with an empty, balled-up crisp packet and a vape pen.

Hannah steeled herself and joined him without bothering to fetch a drink.

'Hi.' She didn't pause to check her pulse rate to see if being near him had set it racing, nor did she wait for an invitation to sit down. 'This is a surprise.'

'Hi.' Dylan set his phone down and ran his fingers through his too-long hair. She could see the jut of his shoulder bones through his army surplus sweater, and the faint hint of spearmint was a clue that he'd not long ducked out the back to vape. 'No drink?'

'No, not for me.' She was still hopeful about that hot chocolate with Tom. If she was game to knock on his door and invite him to join her, that was. There was no need to stretch out what she had to say over a drink with Dylan.

'This is a grand little pub. Your mam and dad made me welcome.' Dylan's eyes swept the space around him like he'd not already had an hour to soak it up.

'It's home,' Hannah replied, trying not to sound terse. 'These are the takings from the seed cards so far.' She slid a fat envelope toward him.

Dylan peeked inside and raised his brow slightly, then gave a low whistle. 'Well done.'

The praise made her sit up straighter, and she remembered how she'd planned to tell him about her secret sales weapon, Princess Leia. Now wasn't the time, though. Nor was she a puppy grateful for a pat, so she needed to stop behaving like one, she told herself firmly, getting to what was on her mind. 'Dylan, why are you here?'

'I said I would help, so here I am.'

'I appreciate it, but I wish you'd called first because I'd have told you things have changed.'

Dylan picked up his pint and supped. His face was an annoying blank page.

Hannah looked away, staring instead at the ring mark left behind on the Guinness coaster. She gave herself a once-over. There were no butterflies or jelly legs to deal with, and her palms weren't clammy either. It was like a plug had been yanked out of a socket, cutting off the source of her attraction to him.

'Your mam said you were with your man down from Dublin this evening.'

She hoped Mam hadn't elaborated on what she and Tom were doing. Knitting would ruin her street cred.

Actually, no. On closer examination, she realised she didn't care what he thought.

'You're not taking it literally, are you? What I said about keeping your enemies close?'

Wasn't there an old movie called *Sleeping with the Enemy*? Hannah thought then snapped, 'That's not your business. Things have changed.'

'Be careful. That's all I'm saying. Have you not heard of a wolf in sheep's clothing?'

Janey Mack! Who said things like that? Hannah thought, inwardly cringing. It dawned on her that the very thing she'd thought she loved about Dylan, the way he took himself seriously, she was now seeing through a different lens, and the urge to laugh rose in her throat. He'd be the sort to use the melting-chocolate bedroom voice! *Was it good for you, baby?* Ugh.

Somehow, she kept a straight face as she stood up. 'Look, I'm sorry you've had a wasted trip, but this was one instance where words did work.' A white lie, given she was only hoping this was the case, but there was no room for Dylan's agitating tactics in Emerald Bay.

Dylan lowered his pint slowly and stared at her, looming over him like a nightclub bouncer. His expression said he was unsure if this was the same person who'd left work last Friday.

'Are you feeling OK?'

'I'm feeling grand as it happens.' She mustered a smile.

'I don't know... You seem different.'

'I'm still me.' She shrugged, even though she knew Dylan was right. She was different.

After apologising for not being able to keep him company, she wished him all the best for a happy Christmas then left him to finish his pint. Or not, as the case may be.

Pushing through to the kitchen, Hannah grinned because she'd put her finger on what was different.

She felt strong – like someone who finally knew her own mind and was ready to act on it.

34

Today will be a great day, Hannah thought, knotting her dressing gown around her waist. 'Debbie Downer has left the building, and Positive Pauline has moved on in.' She spoke out loud, but her voice was barely audible over the steady thrum of rain on the roof.

Instead of using a comb, she ran her fingers through her hair, stretched and then perched on the edge of the bed to tug on her woolly socks, worn in favour of slippers.

'You're good to go,' she said, getting to her feet and crossing the room to the door, desperate to get downstairs and see Tom. She'd stood with one foot on the top step, the other on the landing last night, torn between the possibility of interrupting his work and wanting to recapture their earlier good-humoured closeness.

In the end, she'd decided she didn't want to butt in on an important meeting and had retreated, contenting herself with cosying up with Nan in front of the tele.

Her step faltered as she reached the door, thanks to the magnetic pull of her rumpled bed sheets.

'Almost good to go.' It wasn't worth not drawing the curtains and leaving her bed unmade because if Mam saw she'd left her room like that, she'd give out all morning about not being her servant and Hannah's slovenly habits.

But as she went through the motions, she resolved that nothing and no one would interfere with her Pauline Positiveness this morning. The reason for this was, as Nan would say, she could feel it in her water that everything would work out fine.

The thought of hearing the good news today that the famine cottage land was no longer under threat put a spring in her step as she bounced out of her bedroom onto the empty landing to skip down the stairs. She sniffed with the expectation of being hit by the smell of sizzling bacon, a sure sign Tom was being fussed over by her mam, but, nope, nothing. Perhaps he was thinking of his arteries and joining Dad in having porridge and wholegrain toast instead. That had to be it, she decided as she slid into the kitchen like Tom Cruise in *Risky Business*, only in a dressing gown and minus a microphone.

Her mam was at the table enjoying a cuppa, Dad was reading the news on the phone, as was his habit, the voice of doom as he read out the direst headlines, and Nan was spooning prunes on her porridge. They all looked up as she skidded to a halt.

'Morning,' she sang out.

'Morning,' they grunted back at her.

Princess Leia barked a greeting, which caused her dad to mutter under his breath.

'There's porridge in the pot when you're ready, Hannah,' Kitty said, sounding a little down in the mouth as she gazed at her prunes.

I'd probably feel down if I had to add a load of prunes to my morning porridge, too, Hannah thought, wishing once more that she could tell Kitty everything would work out just grand.

There was no sign of Tom, but it was too early for him to

have headed out already. He was probably upstairs catching up on some sleep after working late, she figured, pausing to fuss Princess Leia. The chihuahua was overseeing the goings-on at the table from her throne on Nora's lap. Her mam was twisted on her seat so her legs faced the worktop, and her torso was angled toward the table. It struck Hannah as an indigestion-inducing position in which to eat toast as she gave the little dog a final tickle behind the ears and then fetched a mug.

'Tom's having a lie-in then,' she said, smiling as she joined them at the table and helped herself to tea.

'He's not upstairs, love. He's gone,' Liam supplied. 'Dear God, you wouldn't believe what's after happening in the Middle East now.' Shaking his head, he didn't elaborate further as his eyes flickered over the illuminated screen he was reading from.

Hannah's hand, which had been reaching for the milk jug, froze in mid-air. 'What do you mean gone?'

Nora filled in the gaps, toast halfway to her mouth. 'I came downstairs to find he'd squared up and left a note on the table thanking us for our hospitality. He said he'd miss my home cooking.' She took a smug bite of her jam-slathered toast, which sent a shower of crumbs Princess Leia's way.

'*Our* home cooking,' Kitty swiftly corrected her daughter-in-law, shooting Hannah a sympathy-loaded look.

Hannah tried to make sense of what she was being told. 'But he never said anything to me.'

'Well, he was busy last night, wasn't he, love? And I expect he didn't want to wake any of us this morning. He was a very thoughtful lad, Tom.'

'He's only gone back to Dublin, Mam, not died!' Hannah's tone was sharp.

'What's got your knickers in a knot?' Nora asked.

Kitty stopped examining the prune now on her spoon. 'If

things go ahead with the Greenhouse project, he'll be back before you know it.'

'If they go ahead.'

Tom had gone without bothering to say goodbye, so was that it? If he'd talked his client into looking elsewhere, there would be no reason for him to return to Emerald Bay except for Eileen's knitting classes. And how badly did he want that Christmas sweater? She squeezed her eyes shut, knowing she wasn't thinking clearly because his not letting her in on his plans stung.

Wait just a second! Hannah opened her eyes; Mam had said Tom had left a note. Maybe there was something in that she'd missed? 'What did the note say again?'

'Here – read it yourself.' Nora produced a crumpled piece of paper from her pocket and thrust it at Hannah, who held it up to the light as if it might reveal an invisible-ink message before smoothing the note flat on the table then scanning the words hungrily, only to slump back in her chair, aware of curious gazes upon her.

'It doesn't tell me anything.' She'd thought, at the very least, he might have mentioned the Christmas invitation she'd given him.

'I already told you what it said. I'm surprised you're so bothered about what Tom's plans are. His mobile number is written in the visitor's book. You could always call him.'

Hannah was annoyed at the coy tone in her mam's voice. 'I only want to know how things stand.'

'Oh yes?' Liam's eyebrow lifted high on his forehead.

'Not between us, Dad! Nothing is going on between us.' She'd misread everything, eejit that she was. 'I'm talking about the Greenhouse and Christmas tree farm.'

Hannah could see that her protesting had had the opposite effect on her parents. Her mind raced ahead. There was nothing to stop her from telling them what he'd told her yesterday, not now. It would get those knowing looks off their faces, so she spilled it out. 'Tom told me he was confident he'd managed to talk the developer into looking for a site elsewhere, and I thought he might have let me know where things were at before heading back to Dublin.'

The prune plopped back into Kitty's bowl. 'But that's grand news, so it is!'

'It's not confirmed, Nan,' Hannah backpedalled. 'I wasn't supposed to say anything until Tom knew exactly where things sat.'

Nora set Princess Leia on the floor and rose from the table. 'Well, it sounds to me like things will work out just fine. I'll go on up and strip his bed,' she announced as Kitty called Princess Leia over to her.

Nora vanished upstairs, but the little dog ignored Kitty, trotting to the door and giving a few ear-piercing yips and yaps.

Liam put his hands over his ears. 'The sooner that one's mam is out of the hospital, the better.'

They definitely had a love-hate relationship going on there, Hannah thought as a tap at the back door sounded over the cacophonous barking.

'I'll get it,' she said, pausing alongside her dad to tell him, 'She was only letting us know someone was here.'

'That's right, Princess Leia. You're a grand little guard dog,' Kitty was saying as Hannah picked the dog up and plopped her on her nan's knee before opening the door.

She stared in shock at who she found standing there, her hand raised in readiness to knock again.

It was the American woman in the red coat.

35

Hannah hadn't moved from where she was blocking the doorway. Her mouth hung open at the sight of the woman, a splash of colour against the wet, grey day, her hair plastered to her face in dark auburn tentacles thanks to the persistent downpour.

It was like a piece of an abstract puzzle, how like her mam's hair this stranger's was.

The similarity between Nora Kelly and whoever this person was didn't lie in age – she was maybe five to eight years younger than Mam – but in their features. There was something about her eyes, too, and whatever it was, it was pulling Hannah in. They were amber, and when it dawned on her that it was like looking into her own eyes, she took a step backwards, shocked.

'What are you playing at, Hannah? Either invite whoever it is out of the rain or shut the door. It wasn't a tent you were born in,' Nan clucked impatiently, shaking her granddaughter from her trance. She was already setting Princess Leia down in preparation for getting out of her seat to put the kettle on and fetch the biscuits for their visitor. Whether they'd be the best biscuits or not remained to be seen.

The woman seemed unaware she was getting soaked. She stood there shivering, assessing Hannah with equal wariness. At least she was attempting a smile, Hannah thought, stepping to one side. 'Erm, I suppose you'd better come in.'

'Thank you.'

Her smile was grateful but tremulous and eerily similar to her mam's, Hannah thought, keeping a watchful eye as she stepped inside, wiping her feet on the mat. She shut the door against the inclement weather then pressed her back to it as though worried this stranger who'd been trailing her mam might change her mind and make a break for it.

Kitty sank back down in her seat at the sight of their uninvited guest, seemingly twigging instantly that this was Nora's shadow. Meanwhile, Princess Leia trotted over to sniff around the woman's ankles, which were encased in leather boots, then, deciding she was friend, not foe, scuttled over to her basket and began grappling with her bone toy.

'Oh, I'm making a mess, sorry,' the woman said, glancing down at the rivulets of water sliding from the red, shiny, waterproof fabric onto the floor. 'Perhaps if I took my coat off?' Her words fell away.

The arrival of a stranger saw Liam put his phone down and angle himself in his seat to look over his shoulder. His mouth was already open in anticipation of a jovial greeting, but no sound came out when he saw who was dripping on their kitchen floor. He'd obviously been too engrossed in the news to pick up on her accent.

Hannah guessed he'd put two and two together, but Liam Kelly was nothing if not a gracious host even when the guest was his wife's possible stalker, and Hannah's brow knitted as he leaped into action, cleared his throat and said, 'Of course.'

The woman flashed him a grateful smile, unbelting the red raincoat and slipping it off with a thank you as Liam reached for it.

Hannah refused to budge from her post and matched her father's hard look as he made to hang the coat on the back-door hook with one of her own. He quickly gave up and hung the coat over the top of Kitty's pinny on the connecting door to the pub instead.

'We all seem to have forgotten our manners. I'm Liam Kelly.' He thrust his hand out, and the woman shook it back.

'You're frozen, so you are! Here.' He released her hand from his pawlike grip and pulled out a chair, ushering her into it. 'You sit yourself down, and I'll make a fresh pot of tea. That'll warm you up.'

'Dad,' Hannah warned through gritted teeth. They didn't know who this woman was or what she wanted, and there he was, telling her to make herself at home.

'I'm Judy, by the way.' Her teeth stopped chattering as she introduced herself shooting a tentative glance in Kitty's direction and then Hannah's.

'Judy,' Hannah said, trying the name on for size as her hands floated to her hips. 'And who exactly are you, Judy, and why have you been following my mam about?'

'Hannah!' Liam dropped the kettle with a clatter.

'No, it's fine,' Judy jumped in quickly, clasping and then unclasping her hands, which were resting on the table in front of her. 'I do owe you all an explanation.'

'Especially Mam.' Hannah wasn't backing down.

'Yes, especially your mom. I'm afraid I haven't handled this at all well.' She bit her bottom lip and stared at her hands. 'I think Nora and I are related.'

Hannah had already guessed that much. It was an obvious connection, but it didn't explain all the cloak-and-dagger behaviour.

Her dad headed her off before she could demand further answers. 'Hannah, you should probably fetch your mam before

Judy goes any further.' He carried the fresh pot of tea over to the table.

Judy looked like she could use something stronger than tea, and Hannah was tempted to tell Nan to take her place guarding the door as she reluctantly left her post and raced up the stairs.

The door to Room 5, which Tom had vacated earlier, was open, and she stampeded down the hall to find her mam bundling up the sheets she'd pulled off the bed, oblivious to the unfolding drama downstairs.

Nora frowned at her. 'You'll go through the floor thundering about like so. Slow down.'

'Never mind that, Mam. She's downstairs!' Hannah tried to catch her breath. 'The American woman who's been following you. She says you're related.'

Shock flickered across Nora's face, and her lips parted as she shook her head. 'Would you say that again, Hannah?'

'Mam, listen!' Hannah almost stamped her foot but knew it wouldn't hurry things along, so trying to keep her voice calm, she relayed what she'd just said once more.

Her mam seemed to take it on board this time, but all she said was, 'Right.'

The sheets were thrust into Hannah's arms, then Nora smoothed her sweater and headed downstairs with her daughter, who trailed white flannelette sheets behind her, trying not to breathe in the intoxicating, musky scent Tom had left behind.

They found Judy sipping tea while Liam made small talk, and Kitty wore an expression that said she was waiting to hear more from the stranger seated at their table before passing judgment.

Judy's hand shook as she placed her cup back in the saucer upon seeing the woman she'd been asking after and seemingly watching up close standing there. She half pushed her chair back.

Nora held her hand up. 'Please don't get up on my behalf.

I'm Nora Kelly, but I think you already know that. What's this Hannah's been telling me about you being a relative of mine?'

Hannah hurriedly dumped the sheets in the machine and came to stand defensively by her mam's side.

'I'm Judy Carter. My maiden name's Kedder. Hello. It's nice to meet you at last.' Judy hadn't taken her eyes off Nora, nor Nora off her.

Hannah fancied she could almost hear the air between the two women crackling and took a sharp intake of air, signalling that she wished Judy would spit it out – whatever it was.

'You do look like my late mother,' Nora spoke up.

'Do I?' Judy asked softly.

Nora nodded. 'You have the same bone structure.'

'And I can see my late father in you.' Judy cleared her throat and gestured to her rapidly frizzing hair. 'Nora, I'm soaked because I stood on your doorstep out there rehearsing how I was going to say what I should have said to you last Christmas.'

'I generally find the best way to get things off your chest is to come right out with it,' Nora replied, her voice not giving away much.

Judy's lips moved from side to side as though contemplating this. Then she said, 'OK.' She strung the word out. 'Well, here goes. Your maternal grandfather was my father.'

Nora swayed as though slapped, and Hannah reached out to steady her. 'I'm afraid you could have saved yourself a lot of time if you'd made yourself known to me the first time you came to Emerald Bay, Judy. You see, that's, well, it's simply not possible.'

She even looked like she'd been slapped, Hannah thought, keeping a firm grip on her mam's arm.

'My grandfather died at sea when I was young.'

Nora's eyes glittered, but Hannah couldn't tell if it was down to defiance or threatened tears.

Judy's cheeks were also colouring as she shook her head.

'No, I'm afraid he didn't, but I think you already suspected that. William Kedder, your grandfather, my father, sailed on a cargo ship to America from Liverpool and started a new life in 1975. My mom was widowed with two nearly grown sons when they met in New York shortly after he arrived. He was fifteen years her senior, and I imagine it was a shock when Mom found out she was expecting again after so much time. They married that same year.'

What was happening here, and why wasn't Mam shooing this woman out the door? She was mad.

'I think you better sit down, Mam,' Hannah said, needing an excuse to do so herself because she was flashing back to Mam, having told Ava last Christmas how a storm at sea had taken her grandfather, their great-grandfather. The remains of his fishing boat had been found, but not him.

She was running on autopilot as she steered her mam to the table and sank down beside her. When Ava had relayed this story, which was the first any of them had heard of it, to her and her wide-eyed sisters, they'd all agreed it was tragic, but Hannah suspected that, like her, they'd all felt like it was a tragedy far removed from their lives.

Nora Kelly never spoke much about her immediate family, and Hannah and her siblings had little contact with them. There were the occasional letters her brother Tiernan's wife sent from America updating them on their lives or the excruciating FaceTime sessions Mam would drag them in on with Uncle Tiernan now and again. Then, closer to home, the four Nolan brothers, cousins of her mam's, could frequently be found propping up the bar at the Shamrock. The brothers were a familial connection that all five sisters were reluctant to acknowledge, given they were heathens. They'd a sister, too, who used to run a guesthouse in Dublin, but they'd never met her.

'Mam?' Hannah wanted answers as to what was happening here.

It wasn't her mam who spoke next, though; it was Judy.

'This isn't my first visit to Emerald Bay, as you already know,' Judy told Nora, who had a white-knuckled grip on the handle of the teacup Liam had slid silently in front of her.

He was now standing by his wife's side, his hand resting on her shoulder. Across the table, Kitty appeared to be holding her breath while Hannah's leg jiggled under the table.

'My husband, John, and I split our time between Dublin and the States. We have business interests across Ireland. He's Irish, but we met in the States. And I'm sorry I didn't make myself known to you. It was cowardly, and the only excuse I have is I think I was in shock at finding out my father was a bigamist who'd left his first family behind in Ireland.'

It was cheesy, but you could have heard a pin drop, Hannah thought, staring at Judy, not daring to interrupt because even though none of this could be true, she had to hear more.

'How did you find out?' Nora rasped, her face bleached of colour.

Judy licked her lips. 'Dad never spoke about his life in Ireland. I assumed he'd had a hard time here because Mom told me once not to push him on the subject, so I left it alone. He died in 2005 when I was thirty-two.'

'He lived into his mid-eighties then,' Nora murmured, working things out. 'My mother and I weren't on speaking terms, but she died a few years back. Mam was seventy-five. She never spoke about her father after he disappeared because there were rumours.'

Hannah rubbed her temples. It was too much.

Judy replied, 'I lost my mother two years ago. When I was sorting her things, I found my father's passport and decided I wanted to learn more about my Irish roots for my children as much as for myself. That was when I began digging. I didn't have to dig too deep, to be frank.' She delved into her purse and produced an envelope. 'I've some photographs and documentation here if you'd like to see them.'

'Please.' Nora took the envelope.

There was still a chance Judy had got her wires badly crossed somewhere along the way, Hannah thought as Nora pulled a Polaroid out. She leaned in to see it for herself. A fortyish woman was leaning into a grizzled man, while off to the left, a young girl dressed in T-bar sandals, knee-high socks and a tunic dress was smiling shyly. They were standing outside a simple clapboard house. It was a snapshot in time, like looking at a picture from a seventies magazine, because these people meant nothing to her, but seeing the tear trickling down her mam's cheeks, it was clear something had resonated with her.

'It's him, my daideo,' she said, looking up through watery lashes at Liam.

Hannah had read about thunderbolt moments, but she'd never experienced one until now. The realisation that had just hit her took her breath away. Tom had inadvertently dropped that his client was a woman, and a snippet of conversation raced through her head.

'How do you know my benefactor's not connected with the land?'

My God, Hannah thought. Was Judy Carter behind the Greenhouse project? Hadn't she said she and her husband had business interests across Ireland? Or was she connecting dots that weren't there?

36

'Growing up, my mam and dad, your uncle Tiernan and I would pile in the Hillman Hunter – orange it was; my dad's pride and joy – and drive down to see Mam's folks on the coast on the first Sunday of the month.' Nora's eyes misted as she drifted back to her childhood. 'Tiernan and I looked forward to it because we'd always stop at a tea room near Salthill and pick up six cream horns for afternoon tea. Oh, but they were gorgeous. And the cream would squish out the bottom when you bit into them.'

Hannah pictured her mam as a little girl enjoying her treat.

'It was like stepping back in time visiting our grandparents. They lived a simple life in a limewashed cottage overlooking the estuary. My mam's father was a fisherman like his father before him. It was always dim inside their cottage but welcoming, with the peat fire smouldering away. The hearth was deep, and the fire burning away in it was the soul of that cottage. Gran cooked over it; she dried their clothes above it, too, and we'd gather around it when we visited. She was a house-proud woman even though they had no mod cons. Not even a telephone. And they didn't get electricity until the early seventies. Can you imagine?'

No, Hannah couldn't. As a child, she'd thought the world had ended any time a power cut meant she missed the end of the television programme she'd been watching. They were made of hardy stuff, those of past generations. She'd swallowed down what she suspected where Judy Carter was concerned. Her mam had had enough of a shock and needed to talk. It would keep.

'My grandmother reminded me of a bird. She was such a tiny woman who flitted about fussing over us, never settling in her seat for long. As for Granddad, Tiernan and I called him daideo.' Nora pronounced it *dadj-yoh*.

'Irish for grandfather,' Kitty supplied for Judy's benefit.

'Mm.' Nora tucked her hair behind her ears. 'They always seemed old to me. That way anyone over thirty seems ancient when you're small, and the last time I saw Daideo, I was eight. But they weren't old, not at all. Sure, Daideo was younger than I am now when he was declared missing at sea. He was only fifty-four, and I don't think he was a man who was happy with his lot. From what I could glean, his brother had sailed to America when he was still a teenager, and I think he'd regretted not going with him when he had the chance. He'd met our gran by then, though, and they were to be married. She was never interested in emigrating. Ireland was her home, and she was fond of saying she'd not be leaving its shores no matter if the streets in America were paved with gold! Or so Daideo would have us all believe. He could be quite poetic when he wanted to be.

'I've never forgotten the book he had. It was filled with photographs of America, and Tiernan and I were allowed to look through it after we'd finished our tea, but we had to wash and dry our hands first. We'd lie on our stomachs on the rug by the fire in awe of the national parks and city skylines we'd never seen the likes of in our village of Ballyclegg. Those afternoons spent poring over that book planted the seed for Tiernan to emigrate as soon as he was old enough.'

Nora went quiet, and Hannah hoped she wouldn't clam up and dismiss her memories because Nora Kelly was apt to say, 'Sure, it's been and gone. What's there to know?' if the topic of her childhood was ever raised. It wasn't her way to harp on about the past, but all three of them seated at the table wanted to hear her side of the story.

'The day he vanished, there was a storm. It was early evening when word came that Daideo had been out at sea when it hit, and his boat hadn't returned. We had to wait until the morning to drive to the cottage.'

Liam squeezed his wife's shoulder, but she didn't appear to notice, lost in time as she was.

'We huddled down at the harbour with Gran, waiting for news. The sea was still churning, and I remember being frightened of the waves because I'd never seen them crashing in like so. There was this sense of foreboding, too. I think we all felt it.' Nora shuddered. 'I've thought about that over the years, and I think it was knowing things would never be the same again. And they weren't.' Her voice broke.

'Oh, Mam.' Hannah's throat was tight.

'It's all a long time ago now, Hannah, but Gran stopped flitting about after that. She'd sit in her chair, staring into that peat fire as though it held the answers as to why, as an experienced fisherman, he'd taken the boat out, aware of the weather bomb that was coming. It didn't make sense. She couldn't grieve. Gran was in limbo, and the whispered word going about was William Kedder had wanted to take his own life.' Nora hesitated. 'But then there was a sighting of him in Dublin.'

Hannah was struggling to comprehend what she was hearing. It was like listening to an audiobook, only it wasn't fiction.

'A local family was returning from visiting family in England, and they swore they saw Daideo in the melee at Dún Laoghaire, but he'd disappeared into the crowd before they could approach him. I always chose to believe he died because I couldn't equate the grandfather I'd known with a man who'd leave his wife, daughter and grandchildren behind.'

For once in her life, Hannah was lost for words.

'But you suspected?' Judy asked gently.

'There was always a longing in his voice when he'd read us the letters his brother sent him. And then there was the book Tiernan and I used to pore over. I found the America book – or what was left of it – after Gran died and I was helping to clear the cottage. All the pages had been ripped out. I put it in the rubbish bag before Mam could see because the thought of Gran sitting in her chair by the fire tearing them out in anger and burning them was so sad. My mam changed too. There was a hardness to her that wasn't there before.'

'When I found out what my father had done, I struggled to reconcile the dad I knew with a man that could do what he did.' Judy spoke so quietly they had to strain to hear her.

Kitty spoke up. 'Perhaps he had a breakdown. You've both said he wasn't a bad man.'

'No, he wasn't. But he was a coward, and that's hard to come to terms with,' Judy replied.

Hannah watched as a solitary tear tracked down Judy's cheek. Nora's hand reached across the table toward this woman whose life was connected to hers.

'They were his mistakes,' Nora said as Judy clasped her hand. 'Not ours.'

It was only then Hannah realised she was crying, too.

———————

37

Hannah made excuses, leaving her mam, dad, nan, and Judy talking over the top of one another. The two women, strangers but family at the same time, had so much ground to cover. A lifetime in fact. She needed to clear her head because, although she was younger than Mam, Judy was her great-aunt.

What if she was right? Did Judy want to change Emerald Bay, destroying not just the landscape and history but also precious memories. How could she lay that on her mam's shoulders when she'd just learned her grandfather was a bigamist? It was so hard to take it all in.

She trooped up to her room, scrambled onto her bed and pinched herself, needing reassurance that she was awake and not having the most bizarre dream. The red mark was confirmation she wasn't asleep – what her mam had said, what Judy had said, wasn't something she'd dreamed up.

The Kelly family had an enormous skeleton in the closet.

Hannah desperately wanted to speak to Tom because he must have known what had attracted Judy to Emerald Bay in the first place. Her simmering anger threatened to boil and overflow. Who did he think he was keeping a secret that huge and not having the courage to be here when it came out? Under-lying the rage, though, was hurt, which had stopped her from snatching up the visitor's book containing his phone number.

She'd surreptitiously switched her phone to silent when her mam began talking because she hadn't wanted to put her off with pinging messages. A wise move she saw, fetching it from the pocket of her slouchy cardy and checking it. She'd missed several texts, but Tom hadn't reached out, and none of the rest were important. Right now, she needed her eldest sister's calming bedside manner and rang her, hoping Shannon wasn't with a patient.

Hannah relaxed a little upon hearing her sister's voice. 'Shan, we need to get together – you, Imo, Aves and Grace. It's urgent.'

'Twice in a few days. Should I be worried?'

'No. Yes. I don't know.' Hannah hesitated because she didn't want to dump the unbelievable turn of events this morning onto her over the phone. 'Please, Shan, will you trust me when I say I need to see you all?'

Shannon seemed to be thinking this over, and Hannah was relieved when she said, 'All right, but you need to calm down, OK?'

The only person who could get away with telling her to calm down when she was anything but calm was Shannon, and that was only because she was a nurse.

'OK.' Hannah bobbed her head even though her sister couldn't see her and did some slow breathing. She wished she had her sick bag on hand because her heart was racing with a borderline panic attack.

'I was heading home for lunch today anyway. I could meet you at the cottage in an hour. Let me ring the others, OK?'

'Thanks, Shannon. I'll see you there.'

Hannah knew working herself into a state wouldn't get her anywhere. She just needed to take her mind off Tom's betrayal,

Judy's suspected deception and the abandoned farm and famine cottage. If Eileen hadn't insisted they store their kit bags at the church hall, knitting might have soothed her. But that wasn't an option, so desperate for a distraction, she opened her laptop. Her fingers took on a life of their own, and she googled youth mentoring, curious about what jobs came under that umbrella, which calmed and focused her mind.

It proved an excellent rabbit hole to go down because the panic had subsided by the time she made her way back downstairs, sidling past the group still sitting in the kitchen. Only now the best biscuits were open on the table.

Mam and Judy were swapping notes about their childhoods as the initial shock of their meeting face to face wore off. Dad and Nan listened avidly. Hannah hesitated, wanting to blurt her fears about what else had brought Judy to Emerald Bay, but she stayed silent, with only her dad acknowledging her as she slunk past to pick up her keys.

The rain had eased a little, and Doris started with the first turn of the key. 'At least you're on my side, eh, Doris?' Hannah said, flicking the lights on and wrestling the gearstick into reverse.

With the wipers sluicing back and forth, she was soon puttering, a little slower than she would have liked, past the twinkling shop windows and under the festive decorations of Main Street toward Shannon's cottage, wondering how life in the bay could be carrying on like usual after what she'd learned this morning.

Hannah was vaguely aware there was no tour bus disgorging its passengers to take snaps of the picturesque cottages today as she pulled over to the side of the road, performed a quick U-turn and parked behind her sister's yellow Honda Jazz. A beacon on a wet day. She saw Imogen had yet to arrive as she got out and ran to the cottage's front door. It was open, so she stamped her boots on the mat then stepped inside, barely registering her surroundings, before stooping to take off her Docs. 'It's only me, Shan,' she called.

As she dislodged her foot from her boot, Shannon appeared through the door at the end of the passage with chipmunk cheeks and a sandwich in her hand. 'I made enough for you and Imo if you want one.' She waggled her sambo, nearly losing the egg salad filling. 'Whoops.'

'I don't think I could eat anything now; I'm too keyed up. Thanks anyway.' Hannah fiddled with the laces of her other boot.

'Well, I'm intrigued as to what's going on, but nothing affects my appetite these days. Will you give me a clue?'

'No. You rang Imo and the twins, right?'

'Of course. They're as intrigued as I am about what's happened now. I tell you, the excitement never stops in Emerald Bay.' Shannon eyed her briefly then devoured her sandwich like a human hoover. 'I can't stop eating these. Egg salad sandwiches,' she garbled through her mouthful. 'I've even been eating them for supper.'

'Your first craving.' Hannah grinned at her blossoming sister.

'That or I just really, really like egg sandwiches.' Shannon eyed the remaining mouthful with adoration and stuffed it in. 'Mmm.'

Hannah's foot popped free of her boot, and she straightened then, hearing a loud miaow, beamed at the Persian that had appeared alongside his mistress. 'Oh, hello!'

Napoleon stalked regally toward her. Shannon, watching on, gave an eggy smile as Hannah swooped down to scoop him up in a cuddle.

'I've missed you. Yes, I have.' She showered his royal furriness with kisses.

'I wouldn't be doing too much up close and personal. He brought a rat in this morning.'

Hannah put him down, wiped her mouth with the back of her hand and followed Shannon to the living room, where a Christmas tree shimmered in the fire's glow. It was a much more respectable size than the Faraway Tree back at the Shamrock.

'Why does it reek of eggs in here instead of the Vanilla Skies diffuser I bought you?' Imogen called from the hallway.

Shannon rolled her eyes and whispered to Hannah, 'I can't use her stupid vanilla thingamajig. It makes me hungry for Carmel's vanilla cupcakes all the time.'

Imogen's perfume arrived in the room before she did. 'Good, you've got the fire going. It's freezing out there.' She stood in front of the woodburning stove inside the original fireplace to warm her backside. 'So, come on, Hannah, spill. What's going on?'

Hannah was already FaceTiming the twins.

Ten minutes later, the only sound in the little cottage was the stove ticking away and Napoleon washing himself enthusiastically.

Hannah, meanwhile, was relieved to have told her sisters who the woman in the red coat was and everything that had brought her to Emerald Bay including her worry that she was behind the Greenhouse project. They were the voices of reason, telling Hannah to give Judy breathing space and trust that if she was, she'd tell them about her part in the land deal when she was ready. They'd asked her not to spoil things for Mam, and Hannah had promised she would give her the benefit of the doubt, but there was no room in her heart to let Tom off the hook.

When they were done, she looked at Shannon. 'I think I will have that egg sarnie now, Shan.'

It was a miracle Judy survived her inquisition from the Kelly sisters, who'd launched like rockets into the scene in the kitchen. But survive it she did. The entire family – Grace and Ava staring out of Hannah's phone with identical flabbergasted faces – listened as they learned about another branch of their family they'd not known existed until today. Time healed wounds because where once there would have been deep hurt and anger over William Kedder's cowardly betrayal of not just his Irish family but his American family, too, there seemed no point rehashing that now. You couldn't change the past, Kitty had declared. What was done was done. What mattered was how you handled the future.

Sometimes Nan could be very wise.

As questions were fired at Judy, Nora took herself off quietly to speak to her brother, Tiernan, because he'd been part of that shivering vigil at the harbour for their grandfather all those years ago, and Hannah's ears burned upon hearing Judy allude vaguely to her and her husband being investors with business connections in Ireland. Investor was a loose term, but in Hannah's mind, it was further proof she was right about Judy and the famine cottage land.

Liam had gone through to man the bar thanks to Enda tapping on the back door to remind him it was past opening time, so it was left to Kitty and her granddaughters to suggest that Judy check out of the lodgings she'd been staying at in Kilti-caneel to stay in the Shamrock's newly vacated Room 5. It would give them all a chance to get to know her better before her return trip to America. And, of course, it went without saying that she would spend Christmas with them.

Hannah's insides twisted at the thought of the Christmas invitation she'd issued to Tom, but she quickly dismissed the memory. Whatever might have been blooming between them was over now.

Always remember to forget,
The troubles that passed away.
But never forget to remember,
The blessings that come each day.

— *IRISH BLESSING*

38

For the best part of the morning, Hannah had been hiding in her room, having cadged needles and wool off Nan to keep herself busy until Mam and Judy headed off to Galway. She'd had it with everybody's cheeriness as the countdown to Christmas began, only days away now. All the festive goodwill and peace on earth circulating about the place was making her feel worse, and when, at last, she'd heard the two women clattering out the door, she'd rolled off her bed to peer out the window.

Mam and her newfound relation had grown close over the last week in the way you do when you sit up night after night chatting. They were mummified by hats, scarves, gloves, coats and boots, their arms linked as they headed to Nora's car, laughing about something. Hannah watched until the car puttered off, assured she would have the kitchen to herself at long last, with Nan at her craft group and Dad busy in the pub.

She padded downstairs feeling like a shell of the person who'd come home full of vim and vigour for stopping the sale of the famine cottage land. The fire she'd burned with had been stamped out by despondency because a whole week had passed in radio silence from Tom. She didn't have him down for a coward, unable to tell her to her face what was going on. Or without the common decency to at least reach out and let her know he wouldn't be here for Christmas. But then cowards came in all shapes and forms – look at her late great-grandfather.

Judy had remained silent about the land deal, if indeed she was fronting it, and Hannah, thus far, was keeping her promise to her sisters and leaving it alone. For now, at least. It wasn't easy, though, which was why she was tucking herself away in her room. This, along with no word from the Department of Agriculture, had seen the fight seep out of her. She'd told Nan there was nothing more they could do regarding the famine-cottage land except wait.

If Nan sensed she was keeping something from her, she didn't press her about it. Hannah didn't intend to confide what her gut told her about Judy's other motivation for being in Emerald Bay or that Tom might have had a clue all along of her connection to the Kelly family. Nan was as caught up in getting to know Nora's long-lost relative as the rest of the family, and Hannah didn't trust her not to let slip to Nora if she came clean with her thoughts on Judy's business intentions for Emerald Bay. The fallout would almost certainly spoil Christmas. Not that Hannah was looking forward to Christmas anyhow. Not now.

Then there was Dylan. Her feelings for him might be dead in the water, but the thought of returning to work at Feed the World with Bees in the new year left her cold, too. She didn't have the energy to do anything about that, though. It would wait.

Hannah stopped in the doorway because she'd expected to have the kitchen to herself, but Nan had her back to her up at the worktop, sleeves rolled up and a pinny knotted about her waist. She hung back, debating a retreat upstairs.

'Hannah Kelly, would you stop loitering and decide whether you'll come in and keep me company or go back to whatever you've been up to all morning locked away in your room?'

Kitty had obviously used those special eyes in the back of her head.

Hannah decided it was safe to hang out with her; with everyone else otherwise engaged, it was unlikely she'd be subjected to an overdose of Christmas spirit.

'I thought you were going to your craft group,' she said, crossing the kitchen and hoisting herself onto the free patch of worktop.

'There's only so much origami one woman can do in a year, and this cake won't ice itself.' Kitty was slathering the enormous slab of fruit cake in apricot jam. Kitty's Christmas cake was legendary, at least within the Kelly family, and she was a stickler for tradition, too, baking it on Stir-up Sunday, the week before Advent. She would have lovingly fed the cake each Sunday since by spooning whiskey over the top, and now, with only days until Christmas, it was time to ice it. The decorating would be done once the icing had set.

Hannah's eyes had begun to sting, and she blinked rapidly. 'Jaysus, Nan, how much whiskey's in that thing?'

Kitty ignored her and didn't pause in her task. 'Now listen to me, Hannah. I know you're enjoying the knitting, and you've always tended to throw yourself wholeheartedly into whatever you've set your mind to doing, but holing up in your room like you've been doing these last few days isn't healthy. Are you planning on going into the woollens business and competing with Eileen? Is that it?'

Nan had a point. She'd moved on to cosy coffee cup warmers with a different coloured rosette for each of her sisters' stockings, having finished knitting the glasses case she had earmarked for Nan. 'It's the knitting keeping me sane, Nan.'

'And a tendency to be dramatic as well as throw yourself into things,' Kitty added to the list.

'No. That's Imo.'

'Is that right?' Kitty shot her granddaughter a look that said she wasn't convinced by her passing the buck. 'So come on then. What's got you so your chin's scraping the ground your face is so long.'

Hannah hefted a huge sigh. 'I'm a terrible judge of character.'

'Why do you say that? And don't be sticking your finger in the jam like so.'

She was too late. Hannah popped her finger in her mouth, enjoying the fruity sweetness, then said, 'Tom kept saying I was. I didn't believe him, but now... I read him totally wrong. I believed him when he said he'd help us and let him string me along by telling me what I wanted to hear. He hasn't even both-ered to phone me to say he's not coming for Christmas.'

'I didn't know you'd invited him, love.'

'I wish I hadn't now.'

'Hannah, I once heard a wise old saying that goes like this: time and patience bring a snail to Cork.'

'What's that supposed to mean?' Hannah's hand was inching toward the marzipan, intent on tearing a sliver of the almond-flavoured icing off, but was thwarted by a tap on her knuckles with the back of the jammy spoon. Nan was a fast mover, so she was.

Now Kitty was piously saying, 'I take it to serve as a reminder that the journey toward achieving a goal isn't always smooth, or fast for that matter, and that sometimes a little time and patience is required.'

'Patience, as you know, Nan, is a foreign word to me, and it's not one of your strengths either.'

'Have a little faith. Things will work out in the end. Why don't you go for a walk? You could wander around to the abandoned farm. Just to keep an eye on things like. Some fresh air will do you good, and Princess Leia is due for an outing. James is after letting us know she'll be going home to her mammy tomorrow, so it'll be your last chance.'

Maybe Nan was right. It might make her feel better. She could head to the famine cottage and lay her own ghosts to rest. The sight of Princess Leia's beseeching gaze sealed it. She'd venture out.

'I'll just nip upstairs and throw on a heavier jumper.'

Hannah's phone began ringing. It was a number she didn't recognise. Tom? Her heart leaped. She ran halfway up the stairs, not wanting to be in Nan's earshot when she answered with a breathy, 'Hello.'

'Hannah Kelly?'

It wasn't him, and her shoulders slumped, but she recognised the voice from somewhere. She scrunched her nose, trying to picture the face behind it, and dawdled up the remaining stairs. 'Yes, that's right. Erm, who's this, please?'

'It's Jeremy Jones.' He swiftly followed this with, 'Don't cut me off!'

Of course it was! She slapped her forehead, regretting having answered, but didn't disconnect the call because she was curious why he would be calling her.

'All I'm after is a short quote from you or your nan.'

'About what?' Hannah demanded with no hint of politeness.

'You haven't heard?'

'Jeremy, I will hang up if you don't get straight to the point of this call.'

The reporter sounded gleeful as he said, 'I'm ringing for your response to the news an agreement for the sale of the famine-cottage land has been reached. Did you hear what I said? A one-line quote will do.'

'I've got one for you, Jeremy. Feck off.'

39

Hannah exited quietly, having no wish to rain on her nan's Christmas cake parade with the news of the land sale. At least she'd left as quietly as was possible when you had a yapping chihuahua clad in the Christmas doggy sweater Eileen had whipped up for their temporary charge trotting by your side. She called out her plans to wander up to the abandoned farm as Nan had suggested. Kitty, however, hadn't taken her eyes off the marzipan. She was draping a big sheet of white icing over the cake like you would a child pretending to be a ghost, the hint of a smile on her face.

The smoky smell of the fires keeping Emerald Bay's residents toasty caught at the back of Hannah's throat, making her cough. Overhead, the sky was grey and pregnant with the promise of the snow Dad had announced at breakfast was forecasted any time now. She paused to sniff the air, then, feeling foolish, began to walk. She was conscious Princess Leia only had little legs as she tried to keep pace alongside her, so she slowed a little.

At least Jeremy Jones's smug call had given her perspective where Tom was concerned. And when he next dared show his face in Emerald Bay in his role of architectural arse once the project got underway, she'd be sure to tell him what she thought of him. He'd better not think about staying at the Shamrock. As for Judy, she'd demand the truth as to whether she was involved in the Greenhouse and Christmas tree farm project.

In the park today, a handful of children in colourful puffer coats were making the most of being out and about because the word on the street was that the snow would last, and the residents of Emerald Bay were in for another white Christmas. Every now and again, there was a tug on the lead, and Hannah would stumble to a stop while Princess Leia investigated various bushes.

As she cut through the park, she gave the play area a wide berth. If you didn't know better, you'd think there was an Icelandic thermal spring over there in the far corner instead of a handful of vaping teens, she thought, seeing the clouds of steam billowing over by the holly bush.

That spot had been a place for Emerald Bay's youth to congregate for as long as Hannah could remember, although in her day, it was an illicit ciggy, not vapes, they'd passed around by the prickly bush.

'How're you, Hannah?' a voice from that direction called, and through the mist of berry-and-grape-infused steam emerged Maire of the chin piercing from their evening knitting class.

'Hi.' She waved back with more enthusiasm than she felt, and if she hadn't been feeling so low, hearing the young woman say to her pals, 'Hannah's cool,' might have put a spring in her step. It was high praise from a teenager, let alone an attitude-filled one like Maire, but Hannah kept putting one foot in front of the other toward the abandoned farm. She didn't even know why she was going there. She just knew she had to.

. . .

Princess Leia was tucked under Hannah's arm as she carefully picked her way over the rutted earth to the famine cottage. The sky was so low she thought she might be able to touch it, and out the corner of her eye, she saw the bounding movement of a rabbit. The fury festering inside her was beginning to dissipate with each puff of white frigid air from her mouth to be replaced by sadness that this land and the cottage would soon be gone. In its place would be a modern glass garden centre with rows and rows of baby fir trees that didn't belong in this landscape, all likely thanks to their long-lost American relation who might well split her time between Dublin, but that didn't mean she belonged here.

She squeezed her eyes shut against the tears blurring her vision, trying and failing to envisage it – perhaps because she didn't want to.

Her foot caught on a rock, and she stumbled. Princess Leia whimpered.

She whispered a ragged apology as the pent-up emotions surged and her throat squeezed tight. The idea of a bulldozer rumbling over the land and razing the cottage, once a home, now a reminder of the past filled with its spirits and its memories, some heart-breaking, some heart-warming, was appalling. She was almost oblivious to the tears tracking down her cheeks as she stepped into the shadowy interior of the cottage.

Hannah's scream pierced the silence, reverberating across the field as a figure emerged from the shadows in the far corner of the room. The chilling sound echoed, but there was no one else around to hear it.

40

'Hannah, it's me, Tom.' The tall, lean figure, clad in a Burberry coat, approached her with both hands in front of him. His glasses glinted in the light, and his hair needed a trim, but it was Tom all right.

The scream, still bouncing off the stone walls, died in her throat as Hannah, in fight or flight mode, automatically stepped backwards into the doorway, ready to run. It took a moment for her thumping heart to catch up with her brain and communicate she knew this person.

'Shush,' she soothed Princess Leia, whose barking was ear-splitting for such a small dog. She swallowed, moistening her throat as she cuddled the trembling chihuahua. 'It's all right. You know Tom.'

When she could no longer feel her shaking, she set her down on the ground and squared up to him.

He stopped in his tracks.

'It would serve you right if she did bite your ankles,' Hannah rasped, assuming it was Princess Leia he was wary of. However, she could be equally ferocious when she wanted to be. He should be afraid of them both.

'I'm sorry. I didn't mean to give you such a fright.'

'Oh, I see, so lurking in dark corners of haunted cottages wasn't supposed to frighten me?'

'Fair play.' Tom kept a watchful eye on Princess Leia as she sniffed around his legs.

'And you could have given Princess Leia a heart attack. She's only got a tiny one, you know.'

'Sorry.'

'You already said that, and you should apologise to her.'

'Erm, sorry, Princess Leia.'

Princess Leia didn't accept the apology gracefully, growling her response.

'What are you even doing here, Tom?'

'I came to see you.'

Hannah wasn't sure what question to roll with first – why he wanted to see her or how he knew where she was. She ran with, 'But how...' her voice trailing away as the answer dawned on her. It had to have been Nan. It didn't explain how he'd got there so quickly, though. She hadn't seen a car in the lane. Why was he back in Emerald Bay in the first place?

Tom pre-empted the question. 'I was driving into the village when Kitty rang me to say you were on your way here, so I came in the back and parked out of sight around the bend in the lane. I knew if you saw the car or if I were to wait outside the cottage, you'd turn around and walk away when you saw me.'

Hannah couldn't believe Nan could go behind her back like so. What was she playing at? And Tom was right. She would have walked away if she'd had an inkling he was here.

'So you've come all this way to gloat, is that it? Because I can't imagine you've much work to be cracking on with here until after Christmas. Or are you chomping at the bit for the diggers to break soil?' She hoped he hadn't rechecked into the Shamrock – that would be too much to bear. She'd pack her bags and go and stay with Imo or Shannon if he had.

'What?' Genuine bewilderment clouded his face.

'You heard me.'

Weak light streamed in through the entrance where Hannah stood, and Tom moved closer, ignoring Princess Leia. Frowning, he scanned her face. Then his hand reached out and gently stroked her cheek. 'You've been crying.'

Hannah was taken unawares, and it took her a second to respond. 'Don't.' She shoved his hand away and swiped her cheeks with the back of her hands. 'They're tears from the cold, is all.'

'Hannah, let me explain.'

'Is Judy your client? Is she behind the Greenhouse project?' His expression told her she was.

'Did you know she was related to us?' she demanded. His eyes shifted away from her momentarily telling her all she needed to know. 'I thought so. But you said nothing. I don't get how she can inveigle her way into my family without mentioning her business interests. She's a wolf in sheep's clothing.' Hannah pulled out Dylan's turn of phrase, but there was no hint of melting chocolate in her voice. 'Why couldn't you tell me the truth? I trusted you. Why did I have to learn that the sale's going through via an arsey reporter ringing me for my comment?'

Princess Leia, seemingly bored, trotted off with her lead trailing after her to investigate the other room in the cottage, leaving Hannah and Tom facing off. A fine guard dog she'd make, Hannah thought, abandoning her post like so.

'OK. So, firstly, I'd signed a confidentiality clause. I couldn't tell you about Judy. And, believe me, Hannah, I wanted to.'

'Don't try to soft-soap me. Just say what you've come to say, and then go away and leave me alone. I don't want to see you ever again. Oh, and I'm formally revoking your invitation for Christmas dinner. You're not welcome.'

Tom stood his ground. 'I wasn't in contact with you because

I didn't want to get your hopes up. I knew it would be a miracle if I could pull it off. I've been working round the clock since I left the bay to make it happen. But I can see not getting in touch was a mistake.'

Hannah was about to wade in again with a sarky 'bully for you' remark.

'No, don't interrupt. You've had your turn. It's mine now. So I made what clearly was an ill-advised decision to come back to Emerald Bay and surprise you in person with the good news.' He held his hands out, palms up, speaking with his body as much as his mouth as he added, 'And obviously it's backfired. Kitty did warn me you're not good with surprises.'

She was definitely having words with Nan when she got home.

'I'm lost.' Hannah risked a glance at him, not wanting to be swayed from her moral high ground by his silver-grey eyes, intense in the dim light, or that mouth that tilted a little on the right-hand side.

'This here' – Tom's arms swept around the cottage – 'and the land, your reporter man was right. It has been sold.'

Hannah's shoulders tensed.

'But it hasn't been sold to Judy and her husband's company or any other developer.'

Now she was holding her breath.

'A private trust for preserving these famine cottages has bought it.'

Hannah couldn't believe what she was hearing and had to remind herself to breathe.

'The cottage and the land will stay as it is. A testament to the past. You, Kitty and Freya did it. I can't speak for Judy. You need to talk to her yourself, but I suspect her interest in this site was an excuse to be here in Emerald Bay. She'd already decided to pull out before she knocked on your door.'

It took a moment for the meaning of Tom's words to sink in,

and Hannah's hands steepled in front of her mouth. Finally, she found her voice, still husky from the scream. 'No, Tom. *You* did it. How, though? I mean, this is incredible.'

'The honest answer to how would be Google initially. Then I pulled every string I could to get things signed, sealed and' – he opened his Burberry and retrieved an envelope from the coat's inner pocket – 'delivered.'

'So cheesy.' Hannah couldn't stop her smile as the last words of that line in the song rang out in her head – 'I'm yours'. She took the envelope, shaking her head, still unable to believe what Tom had done.

'There'll be a celebratory hoolie in the Shamrock tonight,' Hannah murmured, opening the envelope and scanning the copied document hungrily. It confirmed everything Tom had just said. She folded it up once more and passed it back to him. 'This is incredible. Thank you.' She wanted to say so much more as she shifted awkwardly from foot to foot.

'So am I forgiven?'

'I think it's me who should be asking you that.' Hannah swallowed hard. She didn't apologise often, but she'd already done so once before to Tom, and when she did, it came from the heart.

'Tom, I'm sorry I didn't have more faith in you, but when you went silent' – she raised her shoulders and then let them drop – 'I assumed you'd written us off, me off, because the project was going ahead. But it was Judy's connection I couldn't wrap my head around. I felt betrayed, I suppose.'

She didn't flinch when he tilted her chin, leaving her no choice but to meet his gaze. His pupils pulled her in, seeming to stare deep into her soul. Then she saw the sparkle in those silvern irises, lightening the moment.

'So, am I allowed to come for Christmas, after all?' Tom let go of her chin, and Hannah's laugh sounded giddy.

'Nan and Mam wouldn't have it any other way.' She began

to babble then, a nervous reaction to his proximity. He was so close she could feel the warmth of his minty breath, making the pulse at the base of her neck flutter madly. She gabbled on about how he could expect a full table at the Shamrock this Christmas.

Tom interrupted, his schoolboyish cheekiness replaced by an earnest expression. 'And what about you, Hannah? Would you have it any other way?'

Hannah knew what he was getting at. Suddenly, that piece of elastic stretched taut between them snapped, and she flung herself at him, her lips landing clumsily on Tom's cheek.

'Oh wow!' he mumbled, honing in on her lips only to bump her nose with his glasses. They stayed there, the tips of their noses touching, and laughed over the clumsy encounter.

'Maybe we should start over and slow it down,' Tom suggested, reaching out to cup her face.

Hannah nodded, her lips parting in anticipation as he pulled her gently toward him. This time, it was perfect.

'Ouch!' Tom pulled back. 'The little madam bit me.'

Princess Leia, the picture of innocence, sat at their feet, and Hannah began to giggle.

'It's not funny. I was enjoying that kiss immensely.'

'Me too. You're a very naughty girl, Princess Leia.' Hannah could have been saying, *Would you like milk in your tea?* for all the strictness her tone conveyed.

Tom raised one brow. 'Well, that told her.'

'I don't think she meant it. I think she was just letting us know she was back.'

'If you say so.' Then, pushing his glasses back up to sit on the bridge of his nose, Tom said, 'Do you think we could do it again? Kiss, I mean.'

'I think I'd like that very much.'

The second kiss was bolder. This time, Tom gripped Hannah's waist while her hands were wrapped around his neck.

His lips were soft, his breath sweet and hot. It was a kiss Hannah wanted to go on forever, and they only came up for air when Princess Leia began to yip impatiently. She was standing in the doorway by their feet, looking out the entrance to the land beyond, and Hannah swivelled to see what had set her off.

'Well, would you look at that.' Tom moved alongside Hannah, putting his arm around her shoulder. She leaned in close.

It was snowing.

Through the swirling flakes, Hannah saw movement and, squinting into the soft light, glimpsed a tall, broad-shouldered young man wielding a *sléan* as he cut into the earth. He paused in his task, wiped his brow and looked at Hannah. He was smiling and raised his hand. She held hers up, mirroring the gesture. 'Granddad,' she whispered. 'Tom, look over there!'

But of course, when Tom followed the direction of her pointing finger, there was nothing but swirling snowflakes to be seen.

'It's nothing. I must have imagined it.' She touched her index finger to her lip. They'd shared two kisses that had been interrupted. 'You know I firmly believe in the power of three.'

'An amazing coincidence because so do I,' Tom replied, grinning as he spun her round gently to face him. He hesitated, glancing down at Princess Leia, who was hypnotised by the falling flurries. 'This time, you're not to interrupt, got it?'

41

The snow was falling like fairy dust as Hannah and Tom exited the Shamrock on Christmas Eve, smiling a greeting over to where older members of the Emerald Bay community perched on the chairs brought outside from the pub earlier. They'd blankets draped across their laps and had mugs of mulled wine clasped between their hands in anticipation of the carolling. It would start at 5 p.m. sharp, in ten minutes' time.

Her boots sank into the powdery snow coating Main Street as she joined the villagers beginning to congregate in the square, enjoying the solid feel of Tom's hand wrapped around her mitten-clad one.

The citrus-and-spice scent of mulled wine still filled her nostrils. At two euros a cup, it was a nice little earner for the Keep Emerald Bay Beautiful fund, which Isla Mullins had enlisted Nan, Mam and Judy to help with. Nora had told Judy that Isla delegating her with a fundraising task was a sign that the community had accepted her.

Seeing her nan giving Enda Dunne short shrift as he tried to con her into a free refill, Hannah smiled. She might have meddled where Tom was concerned, but it had all worked out.

Hannah had cleared the air with Judy, who, as Tom had said, confessed she'd been terrified of how she'd be received by Nora and the family. Given her and her husband's line of business, purchasing land and embarking on the Greenhouse project gave her a legitimate reason to be in the bay. She'd never intended for it to cause the upset it had, and they'd agreed there was no point in bringing any of it up with Nora, Liam and Kitty. Once Hannah had told her sisters the rest of the story, they'd wholeheartedly agreed, too. Now she'd relaxed her guard and allowed herself to get to know her, Hannah had warmed to Judy as much as the rest of the family had.

Their American relation had been thrilled to meet Ava and Grace along with Shane and Chris when they'd arrived home for the holidays yesterday, as they had been her. The twins and their beaus had been equally eager to meet Tom, and he'd received a thumbs-up from all four. Her sisters had gone the extra mile with waggling eyebrows and kissy-kiss faces. They might all be grown up, but the years fell away as soon as the Kelly girls got together. James had nudged Tom and told him not to sweat it; he'd get used to his girlfriend behaving like a ten-year-old when she was around her sisters. Overhearing the word 'girlfriend' had given Hannah a gorgeous shiver of delight.

The Shamrock would be fit to burst with love and laughter until 2 January when Ava and Shane would return to New York, and Grace and Chris to their canal boat in London.

'How're you, Hannah, Tom? Would you care for a mince pie?' Eileen Carroll bustled her way into Hannah's thoughts by offering them a container filled with the sugar-dusted treats. The local shopkeepers were treating Tom like royalty because, so far as they were concerned, he'd saved their businesses. 'You can take two, Tom,' Eileen added.

'Thanks, Eileen. I don't mind if I do.' Tom helped himself while Hannah, whose hand hovered over a second pie, received a 'don't even think about it' look from her knitting instructor.

'Maire's just after telling me she's going to look into a baker's apprenticeship.'

'That's fantastic!' Hannah grinned, hoping she didn't have pastry crumbs all over her mouth. With the help of Carmel Brady and the use of her industrial kitchen at the Silver Spoon cafe, Eileen had given the teens from the knitting class a crash course in Christmas baking. By the taste of the pies, it had been a resounding success.

'And how are your plans coming along?' Eileen asked.

Hannah had decided to apply for a youth support course in the new year. The added bonus was that the course was in Dublin, the same city as Tom.

'Well, I've sent the applications off.'

'Good for you. Kitty was after telling me how proud she is of you.'

She moved off with her wares, and Hannah, feeling pleased, let the festive vibe filling the late afternoon air wash over her. Snow was landing lightly on the woolly hats and shoulders of the people she'd grown up around, and she was filled with a sense of belonging that made coming home to Emerald Bay so special. Glancing up at Tom, she could see he felt right at home here, too. He might not be from these parts, but the villagers had welcomed him and made him think he was right where he should be this Christmas.

Hannah and Tom accepted the candles being passed around then jostled their way over to where the twins and Imogen were snuggled into their other halves.

'What's going on over there?' Tom gestured to a kerfuffle that had broken out on the square's edge.

Ewan Kennedy, standing behind them, tapped him on the shoulder and leaned in to say, 'Mrs Rae's fox fur was after getting singed with the candle she was holding, but mercifully, Father Seamus came to the rescue by stamping on the poor fox's head. So all's well that ends well.'

'Not for the fox, it doesn't!' Hannah laughed and then, seeing Tom's bewildered face, explained Mrs Rae's attachment to her faux-fox-fur stole.

Tom joined in her laughter, shaking his head. 'It's really something, this place, you know, Hannah.'

'I know.' The smile she shot back was full of pride and interrupted by Tom kissing her. The featherlight brushing of their lips deepened, and they were both careful to keep their candles at arm's length. A disapproving tut saw them break apart.

'I don't know what this place is coming to with people carrying on in public, and you're fire hazards, so you are, waving your candles about like so.' Mrs Tattersall, clad in her Emerald Bay Elves tunic – which did her bony knees, visible beneath her green tights, no favours – glared at them. The elf ears stitched to the striped bobble hat she wore twitched indignantly.

'Isla's beckoning you over, Mrs Tattersall.' Hannah's fib was rewarded by the older woman hurrying over to join the rest of the gathered Emerald Bay Elves.

'What were you just saying about this place?' Hannah grinned up at Tom.

'I stand by it.'

Suddenly, there was a hush in the crowd, and then the Elves, a motley crew of Emerald Bay residents – some of whom could hold a tune, some of whom could not and most of whom should not have been seen in public in short tunics – led by Isla Mullins, launched into 'Hark! The Herald Angels Sing'. The Christmas Eve carolling always got underway with this uplifting number.

Hannah, humming along, stood on her tiptoes for a peek at Shannon, with her burgeoning bump, in full song. James, a surprising baritone, was next to her. Their lives would change forever in five months, and she couldn't wait! Tom squeezed her hand then, and she thought how much her life had changed in just a few short weeks.

The Emerald Bay Elves were three-quarters of the way through their repertoire, singing crowd favourite 'Curoo Curoo', when Hannah decided she couldn't wait until tomorrow. She was desperate to give Tom the Christmas present she'd squirrelled away under the tree in the Shamrock.

'I want to give you your present early,' she shouted into his ear.

'Oh yes?'

'Don't you be starting with the waggling eyebrows!'

Not giving him a chance to argue, she tugged him away from the hub and inside the pub, which was empty now with everyone outside watching the carolling. The tree they'd decorated glowed invitingly in the corner, and Hannah weaved past the tables, pulling Tom behind her.

'Isn't opening a present before Christmas morning bad luck?' he was asking.

'Where'd you hear that? Sure, it's traditional to open one gift on Christmas Eve.' Hannah was so earnest she convinced herself it was true. She bent down and picked up the soft package wrapped in last year's recycled Christmas paper, thrusting it at him shyly. 'G'won – open it.'

Tom's face was alight, but he didn't tear into the gift. Instead, he carefully unwrapped it, smoothing the paper so it could be used again, further etching himself onto Hannah's heart. Then he unfolded the woollen garment, holding it up for inspection, his face splitting into a wide grin of delight.

It was a gilet with a reindeer on the front.

EPILOGUE

Nollaig shona dhuit!

Happy / Merry Christmas

Soon, it would be time to push the tables together in the pub, lay the white cloths, and set them with the Christmas crackers, serviettes and Nan's red origami rose napkin holders. Although the jury was out on it, the holly-pine-cone extravaganza – a supposed family heirloom – would be carefully placed in the centre. It would be all hands on deck with jobs delegated by Nan and Mam, so everyone had a hand in getting ready to serve the Christmas dinner, including the new branch of the family: Judy, her husband, Cam, and their two adult children.

At the heart of the Shamrock was a spirit of community. It was tradition to ensure no one from the village was lonely on Christmas Day, and extra places were always set at the festively laid table. Hannah knew the air would fill with toasts, terrible Christmas cracker jokes and food – too much food!

For now, hands were resting on bellies, letting the enormous brunch of eggs Benny with wild Atlantic salmon or bacon go down as the gathered group sat in the shadow of the world's biggest indoor Christmas tree. Ava had joked upon seeing it that someone should put in a call to the Guinness World Records. At their feet, wrapping paper was strewn about that Hannah would sort through, folding away the salvageable pieces to be recycled next year.

Full they may be, but they'd all found room for the cinnamon-vanilla creamy eggnog Nan had brought out, and even the Quality Street chocs were doing the rounds.

'I love your vest, Tom. It's very, erm...' Shannon grinned, one hand resting on the small of her back, the other dipping into the box of sweets.

Mam had half-heartedly said chocolates before dinner would spoil appetites. Of course, no one had listened because everyone knew they'd miraculously find room. Noses were already twitching at the smell of the roasting turkey, which was sweet and smoky as it wafted into the pub through the open kitchen door.

'Christmassy is the word you're looking for, I believe,' Hannah supplied on Tom's behalf, smiling. 'And it's a gilet, not a vest.'

Shannon laughed. 'Ooh, gilet – get you.'

Hannah's hand-knitted Christmas gifts had gone down a treat, with her sisters putting their cup cosies around the eggnog-filled mugs. She couldn't take credit for Tom's gilet, though, which he wore proudly over a long-sleeved shirt. That was down to Eileen Carroll, who'd worked through the night to ensure Hannah could present him with his longed-for gift. She'd had to wait until morning for Tom to give her the gift he'd bought her, a thoughtful hand-crafted knitting bag made of hemp, stuffed with a rainbow of wool and personalised needles. She loved it, although the best present was when Tom slipped his arm around her, the laughter around them blending into the background and whispered, 'I dreamed of a Christmas morning like this when I was a lad.'

Hannah snuggled into him and looked around her big, ever-expanding, boisterous family. There was so much to look forward to! A new baby, a new career, a whole new life to be explored with Tom.

Tom gently lifted her chin and their lips brushed, sealing the deal for the year ahead.

He broke away with an 'Ouch!'

There blinking up at him was the guest of honour, Princess Leia, with a Christmassy red bow on her head. Mrs Tansey, home from hospital, was delighted to have been invited to spend Christmas Day with the Kelly family.

Hannah laughed on seeing the little dog, the picture of innocence.

'It's not funny!' Tom rubbed his ankle.

'Should we get a chihuahua when I move to Dublin?' she cheekily asked. 'Small dogs are perfect for apartment living. A little boy we could call Luke Skywalker.'

'No comment.'

A LETTER FROM MICHELLE VERNAL

Dear reader,

I'm thrilled you chose to dive into *Saving Christmas in the Little Irish Village*. Your support means the world to me, and I can't express how grateful I am to have readers like you. If you did enjoy it, and want to keep up to date with all my latest releases, just sign up at the following link. Your email address will never be shared, and you can unsubscribe at any time.

www.bookouture.com/michelle-vernal

I've had such a wonderful time writing about the Kelly family and the residents of Emerald Bay. I hope you've enjoyed getting to know them just as much. Bringing these characters to life on the page has been a joy.

Hannah's character was so much fun to write. I hope you were as invested in her story as I was, especially when she and Tom finally found each other.

Another highlight for me was Kitty Kelly's storytelling about how she met her husband, Finbar. I loved weaving her past into the fabric of present-day Emerald Bay.

The world of Emerald Bay has become like a second home to me, filled with characters who feel like old friends. I hope they've started to feel the same way to you too!

Thank you for being a part of this journey. Readers, like you, make it all possible, and I always remember that.

I hope you loved *Saving Christmas in the Little Irish Village*, and if you did, I would be very grateful if you could write a review. I'd love to hear what you think, and it makes such a difference helping readers discover one of my books for the first time.

I love hearing from my readers – you can get in touch on social media or through my website.

Thanks,

Michelle Vernal

KEEP IN TOUCH WITH MICHELLE

www.michellevernalbooks.com

facebook.com/michellevernalnovelist

x.com/MichelleVernal

goodreads.com/goodreadscommichellevernal

ACKNOWLEDGEMENTS

Thank you to team Bookouture for all their hard work ensuring my readers receive the best book package worldwide. Also, thanks to my amazing Editor, Natalie, for her invaluable insights into this story. Bookouture is fabulous to work with, and I appreciate each and every team member for all that they do.

Lastly, thank you, Paul. I really couldn't do what I do without you. You and the boys are my world.

PUBLISHING TEAM

Turning a manuscript into a book requires the efforts of many people. The publishing team at Bookouture would like to acknowledge everyone who contributed to this publication.

Audio
Alba Proko
Melissa Tran
Sinead O'Connor

Commercial
Lauren Morrissette
Hannah Richmond
Imogen Allport

Cover design
Debbie Clement

Data and analysis
Mark Alder
Mohamed Bussuri

Editorial
Natalie Edwards
Charlotte Hegley

Copyeditor
Laura Kincaid

Proofreader
Maddy Newquist

Marketing
Alex Crow
Melanie Price
Occy Carr
Cíara Rosney

Operations and distribution
Marina Valles
Stephanie Straub

Production
Hannah Snetsinger
Mandy Kullar
Jen Shannon
Ria Clare

Publicity
Kim Nash
Noelle Holten
Myrto Kalavrezou
Jess Readett
Sarah Hardy

Rights and contracts
Peta Nightingale
Richard King
Saidah Graham

Printed in Great Britain
by Amazon